THE BRIDAL PARTY

BOOKS BY MARIA FRANKLAND

Last Christmas

I Let Her In

MARIA FRANKLAND

THE BRIDAL PARTY

bookouture

Published by Bookouture in 2024

An imprint of Storyfire Ltd.
Carmelite House
50 Victoria Embankment
London EC4Y 0DZ

www.bookouture.com

Copyright © Maria Frankland, 2021, 2024

Maria Frankland has asserted her right to be identified as the author of this work.

First published as *The Hen Party* by Autonomy Press in 2021.

All rights reserved. No part of this publication may be reproduced, stored in any retrieval system, or transmitted, in any form or by any means, electronic, mechanical, photocopying, recording or otherwise, without the prior written permission of the publishers.

ISBN: 978-1-83525-036-5
eBook ISBN: 978-1-83525-035-8

This book is a work of fiction. Names, characters, businesses, organizations, places and events other than those clearly in the public domain, are either the product of the author's imagination or are used fictitiously. Any resemblance to actual persons, living or dead, events or locales is entirely coincidental.

*I dedicate this book
to the fabulous ladies who
attended my hen party
in 2020... without
such deadly consequences!*

PROLOGUE

It takes a moment for my eyes to grow accustomed to the darkness. My heart rate quickens and I hear the hiss of my breath in my ears. As I tiptoe to her side, she doesn't stir.

I hold the pillow, my hands gripping either edge as I prepare to lower it.

She barely flinches to start with. I wonder if she'll just drift into an eternal sleep without waking first.

Her body becomes rigid, but then, some fight must kick in, her arms and legs flail in all directions. Taken aback, I press down. Hard. I hear her gasps beneath the pillow. She doesn't thrash for long before going limp. Then. Silence.

I hardly dare move the pillow for a moment. When I do, I know there's no going back.

She's gone.

ONE

JEN

I try to make out what's below us as we descend through the clouds. 'Here we are, ladies.'

'Thanks for organising all this.' Caitlyn squeezes my hand. 'This is going to be a hen party that will never be forgotten – I just know it.'

'At least you made it.'

'I know! I'm sorry. I live a stone's throw from the airport and I was still the last one to get there.' She lapses back into the silence we've spent much of the flight in.

I must try to pull her out of it. 'Are you OK? You seem quiet today.'

'I'm fine. It's not exactly easy to get a word in edgeways with that lot, is it?'

We're taking up two rows of the plane. Caitlyn's got the window seat beside me. There's two behind us and the rest are at the other side of the aisle. Their side has been quite rowdy throughout the flight. They've had a noisy game of charades – fuelled by the hugely expensive bottles of Prosecco we bought from trolley service. I imagine the other passengers are glad the flight was only fifty-five minutes, especially the poor man who has found himself in the middle of them. He couldn't even have asked to be moved – the plane is packed.

I notice Emma, Caitlyn's younger sister, gripping the armrests for dear life.

'I don't enjoy landing.' She must see me smiling at her.

'You're such a wuss.' Annette, the middle sister, narrows her eyes.

It's the smoothest landing I've ever known. We're told we can unbuckle but as I rise to pass the hand luggage down, Michaela, Caitlyn's sister-in-law-to-be, pokes her head above the seats. 'We might as well wait until the stampede has passed. We'll only be standing around in the aisle if we move now. I, for one, am going to enjoy the rest of the bubbles.' She refills her glass with what's left in the bottle.

'So you should.' I sink back into my seat. 'They cost enough.' It doesn't go past me that she drains the bottle without bothering to see if anyone else wants to share what's left.

'Right, come on, bride.' I smile at Caitlyn. 'And get that hat back on your head. Now!'

'Do I really have to wear this?' She strokes the green hair hanging beneath the equally green sparkling hat. 'Why couldn't you have got me a nice veil or something?' It's good to see her smile. She's been so subdued since we all met at the airport.

'Get it on, Caitlyn,' Michaela barks across the aisle. 'Stop being so vain.'

We file onto the tarmac, all ten of us, dragging our wheelie cases behind us. It's a miracle that I've packed my requirements for two nights into such a minuscule case. We've all assumed responsibility for the adornments needed to decorate the hen's apartment. Booze and food, we decided, could be bought in Dublin. Though I'm told it's extortionate here. Adele, Caitlyn's old school friend, has already been pleading poverty. I know she's a single mum, but she didn't even tip in when we were buying Prosecco. *Why come to Dublin if you're skint?* I wanted to say. She's had a bit of a face on since we set off, to be honest. I know she wanted to be a bridesmaid, but as Caitlyn has tried to explain to her, she couldn't choose everyone.

By the time we reach passport control, we're divided into our cliques. It seems the lines of separation are drawn. I'm with Caitlyn. Her two sisters, Annette and Emma, walk arm in arm. The noisiest clique of all is Ben's side of the family – his sister Michaela, his mum Karen and his daughter Lucy. It surprised me when Lucy said she wanted to come. She's struggled to accept Caitlyn from the get-go. She's only seventeen, but she's got fake ID so hopefully her presence won't curtail anything, though with her height and impeccable make-up, she looks much older than she is.

Shelley, the third bridesmaid, Caitlyn's former colleague, tails Emma, looking like she's trying to break into whatever conversation Emma is having with Annette, but they don't acknowledge her. The last two members of our party, Caitlyn's neighbour Mari, and her old school friend, Adele, look out on a limb. They're unknown to each other but are forced to walk together. Neither of them look happy about it.

We get through passport control without incident. They've introduced self-service at some exit points, the same as our airport in Leeds. A scan of the passport, a look into a camera and we're on our way. It's better than queueing. I don't know why it's not available at all of them.

'We're here,' Emma shrieks, looking around, her blonde plaits swinging with the motion. 'And since we're in Dublin, we should go for a pint of Guinness before anything else. It's supposed to taste much better in Ireland.'

'Yuk. I'm glad I'm not drinking.' Shelley screws her face up.

'I don't like Guinness either.' Caitlyn stands her case up whilst she lets her blonde hair out of its ponytail to fall loose around her shoulders. Though since she's been ill, her hair has lost its former lustre. I'll have to help her get something done with it before the wedding.

'I hope you're having something to drink, Caitlyn.' I laugh, whilst injecting a mock sternness into my voice. 'You hardly touched your Prosecco on the plane. I can't spend all weekend finishing your drinks for you – it's *your* hen party – I'll be wrecked!'

'Trust you to be so well behaved, Caitlyn.' Annette's voice has a hostile edge as she surveys her sister. 'Why don't you let yourself go a bit? Enjoy yourself for once.'

'Why do I need to get drunk to do that? No, thank you. I've had enough feeling ill to last me a lifetime.' Caitlyn sets off again and, like lemmings, so do the rest of us.

'Don't we know it?' Annette sounds irritated, but then she always does where Caitlyn's concerned. It's possibly something from childhood – there's always an atmosphere between them. 'Just put it behind you, Caitlyn. Your illness is in the past now. It's time to look forward – you're getting married, for God's sake.'

'I don't see why it should matter to you how much I drink or don't drink. I'm not stopping the rest of you getting as blitzed as you want to. I can have a good enough time without it, thank you very much.'

'Too right,' Emma says as we head towards the exit. 'And you deserve to, especially after what you've been through. Get off her back, you.' She wags her finger at Annette, then turns her attention back to Caitlyn. 'You'll have a fab time, sis – we've been planning this for ages.'

'So, what's the plan then? I could do with some food,' Shelley calls from the back of our entourage.

'Eat? It's a hen weekend!' Lucy, Ben's daughter, therefore Caitlyn's stepdaughter-to-be, pipes up. I glance at her, hoping that at her age she's able to deal with her drink. I don't fancy mopping up after her this weekend. Having said that, her grandma and auntie are here to look after her. It also surprised me when *they* confirmed they were coming – they were very late in letting me know.

'Shelley and I are going to get the apartment ready.' Emma pats the top of her case. 'Ladies, we need to pool our decorations. Caitlyn, do you need to go to the loo or something? This little lot is not for your eyes – yet.'

'Actually, now you come to mention it – I do need the loo.' Caitlyn heads off and I watch her retreat. Though it's more of a trudge, and there's a definite droop to her head and shoulders. As soon as she's walked away from us, she slides her green hat from her head and stuffs it into her pocket. I'll be having words with her.

The rest of us pull balloons, banners and lots more besides from our cases. We pile it all on the floor in front of us. I'm pleased everyone has got on board with this – from the tone of the messages when I was trying to pull it all together, I thought I might have to go shopping when we got here.

'We'll never get all of this in our cases.' Shelley unzips one end of hers and shakes her head. 'No way. I'm already packed to the rafters. Has anyone got a carrier bag?'

We all look at Ben's mum, Karen, the oldest member of our hen party. We've already discovered she's good for headache pills and plasters. Both required by Caitlyn. So I'm not surprised when she produces a folded up carrier bag.

'Quick.' I look towards where Caitlyn is emerging from the ladies'. 'Put it away. Right, you two. Do you know where you're going? That one needs to put her hat back on!' I point at Caitlyn.

'We'll get a taxi.' Emma takes hold of the bag. 'We'll be fine. And we'll have the place looking amazing by the time you get there. Are you going to go for some food?'

'We should leave that decision to the bride,' I say as Caitlyn rejoins our group.

'Why don't we compromise.' She picks her case up. 'Let's go somewhere where we can either eat or drink – or both. I'm not sure I'm fussed about either.'

'Ah, come on, you. We need to get you built up again. You need some boobs to fill that wedding dress of yours. How about an Italian?' I start our group walking again. 'What does the bride think?'

'Stop calling me the bride, will you?' Caitlyn appears to be forcing a smile. 'You make me sound like Bridezilla!'

'Just get that hat back on.'

Shelley and Emma join the taxi rank queue outside the airport entrance. 'Do you want some food bringing back?' I ask. 'A pizza or something? If we end up being a while, I'll look at getting something delivered for you.'

'That would be great. Can you pick up nibbles and beverages as well?'

'Just some cordial for me.' Shelley looks peaky. 'I've mentioned I can't drink this weekend, haven't I?'

None of us really know Dublin, so we wander about aimlessly, peering into cafés and restaurants that might have some space. I'm underwhelmed. Dublin seems much like any other major city with its chain-like shops, restaurants and coffee bars. Until I notice a man playing a violin, dressed from head to toe in green.

'Get your hat back on.' I nudge Caitlyn towards the man. 'It'll make a great photo to post on Facebook.'

She shrinks back. 'No chance.'

'Ah, go on. Rumour has it that the men in Dublin are lovely. They're proper gentlemen with impeccable manners and everything.'

'I don't want my picture taken.'

Annette looks at her. 'Boring sod. Come on, liven up a bit.'

'You never miss a chance to have a dig at me, do you?' Caitlyn bites back. 'And you wonder why I keep my distance from you.'

'Ladies! Ladies!' They've always been like this. But to be fair, it is usually Annette who is the sniper and Caitlyn who's defending herself.

'Come on, Auntie Michaela.' Lucy grabs her auntie's arm. 'We'll get a piccie taken with him instead. I'll stick it on Insta.'

We watch as they pose with the green man. Lucy shakes her strawberry-blonde hair behind her shoulders and sticks her chest out. Michaela rests her arm on her niece's shoulder and pouts. Pouting is the new smiling.

We go on a bit further, eight of us now, heels clip-clopping on the pavement, the wheels of our cases rhythmically clicking as we walk. Caitlyn is so quiet – I wonder if it's being around Annette that's bothering her. 'What about here?' I point at Bella Mia. 'It looks quiet enough.'

'Do we really want *quiet*?' Michaela pushes her way up to the front.

'You'd better ask the bride,' chimes Annette.

TWO

JEN

We seem to make our presence felt in Bella Mia, filling the foyer with our eight suitcases and coats, before taking over a long table in the centre of the restaurant.

'Special occasion?' asks the waitress.

'She's getting married in three weeks.' I point at Caitlyn. 'So, we'll start with some bubbly please.' I'm determined that she'll have a good time this weekend. Caitlyn really should look happier. She's in remission, getting married, and here with us, for the weekend.

'Cheers, ladies.' Karen holds her glass aloft.

'Speeeeeech.' Michaela looks at Caitlyn. 'Come on, future sister-in-law. You've dragged us all the way to Dublin.'

It's nice to hear her being friendly for a change.

'I don't do speeches,' Caitlyn says.

'Ah, come on.' I join in now. Between us all, we must be able to bring her out of herself.

'You've all got a glass of fizz in your hand – what more do you want?'

'A speech from the bride-to-be.' It's the first time Adele has joined in with anything. Her voice is so quiet that I think only I heard her.

'Speeeeech!' Michaela taps the side of her glass with a spoon.

'All right, all right.' Caitlyn stands. 'Anyway, yes, I'd just like to say thank you all for coming...'

'Booooring.' Lucy sips her Prosecco, smearing the glass with red lipstick. She's got fully-laden Pandora bracelets on each wrist and seriously big hair. I can't believe she's only seventeen.

'Don't forget, Lucy – I'm going to be your wicked stepmother before long.' Caitlyn's face bears an expression I can't quite put my finger on. So does Lucy's. It seems to say, *Yeah, right*.

Strained laughter rises amongst us. Caitlyn places her hands on her hips and appears to be waiting for a pause. The whole restaurant falls quiet. 'Oh gosh, everyone's listening.' She colours up. She's been looking pale throughout the journey, so the colour makes her look better. 'Anyway, as I was saying... I've got all the ladies here this weekend who have made the most impact on my life.'

There's an edge to her words which appears to be lost on the others.

'To those of you who've supported me during my illness – thank you. I know I haven't been easy.'

Annette coughs, and Caitlyn glares at her.

'But you're all here this weekend to celebrate with me, and I'm glad you've all come along. We'll have a weekend never to be forgotten.' She raises her glass. 'I'd like to propose a toast... to my hens.'

'To us hens.'

I stand now and Caitlyn immediately drops back into her seat. 'As chief bridesmaid,' I begin, 'I'd firstly like to acknowledge the awful time Caitlyn has had lately. I know I speak for all of us when I say how much I've been in awe of her battle, without complaint, to get into remission.' I ignore Annette's comment, something to do with how Caitlyn's never stopped moaning. I raise my voice a notch to drown her out. 'Which is why it's so important that we need to give our lovely Caitlyn the greatest send-off imaginable. I'd like to thank you all for helping me organise this weekend. Our blushing bride will not know what's hit her.'

Everyone laughs again as the waitress reappears to take our order. It's more genuine laughter this time.

'I'll find out what pizza Emma and Shelley want.' Caitlyn slides her phone from her bag. 'It's good of them to get the apartment ready.'

'You sure? I don't mind sorting the pizza.'

'You've done enough.' She places her hand on my arm. I glance at her skinny wrist, unable to believe how much weight she's lost.

On the way to find a taxi, we call at a supermarket to load up with essentials. Our haul, comprising mainly wine and gin, comes to over a hundred and fifty euros.

There's an air of anticipation as we arrive at the apartment block. I climb out of the taxi I've shared with Caitlyn, Mari and Adele, and tip the driver. It was a silent journey. Mari and Adele have attempted to engage Caitlyn in conversation, but she's in a world of her own. I wonder if she's argued with Ben or something. On the face of it, some might think she's lucky to have met him. To look at, he's drop-dead gorgeous but there's more than a grain of truth in the saying, 'beauty is only skin deep'. 'You OK?' I whisper to her as we wait on the pavement for the other taxi. 'You really don't seem yourself.'

'We'll have a chat later.'

I squeeze her arm. That sounds very ominous indeed. I knew

there was something up with her. Thank goodness she's planning to talk about it.

The other four step out of their taxi, making so much noise that the driver's ears must be ringing. At least *they're* having a good time. Our lot looks more like we're arriving at a wake than a hen party.

'Right. Where are we?' Caitlyn looks at the building in front of us.

'Top floor, I think.'

'I hope there's a lift.' Annette looks up. 'Especially with all this stuff we've just bought.'

With no sign of a lift, we go in convoy up ten flights of stairs. By flight five the talking and cackling has quietened – everyone is huffing and blowing instead.

'You ought to stop and have a rest?' I look at Caitlyn who seems to be struggling. 'You shouldn't be overdoing it.'

'I'm so out of condition,' she gasps. 'I could have run up and down these stairs fifty times before my diagnosis.'

'I know. You'll get back to where you were. A jog in the morning, methinks – get you moving again now you're in remission. You've no excuse now.' I smile as we reach the top. 'Oh, look. A sign for the lift!'

Everyone groans. 'As if we missed that,' Adele says.

We wait for Mari who is *very* out of condition.

She arrives at the top a few minutes later, clutching her side and gasping, 'I've got a stitch.'

'We're here,' I call into the darkened hallway of our apartment.

'Hellooooo.' Emma snaps a light on and looks expectantly at her sister. 'Welcome to your hen party.'

'Gosh, you've been busy.' Caitlyn wanders from room to room, taking in the party games that have been set up, the balloons, the streamers, the banners and photographs. 'Thank you all so much.'

I have to say, there's a cloud of sadness in her face rather than joy. I'll have to get her on her own soon so I can speak to her.

I'm disappointed that the apartment doesn't look as it did in the photos. The décor is gaudy and the carpets are seriously tired, but Shelley and Emma have done a great job of tarting things up.

Emma opens a door. 'Being the bride's sister, I'm a reliable authority that she snores, so I allocate this first room as the bridal suite. You wanted your own room, didn't you, Caitlyn? Besides, it's the only one with its own bathroom.'

'She's like a pneumatic drill,' Annette says, drily. 'I had to grow up sharing a room with her.'

'Thanks for giving me my own room.' She steps next to Emma. 'I haven't been sleeping too well, so at least I won't be disturbing anyone.'

I peer in over Caitlyn's shoulder. 'There – you've got your veil and tiara.' I point at it, laid out on her bedside table, and nudge her. 'Happy now?'

Her eyes are shining with what look like tears as she gazes back at me. Her bedroom has been decorated the same as the lounge, kitchen and hallway, with balloons and banners everywhere. 'I don't know what to say.'

'As mother of the groom...' Shelley holds another door open for Karen. 'You've also got your own room. It hasn't got its own bathroom, but there's one right next door.'

'Good stuff. I'll go and assemble myself.' Karen grabs her case and wheels it into the room behind her. She's in her early sixties but doesn't look particularly out of place amongst the rest of us. With her long, dark hair and slim figure, she could be a twenty- or thirty-something from the back. According to Caitlyn, she's recently had a boob job. I couldn't be bothered with all that. *Grow old disgracefully* is what I say.

'Now for the rest of us.' Emma projects her voice with the

sense of importance of an *X Factor* host. We follow her around the corner to where five doors sit on either side of the hallway.

'I will share with my sister here.'

Annette smiles and stands next to her, as though she's been chosen for the best team.

'Auntie and niece will also share.' Emma gestures towards Michaela and Lucy. 'Adele and Mari, I know you've only just met, but there's no better way to get to know each other than to share a room.' Everyone laughs as they move together like two children who've been forced to partner in PE. Adele would be the skinny, unsporty one who can't run, and Mari the overweight one who would drop any ball that came in her direction. 'And lastly, Jen will share with my partner in crime and fellow bridesmaid over there. Oh, and that door right there – is the bathroom.'

I'm glad to be sharing with Shelley although she's strangely quiet too. I'll have to have a chat with her as well – see what's bothering her.

'And that concludes the tour of your party apartment.' Shelley enunciates every consonant as she speaks, but sounds as though loading enthusiasm into her voice is an effort. I wonder if Shelley and Caitlyn have had some sort of fallout that I don't know about. They're both subdued and I've noticed that they've not spoken to each other a great deal.

'As chief bridesmaid—' I begin.

'I think we're going to hear this a lot.' Emma laughs. At least Emma is her usual jolly self. She's a breath of fresh air compared to some of them here.

'As chief bridesmaid,' I say again, 'I think we should get settled in, set up the kitchen with our refreshments, then convene in the drawing room.' I gesture towards the lounge.

'The drawing room.' Emma laughs, showing her perfect teeth. 'Get you!'

. . .

Within half an hour, everyone is in the lounge, gathered in a circle around the walls. Except Michaela. Everyone is quiet and the scenario strangely reminds me of my dentist's waiting room.

'I don't think Auntie Michaela's too thrilled with her room. She wouldn't tell you herself though.' Lucy speaks in a hushed voice. 'The window is broken, so it's cold in there, and she doesn't like having to share a bathroom with so many people. She says her bed is lumpy and that there's a funny smell.'

'It's only for one weekend.' I keep my voice airy. It's impossible to please everyone. But I've spent hours arranging things so can't help feeling a little disgruntled. However, I smile as she walks in; she heads towards the only empty seat, next to the window.

'I can't sit there.' She gasps as she glances out of the window. 'I didn't realise we were so high up.'

'She's always had a thing about heights.' Karen laughs as she stands. 'Ever since she was a little girl. You sit here.' They swap around.

'Thanks, Mum.'

'You can share my bathroom,' Karen says to her as they pass. 'I thought you would have done, anyway.'

'And me, Grandma.' Lucy pouts, as usual.

'Put that phone down,' Caitlyn says to Annette. 'You've not stopped texting since we got to the airport.'

'I agree.' Emma pokes her.

'Yes, *Mother*.' Annette stands. 'It's work. They won't leave me alone. I'll get the drinks.' Emma follows her sister out of the room.

Moments later, they each return with a tray. Annette's is laden with shot glasses and Emma's with Prosecco glasses. 'Let's get this party started.' Emma and Annette follow one another around the group, giving the glasses out.

'Not for me.' Shelley has been madly texting too, but places her phone in her lap and holds her palm towards Annette as she offers her a drink. 'I'm not drinking this weekend, remember.'

'Why not? Drinking at a hen party is the law.'

'I'm on some really strong antibiotics.'

'That's not good timing.' I look at Shelley who glugs from a bottle of water. 'What's up?'

'Just an infection. I won't bore you with the details. I'll be back in a minute.' She snatches up her ringing phone and lurches towards the lounge door.

'You'd better go easy on it, sis, as well.' Emma hands Caitlyn a glass. 'You haven't drunk properly for ages.'

'Don't worry. I won't have you dealing with projectile vomit.'

'Just have a few drinks like the rest of us,' Michaela says. 'Don't worry, Caitlyn, you'll still be the centre of attention as always. Loosen up a bit.'

I search Michaela's face for a trace of something, hoping that she's joking. She and Caitlyn have always been up and down. Caitlyn has confided in me a time or two about her. Michaela lives in her brother's old flat, rent-free, and is always sponging off him. She's still on his company payroll and has been since she worked Saturdays there in her teens. Apparently, she doesn't lift a finger to earn the income that hits her account each month.

Caitlyn reckons Michaela's threatened by her being around. The difference as well is that Caitlyn is a grafter. Not only is she a physiotherapist, she also helps on the contracts and investments side of Ben's business. And she's good at it. She's been away from her physio job whilst she's been ill but has tried to stay as involved as possible with the company she'll soon be marrying into. They manufacture some gorgeous clothes – the dress I'm wearing today is from them. They used to have some amazing designers free-lancing for them, but I gather from Caitlyn that it has been necessary to cut some of them back. As they've grown in popularity, so have their fees.

And Ben's mum, Karen, is just as bad. When Caitlyn and Ben got engaged, rather than congratulate them, she said, *I don't know why you can't just live together – why do you have to get married?* And that's coming from someone who got a *huge* payout when she divorced Ben's dad. Even with all the Botox and beauty treatments Karen was having, he still ran off with a younger model.

I thought Ben's family would have all warmed more to Caitlyn whilst she's been fighting cervical cancer, but they have kept their distance even more. I guess some people are like that and struggle to deal with serious illness. Also, Michaela seems territorial with her mother, and I doubt she would allow Caitlyn into their inner circle, anyway. She's been peeved enough sharing her brother with Caitlyn, by the sounds of it. When Ben left her in the flat they shared together to move in with Caitlyn, she was said to be heartbroken.

'Cheers, ladies.' Emma's voice cuts into my thoughts as she holds her glass in the air. 'To Caitlyn and Ben.'

'Caitlyn and Ben.' Everyone raises their glasses – some with more enthusiasm than others.

'Oooh, it's so exciting.' Emma sips her Prosecco. 'I can't believe my big sister is actually getting married. You're so lucky.'

'It'll be your turn soon enough.' Caitlyn smiles at her, but there's a sadness in her smile that I can't decipher.

The conversation in the room is faltering. From the initial high on arrival, everyone is just looking at each other. I've done my research into hen party activities and luckily have something up my sleeve for this. 'I think we all need to get to know one another better. Let's do an ice-breaker. Caitlyn has to introduce each hen and give an interesting fact about them.'

'Oh no!' She shuffles in her seat. 'That will be too hard!'

'Are you saying we're not interesting?' Karen sniffs and flicks her hair behind her shoulder. She flicks her hair around a lot – it seems to be her pride and joy. I notice that as well as her boob job, she's had some fillers in her eyes. Her skin hardly moves when she smiles or frowns.

'OK, OK, I'll do it.' Caitlyn straightens up in her seat, and it's good to see her look more animated. 'I'll start with you then, Karen. Karen, Ben's mum, erm, interesting fact... she did a bungee jump for charity to celebrate being single again.'

A collective gasp and exclamations of *brilliant* go up around the room. Shelley slips back in and retakes her seat.

Karen smiles. 'I'll have to show you all the video.'

'I'll go around the room, shall I?' Caitlyn's looking like she just wants to get this ice-breaker task over with. 'Next – Lucy. Ben's daughter. Interesting fact? Erm. She's the only person I know who can spend hundreds of pounds on clothes without even leaving the house.'

It's Lucy's turn to frown. Clearly she was hoping for a different interesting fact.

'Moving on. Shelley.' She stares at her for a few moments before speaking. 'Shelley gets a bit mixed up. She's not quite as perfect as she'd let you believe.'

'What's that supposed to mean?' Shelley stares at her and crosses one denim-clad leg over the other.

I hold my breath and will the long pause to be over, but then Caitlyn becomes animated again. 'What I mean is that Shelley doesn't know her left from her right. When we were training, she treated a patient's knee. He was too polite to tell her until the end that she had treated the wrong knee.' Everyone laughs. 'Oh, and how could I forget?' Caitlyn holds her ring finger towards Shelley. 'Adept at undercover ring shopping and keeping secrets with my husband-to-be.' Caitlyn winks at her. There's still a strangeness between them I can't put my finger on. There has definitely been a falling-out between them, but I'm sure I'll get the chance to find out soon enough.

'Next, Mari, my neighbour, and friend, of course.' Caitlyn adds the second part of her sentence as though it's an afterthought, then closes her eyes as if really searching for something. 'Erm, she makes the best cup of tea in the whole of Yorkshire.'

'And a chat to go with it,' Mari adds. She's been literally silent up to now, but visibly lights up when Caitlyn uses the word *friend*. Mari wasn't originally on the guest list and had reportedly been really upset when she found out about this weekend. Caitlyn says she never normally goes out, which is why she didn't think to ask Mari. She's very overweight and apparently suffers with anxiety and depression. However, she looks to have made an effort for this weekend. Her hair looks like it's just been cut and her outfit of leggings, black sparkly pumps and a patterned tunic top look to have been recently shopped for.

'Jen next.' Caitlyn smiles at me.

I wonder what's coming. No matter what she says, I'm pleased that she's engaged with this game.

'My chief bridesmaid who I've known since sixth form. Good at secretive organisation of hen parties. An interesting fact? Hmm. We were once in the Upstairs Downstairs nightclub and Jen here was entertaining one gentleman upstairs and another one downstairs. She spent the night disappearing to the loo or the bar. Neither were aware of the other's existence the entire evening.'

'That was so funny.' I remember it well. 'It was New Year's Eve. I'd invited them both to make sure I wasn't without a date that night. I had no idea they'd both turn up. I didn't see either of them after that though.' I'm glad I had the idea of this icebreaker. It seems to have brought Caitlyn back to life. There's a light in her eyes that wasn't there before.

Everyone laughs again. Apart from Annette as Caitlyn turns to her. She's probably worried about what could be to come.

'Annette. My younger sister. Middle child. What can I say? Interesting fact. Yes, I know. Used to stuff pillows into her bed so it looked like she was sleeping when really, she was sneaking out into the night via the shed roof, meeting boys.'

'Annette!' Emma's eyes widen in mock-horror. She and Caitlyn are so alike. Their eyes are the same blue and their hair's similar apart from Emma has a fringe and always wears hers in plaits.

'And you can talk.' Caitlyn moves to Emma. 'Emma. Baby of the family. You've been a fab sister.'

'You make it sound as if you're going away forever, rather than just getting married! And I sense a *but* coming!'

'Anyway. Emma once brought two mice home, and they did the obvious. We ended up with a mouse infestation within a few months and had to get pest control in. Even our dad was furious, and usually Emma can do no wrong in his eyes!'

'It devastated me.' Emma pouts. 'All those mouse traps and poison.'

'Next. Adele. Interesting fact.'

'Are you OK, Adele?'

Her head jerks up from gazing at the floor. 'Erm, yeah. Just thinking.'

'Adele always looks miserable when she's thinking, Jen. Don't worry.'

Adele smiles, possibly pleased at this observation Caitlyn has made of her which shows how well they must know each other.

'Well,' Caitlyn begins. 'I've known Adele a long, long time and have it on good authority that she once left her little girl at the wrong birthday party. It was only when she collected her and Louisa said she hadn't known anyone there, that Adele realised she had the wrong week.'

'Whoops!' I laugh. 'Anyway, this is turning into more of a divulging of everyone's secrets than the giving of interesting facts.'

'And last but not least. Michaela. Now, what dark secret or

interesting fact can I think of?' Michaela has a look on her face as if to say, *Don't you dare.*

Lucy pipes up. 'I can tell you a story about Auntie Michaela – the one where she got married, and it lasted one week.'

All eyes turn back to Caitlyn, but she says nothing. Evidently, Lucy's taken care of the *interesting fact* for her.

The windows are steaming up with the amount of bodies in the room and another awkward silence descends over us all. Clearly, more alcohol is required. 'All right, all right.' I reach under my chair for where I've put my shot glass. 'Ladies, it's shot time.'

Everyone grapples under chairs to retrieve theirs.

'Raise your glasses – to the bride.'

'To the bride.' Everyone choruses, grimacing at the burn of tequila. Apart from Shelley who swigs from her water bottle.

We'll all be suffering in the morning and she'll be fresh and full of energy.

THREE

JEN

Caitlyn clutches her latest prize to her chest. A handbag. 'I like this Mr and Mrs game. I'm getting them all right. What's the next question?'

She seems to have put whatever was troubling her earlier to one side. We've all changed into pyjamas and slippers which has provided some decent photo opportunities.

Shelley has disappeared with her phone again. She's missing half the hen party. I wonder if she's got something up her sleeve – some sort of surprise for Caitlyn that she's having to organise on the phone. I'll have to ask her.

'Your turn to ask a question.' I pass Adele a card, noticing her stumpy nails as she takes it. Everyone else has had their nails done for the weekend, however Adele is small and quite boyish with short hair. I've barely heard her speak since we assembled in what I dubbed 'the drawing room'. She hasn't seemed happy to be part of all our so-called celebrations, but now she smiles as she takes centre stage. 'What place does Ben most want to visit in the world?'

'I know this. I know this.' Lucy jumps around in her seat.

'I'm not sure.' Caitlyn pauses then eventually says, 'India.'

'I thought you were supposed to know my dad!' Lucy laughs. Her laugh has a nasty edge to it but it's still better than her scowling and pouting.

'How can she? They've only been together a couple of years.' Michaela's voice bears a trace of contempt. 'Nobody knows my brother like I do. He wants to go to Egypt. He used to have a book about it when we were kids.' She rolls her pyjama sleeves up, her bracelets rattling against each other.

'Shall I open the window?' I ask no one in particular as I move towards it. 'It's getting stuffy in here.'

'Oh.' Caitlyn holds the prize that she hasn't won in the air.

It's a scarf. I resisted the temptation to keep this one when I was assembling the prizes – it's rather nice.

She looks around at everyone. 'I nominate Karen to have this prize.' A collective buzz of disappointment echoes throughout the room.

'Thank you.' Karen beams as Caitlyn passes her the coveted prize. It's the first time I've seen Ben's mum show any warmth towards Caitlyn. She holds the scarf up first, then smooths it over her lap.

'Which means it's your turn to ask the next question.' I offer Karen the cards and Caitlyn chooses the next prize from the lucky dip – a make-up bag this time.

'Right, Caitlyn.' She turns the card over. 'No. I'm not asking that. I can't! He's my son, for God's sake. Not that you'd know that because obviously I don't look a day over forty.' She pats the side of her cheek with her hand.

'Pass it here.' Michaela plucks the card from her mother's hand. 'OK.' She grimaces but is laughing at the same time. 'How many dates would Ben have said you had before you did *the deed*?'

There's a stunned silence in the room, which then dissolves into laughter.

'I've never seen you go so red!' I laugh at Caitlyn.

'As if you've put that question in.' Caitlyn shakes her head. 'And I can't believe you got it, Karen. Sorry!'

Shelley reappears in the room. 'What's so funny?'

Annette gives her one of her looks. 'Well, if you'd care to join us instead of being on your phone all evening, perhaps you'd find out.'

'Well, answer the question then!' Adele says when there's a lull in the laughter. 'We're all dying to know.'

'Noooo! Ugh!' Lucy screws her face up in the same way her auntie did. She can't be blamed, really. After all, it's her dad we're laughing about.

'All right, all right... seven.' Caitlyn keeps her head in her hands.

'Wrong!' I wave the card in the air. 'The answer that Ben gave was, in fact... four!'

Everyone shrieks with laughter again – apart from Lucy, Karen and Michaela, who clearly aren't amused. Michaela seems to stifle a smile though.

'So who gets the prize?' I ask.

'I think I'd better give this one to Lucy. It's got some make-up in it too. It's a very good prize.' She passes it over. Lucy takes it without acknowledgement.

The next two questions are tamer. *What is your song? What would Ben say your worst habit is?* Caitlyn gets them both right and receives a purse and a shot, which she passes to Annette to do the honours with.

I give Shelley a cursory glance. She's barely put her phone down all evening and has been texting madly. Her expression keeps ranging from annoyed to smiling. I suspect she's got a new man on the go. Work doesn't make you smile like that.

'Mr and Mrs' is soon over with. Everyone refills their glasses apart from poor Shelley who has finally put her phone down and is sipping a glass of water. The next game is 'Pin the Appendage on the Man'. We have David Beckham's body with Ben's head superimposed. Everyone's laughing this time, even his mum, his sister and his daughter. Then, when Caitlyn leaves the room, saying she's off to the loo, we're all wearing 'Ben' masks when she returns. I got the photo from his Facebook page, then sent it away to have the masks made.

I get her to take a photograph. 'It looks very odd to see Ben's face everywhere. Speaking of which – I'd better give him a ring before I get sat down again. I won't be long.'

'Oh, lover boy... Ben... I'm missing you!' Two or three people yell after her. Adele and Mari are still very quiet. Maybe they'll join in more tomorrow after they've got to know one another. I'd have thought they would have loosened up, now that the drink is flowing. I should, as chief bridesmaid, probably be trying to bring them out of themselves more, but there's enough politics and undercurrents here to be going on with.

'He's not answering.' Caitlyn returns a few minutes later. 'He must be busy.'

'Dad's got that meeting in London tomorrow, hasn't he?' Lucy directs the question to her grandma, then looks at Michaela with a sly edge to her expression. 'That's the only reason I'm here. I'd have stayed with him otherwise.'

Charming. Luckily Caitlyn doesn't react. She folds her arms and I wonder what is going through her mind.

'Fancy ringing your bloke when you're away on your hen do.' Annette drains her Prosecco, a look of disdain etched across her thin face. She looks nothing like Caitlyn and Emma. She's as dark as they're fair – looking at her eyes, it's difficult to see where the brown stops and the black begins. She's very different to Caitlyn and Emma in personality too. 'He's probably living it up – enjoying the freedom.'

'What would you know?'

'Sisters, sisters,' I say in my most authoritative voice. 'This is a hen party. Let's leave the domestics. Anyway...' I'm trying to crack the tension I can see on their faces. 'We've got a lovely spa day to look forward to tomorrow, then a meal, and then we're off clubbing! It's going to be fabulous.' I say this with an enthusiasm I don't feel.

I watch as Shelley walks to the door. She really doesn't seem herself – maybe because she can't have a drink due to the antibiotics. It must be boring for her.

Karen is the first hen to retire. She yawns as she gets up and slides her feet into fluffy mule slippers. 'Well, that's me, ladies. I'll leave you youngsters to it. I might look young, but tonight I feel old and weary.' She is soon followed by Michaela. One by one the rest of the hens depart, eventually leaving me in the room with Lucy and Caitlyn. I wonder why Lucy hasn't followed her auntie and grandmother.

'Did you mean what you said before, Lucy?'

I'm taken aback by Caitlyn's hardened tone of voice.

Lucy looks up from her phone. 'About what?'

'About only coming because your dad's working? I'd rather you hadn't bothered coming, to be honest. Or at least you could have had the decency not to have told me the truth.'

'Like you have the decency to ever let me have some time on my own with him?'

'Then why don't you make the time? Both of you. Stop bloody blaming me for everything. You probably wouldn't spend any more time together even if I wasn't around.'

'You wouldn't be if I had my way.' Lucy mutters this low enough for Caitlyn not to hear, but I do. Caitlyn's attention has been diverted to the shadow in the doorway. She stands and marches over to it.

'What are you doing, just lurking there?'

Michaela strides past her. 'I wanted to listen to what you were saying to my niece. You've done nothing but bully her.'

'*Bully her?* What are you talking about?'

'What are you... twelve years older than her?' Michaela points at Caitlyn as she speaks. 'Why don't you act it?'

'Michaela, I was sticking up for myself.'

'And about time,' I butt in now.

'And what's it got to do with you?'

'I'm her friend and I've seen and heard quite enough of her being ganged up on by your family.'

'Well, I've heard quite enough of you ganging up against my niece whilst I've been standing in the doorway. You just waited until you got her on her own, didn't you, Caitlyn?'

'Of course not. I'm not cut from the same cloth as you lot.'

Michaela steps closer to Caitlyn. I'm ready to pounce if she moves one step closer. Especially with Caitlyn having been so compromised lately. 'You come across as being nicey-nicey, but we can all see right through you. And Ben's getting that way too.'

'Why don't you just go to bed. I can't do this right now. I don't want to talk to you. In fact, I wish you hadn't even come.' Caitlyn looks exhausted.

'Come on, Lucy. Let's go.' Michaela turns to walk away but then swings back around to face Caitlyn. 'Let me tell you something.'

Caitlyn is trembling, but she's holding her own. I don't need to intervene... yet. Let Michaela say what's she's got to say, then hopefully she'll bugger off.

'What?'

'Over my dead body are you going to marry my brother, have you got that? Over my dead body.'

. . .

'Oh, my bloody God.' Caitlyn sinks into her chair and drinks her wine straight down. I grab the bottle and cross the room to refill her glass.

'Aren't they awful? Even more reason not to marry into their family, if you ask me.'

'They shouldn't have come.' She drops her head into her hands. 'I knew they didn't much care for me, but I didn't realise they felt so strongly.'

'Come on. They've probably had too much to drink. They'll be apologising to you in the morning.'

'They won't.' I'm shocked by how quick and how definite her response is. 'And I wouldn't want to hear it, anyway.'

We sit quietly for a few moments, both, I think, taken aback by the altercation.

'Thanks, Jen. Thanks for organising this.' Her voice is downbeat as she gestures around the room, to the discarded party paraphernalia and empty bottles and glasses strewn all around. 'Even if it is turning into a disaster! You're an amazing friend. Never forget that.'

'You'll have to keep reminding me, so I don't! Anyway, you're very welcome. You've enjoyed *some* of it, haven't you?'

'Apart from what's just happened with Lucy and Michaela.' Her expression darkens. 'That came out of the blue, to be honest. We're a right mix here this weekend, aren't we?'

'I know what you mean.' I sip my wine. 'Your sister and Shelley haven't stopped texting all night and both have faces like a bag of spanners.'

'They're not as bad as Ben's family.' Caitlyn lowers her voice to a whisper. 'I've never been good enough for him in their eyes.'

'Adele and Mari don't look over the moon either.' Normally we'd dissolve into laughter, but Caitlyn looks more like she wants to dissolve into tears. 'Come on, you, at least me and Emma are celebrating with you.'

'Shame about the other bridesmaid.' She gathers up glasses.

'Well, Shelley doesn't seem too great, does she? Maybe whatever infection she's got is getting on top of her. Leave that. I'll sort it in the morning.'

'I'll just put these in the kitchen.'

I follow her in. 'You must have caught whatever she's got, Caitlyn. You've been on the quiet side today as well. Even before all this. What's up? You're feeling OK, aren't you?'

'I'm OK but... it's Ben.' She walks back into the lounge and sinks to a chair. 'I think he's going to call off the wedding.'

'Why would he do that?' I pull up a chair and sit facing her.

'I've been moaning at him. I'm sick of him working away all the time.' She twists her engagement ring. 'He's so distant when he comes home. I know I've been hard work lately – really needy whilst I've been ill. He says I depress him.'

If Ben was in front of me now, I think I'd lamp him. 'If you can't be needy when you're fighting cancer, when can you be?'

'He's seeing someone.' Her voice is flat.

'What makes you think that?' I look at her miserable face. 'Have you asked him outright?'

We're both drawn again to a shadow looming against the lounge wall. Someone seems to be listening. We both jump as Adele appears in the lounge doorway, clutching a picture frame.

'I heard voices.' She shuffles towards us in her slippers. 'I wanted to give you this, Caitlyn.' She gives me a look as if to say, *Shove off*.

'Oh, erm, thank you.' Caitlyn stands and takes the picture but with barely a glance at it, stands it against the wall.

'It's a collage of photos from when we were younger.' Adele points at it and runs her fingers through her mousy hair. 'Aren't you going to look at it?'

'It's lovely.' Caitlyn glances towards it. 'Thanks, Adele. I'll have a proper look at it soon.'

'Why not now? What's the matter, Caitlyn? You've barely managed two words towards me all evening. I might as well not have come.'

Oh God. Adele's going to cry. Can this evening get any worse?

'If you don't mind, Adele.' I can tell from her face that Caitlyn feels uncomfortable. 'Jen and I were just having a private chat about something before we go to bed.'

Adele is poised to sit down but springs back up again. 'Oh. Like that, is it?'

'Please don't take it the wrong way. I'm not being rude. I'm sorry.'

'Thanks a lot, Caitlyn. We've been friends for years.'

Caitlyn closes her eyes. 'I need to speak to Jen at the moment, that's all, Adele. It's important.'

Adele stands, hands on hips, her lip curled in anger. 'You've ignored me all evening and now you think it's OK to send me packing to my room, just because you want to speak to *her*.'

'I haven't ignored you.'

'I've got a name, and it isn't *her*.' I look beyond Adele and notice Mari looming large in the doorway. Great. Caitlyn was on the verge of getting things off her chest and now we've got these two to pacify.

'I heard all that.' Mari has a look of distaste on her face as she tightens the cord on her oversized fluffy dressing gown. 'We've come all this way to celebrate' – she draws air quotes as she says the word *celebrate* – 'with you, Caitlyn, and you think treating us, me and Adele, like this, is acceptable?' Mari stands beside Adele. 'You've shoved us in a room when we don't even know each other. After all I've done for you.'

'I can't do this right now.' Caitlyn looks at me, tears in her eyes, as if to say, *Do something*.

'Look. Both of you. This is ridiculous.' They're behaving like kids in a playground. 'We'll carry on our conversation in Caitlyn's room. You're right. Just because we're talking about something *private*, should not mean we can take over the living room.'

'No,' Caitlyn replies. 'I don't want to talk in my room. I'm fine in here.' She sips her drink.

I'm relieved that she's being firm about where she wants to be.

'Let's hope you'll be less ignorant tomorrow, Caitlyn.' Adele's eyes are full of tears and her fists are bunched up at her sides.

'At least you were invited,' Mari mutters to her. 'I was an afterthought.'

'Why do you both have to be like this? Grow up.' Caitlyn won't stick up for herself, so it's down to me to do it for her. I realise I've raised my voice. Any minute now, we'll have everyone else in here to see what's going on. Some party this is turning out to be.

'I'm sorry.' Caitlyn is fighting her tears now. 'If I've seemed quiet. I have a lot going on at the moment.'

'It's not quiet – it's rude. Come on.' Mari tucks a wisp of hair behind her ear and catches Adele's arm. 'I'm used to this sort of treatment from Caitlyn. She's all over me when she's lonely, but the minute Ben turns up, she drops me like a used rag. But don't you worry, Adele. What goes around, comes around.' She turns to Caitlyn then. 'Don't forget that, Caitlyn. You'll get what's coming to you.'

After they've flounced off, Caitlyn and I stare at each other.

I eventually break the silence. 'Bloody hell. Should I shout "next" into the hallway?' I let out a jagged breath.

'Don't.' She half laughs. 'My sister wouldn't need too much of an excuse to have a pop at me. I don't know what I've done so wrong. Isn't everybody supposed to be nice to you when it's your hen party?'

'Come here.' I pull her into a hug. 'It's them, not you.' Then I let her go and look her straight in the eye as I sit down again. 'Anyway... why would you think Ben's having an affair? Men sometimes find illness hard, but he stood by you when you were ill, didn't he?'

Tears roll down her face. 'He's been keeping up appearances.'

'You're getting married in three weeks. You need to sort this. Quickly.'

She looks thoughtful for a moment, as though wrestling with what she's going to say next. 'He actually told me yesterday that he wants to call things off.'

I walk over to the door and push it closed in case we get any more visitors. 'Oh, no. You're joking, aren't you – surely?' But her expression tells me she really isn't. 'He's probably just feeling nervous.'

'He's been distant for ages – it's not a new thing. And he's never around anymore. He hasn't been since I first got diagnosed. Why he actually got engaged to me in the first place – I don't know. Maybe he thought it was what he wanted at the time.'

'But that still doesn't mean he's having an affair. Look, I'm not sticking up for him, really I'm not. But I hate seeing you like this.'

'I know. I've had enough. It's killing me. He's so cagey all the time. Especially with his phone and laptop. And he's gone into the garden a couple of times lately to take phone calls.'

'That still means nothing. It could be something private – to do with work.'

'I know everything about that business. Enough of my money has gone into it.'

'Or he could be planning some kind of surprise for you.'

'Well, the only surprise I've had is that since I've started watching him, I've seen him go into and leave a few hotels several times in Leeds, when he's supposed to be working away.'

'Who with?'

'I haven't actually seen him with anyone, but the fact is that he's been staying in a fancy local hotel when he's telling me that he's in London.' She drops her head into her hands, and I can tell by the shake of her shoulders that she is crying. I bolt next to her and put my hand on her back.

'You're going to have to confront him, Caitlyn. Just ask him outright.'

'I don't need to. I heard him telling someone on the phone that they were like a drug to him.'

'Oh God. But I don't understand. Why would you marry someone if you seriously suspect they're having an affair? When you heard him saying that, you should have burst in and confronted him. Caitlyn, look at you – you're gorgeous.' Admittedly, her once-perfect figure has withered somewhat, and her usual peaches and cream complexion has faded to just cream, but she'll bounce back. She's not been in remission for long. 'Why would you even stay with someone, let alone marry them, when you're this unhappy?' I take hold of her hand. 'You can get through this. I'll help you.'

'But he can still be nice when he wants to be. I hang onto this when he's being awful. But he says I depress him and that being around me brings him down. I don't blame him.' She's staring at the floor as she speaks, her voice a monotone. 'I have been hard work lately.'

'Caitlyn. You've had cancer.' I see the weariness in her eyes. She's put a good front on up to now, but she can't hide things from me. 'What the hell's happened to you? Why are you putting up with being treated like this? I know you've not been the same since your mum died but—'

'It's nothing to do with my mum.' Caitlyn shakes her head. 'It's more since I've been ill. I guess I feel more vulnerable. I might as well tell you...' She pauses and sniffs. 'It gets worse. The woman he's been seeing is pregnant.'

At first I think I'm hearing things. 'How can you possibly go through with this wedding? You can't! And how do you know that?'

'His WhatsApp messages.'

'What on earth are you going to do? You've *got* to leave him.'

She shrugs. 'I've got the upper hand because he doesn't know that I know. We've reached a stalemate though. He wants to call things off, but I get on well with so many of his work contacts and his friends that he'd really lose face, and possibly lots more besides.'

'What do you mean?'

'Most of them know I've beaten cancer – I've had some lovely messages during it all. I haven't helped him as much with the business lately, but when I did, it was me who swung his biggest contracts. He's hanging on to things by a thread now, in a business sense as well as a personal one.' She grips my arm. 'Please don't repeat any of what I've told you, Jen. No one else knows a thing.'

'You don't need to say that to me. Of course I won't repeat it. But I think you should take charge and call things off yourself. You've got your whole life in front of you.'

'Have I?'

I look at her pinched and tired face. 'Surely what you've been through has taught you something about how short and how precious life is. I think you should talk to Ben, really talk to him, when you get back. Give him the chance to tell you the truth himself.'

'He won't even answer the phone to me.'

I drain my wine glass as I look at the friend I thought seemed happy and together, especially since going into remission. She's got to think twice before hurtling into this marriage. From what she's saying, it really sounds like Ben's only going through with it to save face and his livelihood. And Caitlyn is only going through with it because her self-esteem is on the floor and deep down she loves him.

'So how bad are things for him with his business?' I ask.

'Put it this way...' Caitlyn stands and sets about picking up the rest of the glasses. 'He's not far away from losing the lot. Things just aren't balancing.'

'Right, you. Time for bed.' I try to take one of the glasses from her, but she turns away. 'You look done in. We'll talk more in the morning.'

'Whatever happens,' she turns back towards me as I follow her to the door, 'I think you're an amazing friend. You've always been there for me and I really appreciate you.' She puts the glasses she's collected onto the coffee table and comes toward me with a hug. She feels like absolute skin and bone.

'I'm really worried about you, Caitlyn.' I feel hot tears prodding at my own eyes now. 'I'll help you sort this out, I promise.'

'I wish you could.' She tries to smile as she picks the glasses back up and they clink together. 'I'll take these through then I'll turn in. Thanks for everything.'

'What are friends for? See you in the morning. Make sure you get some sleep.'

FOUR

JEN

It *feels* late. I reach for my phone – it's nearly ten a.m. What a lazy lot we are – the apartment is still in silence. Having said that, the Prosecco and shots had been flowing. We'd had an alcohol-fuelled journey over from Leeds Bradford, the wine with the meal at the Italian and back to the flat. More alcohol.

I lay awake for a while last night, replaying all the crap with Lucy and Michaela, and then with Mari and Adele. Poor Caitlyn. Some evening it turned into. Then my thoughts had turned to the conversation I'd had with Caitlyn. The Caitlyn I used to know would not have stood for the treatment she's getting. It's as though the last year has put out the fire in her belly.

This bed is so comfy but I'm going to have to move soon. I don't want to get out of it, nor am I too fussed about jumping back into referee mode between everyone. I look across at Shelley whose head will be as clear as a bell after not drinking. I didn't envy her for it last night, but I do this morning. My head feels really foggy.

'Morning.' She turns over, as though she senses me looking at her. 'You came to bed late.'

'I don't think it was *that* late.' I place my phone back on the bedside table. 'I didn't wake you up, did I – you were well gone. I have to let my second in command get her beauty sleep.' Maybe I should warn her that there might not be a wedding for us to be bridesmaids at.

'No, I was awake when you came in.' She tilts her phone towards her face, and an expression which suggests whatever she wanted to see is showing on her screen. 'I was plugged into my relaxation track. I never sleep well in a strange bed.'

'I've been lying awake for half the night myself. I'm so tired this morning.' I stretch my arms towards the ceiling. 'It turned ugly after you left.'

'What do you mean?'

'First, Lucy and Michaela were having a go at Caitlyn, and then Mari and Adele started.'

'Why?' Shelley's eyes are large in her face already, but they widen even more.

'It's all so trivial it's not even worth getting into.'

'But I'm interested.' She sounds more interested in this than anything else since we set off.

'Well, with Mari and Adele it was *really* trivial. Both of them were feeling left out and sidelined by Caitlyn.'

'And?'

'With Lucy and Michaela, it was the usual. Jealousy over Ben.'

'Why would they be jealous?'

'You'd have to ask them that.'

'It sounds like they're all still asleep.' Shelley sits up and twists her dark hair into a knot on the top of her head. She looks immaculate, even though she has just woken up. 'What's the plan for today? I need to get out of this apartment.'

'The spa, of course. Caitlyn said going to a spa was a deal-breaker for her.'

'What time are we supposed to be there?'

'Not until this afternoon. Perhaps, as the bridesmaids, we should sort breakfast for everyone. They might all be in a better mood after a decent breakfast.' I swing my legs out of bed and rifle through my case for something to wear. 'We might have to nip out to the shop. Get some bacon. All we seemed to buy last night was crisps, wine and gin.'

'Well, Emma can help, can't she? Do her bridesmaiderly duties too.'

'Is there such a word?' I force a laugh, though really I don't feel at all like laughing. Shelley doesn't laugh – I realise that she actually seems to be in a similar mood to the one she was in last night.

'Perhaps Lucy should help instead of me.' Shelley stretches her painted toes out from beneath the duvet. 'And I'll stay in bed. She was first choice to be bridesmaid, wasn't she?'

'Only because she's Ben's daughter. She didn't want the job, so you got asked. Anyway, I've just told you – she was a right cow last night.'

'Still second choice. Story of my life.' She looks at her phone again.

'Ah, give over. You and Caitlyn have been friends for ever. I understand why she asked Lucy first. She's going to be her stepmum.' *Perhaps*, I stop myself from adding. I will not say anything to Shelley about what Caitlyn's told me. It doesn't feel like a good move.

Shelley tugs her dressing gown on and gathers her clothes. 'Is it OK if I use the bathroom first? I'm dying for a wee. Then I'll go to the shop – I could do with some fresh air, anyway. It's so stuffy in here.'

'Yeah, go for it – let's get this show on the road.' I point my feet into leggings and pull them up. 'I can't wait for Club Nassau this evening. It should be a laugh. I've got my leg warmers and fluorescent rah-rah skirt at the ready.' I tug them from my case and hold them up to show her. 'What are you wearing?'

'Dunno yet. I might have to go shopping.'

This weekend is turning into anything other than a laugh. There's such an atmosphere. Everyone is sniping at each other, and with Caitlyn admitting that the wedding might not even go ahead – well, I didn't know what to say. Thankfully, no one else appears to know anything either. From being a self-assured, vivacious girl, Caitlyn has been reduced to this whimpering wreck of a woman. As Shelley leaves the room, I sigh and lie back on my pillows, staring at the cracks in the ceiling and wondering what today will bring.

From what Caitlyn said last night, she's hanging on to a man who doesn't really want to marry her. Not only that, he's carrying on behind her back, and he's actually got the woman he's been seeing pregnant! It sounds as though he is still going to allow the wedding to go ahead, but only because of the damage it will do to his professional reputation if it doesn't. Personally, I think there's more to things than meet the eye. There's something else Caitlyn hasn't told me. I don't buy this *feeling vulnerable after her illness* either – if anything, it should have shown her how short life can be.

By the time I've finished in the bathroom, Shelley is standing near the front door with her coat on.

'You realise this door has been open all night, don't you?' She points at it.

'What, do you mean, open? It can't have been!'

'Well, unlocked. Were you and Caitlyn the last ones to go to bed?'

'Well yes, but – I'm certain I locked it. I'm meticulous about it at home so I wouldn't be any different here.' I glance into the lounge to make sure everything's as it was last night. 'Your handbag's in there, Shelley – don't you need your purse for the bacon?'

'I can use the app on my phone to pay. Anyway, there's no harm done.' She smiles for the first time today. 'Stop worrying about the door. You'd had a few shots and glasses of fizz. I won't tell the others that they could have been murdered in their beds.'

After she's gone, I set about tidying up the debris from last night. I hate getting up to a mess and a sink full of washing up. However, events took an unexpected turn, which was why I didn't follow any of my usual night-time routine. I can't believe the door has been unlocked all night – madness, in an area we don't even know. Though, I have to say that everyone we've encountered in Dublin so far has been welcoming and friendly – I can't imagine anyone wanting to get into our party apartment.

I soon hear stirrings from the other rooms. One by one the other hens turn up in the kitchen, making drinks and taking them into the lounge. 'The rest of you can finish tidying up,' I poke my head into the room and put on my most authoritative voice above the music channel that must be something that either Emma or Lucy has put on. I'm not exactly old but it's too much for me.

'Ugh. I feel rough.' Annette slides past me and flops into an armchair in the corner. 'I'm never drinking again.' She does look bad. To say she's a couple of years younger than Caitlyn, she definitely looks like the older of the two of them. I'm not sure why she's so jealous of her older sister though – it must definitely stem from childhood.

She wouldn't be jealous if she knew the truth of Caitlyn's predicament. Perhaps it might make Annette soften towards her. For a moment, I consider taking her into my confidence. Maybe I could do them a favour. But I stop myself. I'd better give it some thought first. Perhaps I should say something to Shelley and Emma though.

'I'll take charge of breakfast if someone wants to volunteer to help me.' I look around the room.

'I will.' Karen rises from her spot in the lounge.

For a moment, I'm taken aback. Caitlyn certainly hasn't painted Ben's mother as someone willing and helpful. Quite the opposite. Still, it might be a good opportunity to fish for more information on what Ben might or might not be up to.

Adele and Mari are the last to get up, looking brighter than they did last night. They've clearly formed an alliance and are getting on with each other.

'Morning.' I pass them on my way back to the kitchen.

'Morning.' Mari's voice is clipped and Adele walks straight past me. I'm obviously still public enemy number one for daring to have a private conversation with Caitlyn.

Shelley bursts through the door and thrusts a carrier bag at me. 'Sorry if I've been a while. I took a wrong turn on the way back.' She slides her coat off. 'What's up with them? They've got faces like smacked arses.'

'Don't ask.'

'Is Caitlyn up yet?' Karen follows me into the kitchen as Shelley follows Mari and Adele into the lounge. I'm glad I'm not in there. They're all very quiet. The ambience of the hen party weekend is even worse than it was last night.

'I haven't seen her this morning.' I slice the bacon packet open and begin laying rashers on the grill. 'Can you whip some scrambled eggs up please?' I pass Karen the box of eggs from the bag. 'She's probably exercising her bridal right to be a lady of leisure this morning. Plus, she'll need more rest – after being ill.'

'She's in remission now, isn't she? She seems pretty much back to normal to me. She might have gone for a walk.' Karen takes a bowl from the cupboard. 'Maybe clearing her head after all that drinking last night.'

'I don't think she had that much. She's trying to take it steady. I'll give her a shout.' I slide the laden pan beneath the grill. 'She can get herself sorted and dressed whilst we're cooking breakfast.' I call into the hallway, cupping my hand around my mouth. 'Caitlyn! Get up, you lazy sod. We're making some breakfast.' I look towards her closed door.

Nothing.

'She must have nipped out, like you say.' I slice the tomatoes. 'Do you want to sort the toast, Karen? We make a good team, don't we?'

'Just think – if things had turned out differently, you could have been my daughter-in-law, instead of Caitlyn.'

'That's all ancient history.' *No! I can't believe she's bringing this up.* 'Karen, it was years ago. I was still a teenager when I was seeing Ben.'

'I know. Don't worry. I won't say anything to anyone.'

'I only went out with him a few times.'

'Well, it must have been *something* for him to bring you to that wedding.' I'll never forget that. I was seventeen and knew his parents were going to be there, but I liked him so much that I went along with it.

'Like I said. It's all in the past.'

'Did you ever tell Caitlyn?'

'I would have done if it had been serious. But in the grand scheme of things, it wasn't.' I just want to change the subject. 'You and Caitlyn seem to get on well.' It's a question rather than a statement. I know it's not strictly true but I want to move on.

'Er, yes, I guess so.' Her voice is too highly pitched to be authentic. 'As long as Ben's happy, I'm happy.'

'Hopefully he'll be at home a bit more after they're married. I'm sure she'll want to keep helping him with the business.'

'What makes you say that – about him being at home more?' Karen turns her back on me and presses the button on the toaster. 'Has Caitlyn said something?'

'No, not at all. It's just whenever I ring or see her, Ben seems to be working away. Hopefully, they can spend some time together after the wedding. Especially after what they've just come through. With her illness, I mean.'

'His work commitments don't stop just because he gets married.' Karen folds a tea towel into quarters.

Karen very evidently has a downer on marriage. Apparently, when hers ended, Ben went into partnership with his dad in his clothing business and Michaela did what she's always done – so Caitlyn has said – nothing. Ben's dad eventually moved with his new family to the South of France and Caitlyn put everything her mum had left her into the pot. To help Ben buy his dad out completely.

I know that Michaela and Ben shared a flat before he moved in with Caitlyn. And as far as I know, she still lives there and she's on the business payroll, but does nothing more strenuous than getting her nails done and going away with her friends. As brother and sister, Michaela and Ben are close; she rings him constantly, another thing that grates on Caitlyn's nerves. She keeps saying, *When's Michaela going to grow up and take some responsibility for herself?*

'I expect you'll be looking forward to grandchildren after they get married?' I turn the bacon over. It's a bold question to ask, but its answer will give me a better indication of how Karen feels about Caitlyn, and how permanently she sees her being in her son's life. I want to see if she's any idea that there's already another grandchild on the way – though not from Caitlyn.

'You must be joking.' She takes four slices of bread from the toaster and inserts four more. 'I didn't want to be a grandmother. Not that I'd swap Lucy, of course.'

'Of course.' She obviously doesn't have a clue that Ben's going to be a dad again.

'Besides, Ben doesn't want any more kids.'

'Does Caitlyn know this?' We're on dodgy ground here, although Caitlyn's already told me that they have compromised her fertility from the treatment she's had. She had the option of harvesting some eggs, but at that point, she just wanted to get on with the treatment.

'You must have heard how Lucy's mother trapped Ben.' Karen purses her lips. For half past ten in the morning, she's impeccably made-up. 'Though obviously he adores Lucy, he's never forgiven her mum. What gives a woman the right to decide whether a man becomes a father?'

'I completely agree. It's women like that who give the rest of us a bad name.' This is the longest conversation Karen and I have ever had. I wonder if whoever he has been seeing has 'trapped' Ben into fatherhood again.

'Which is why I'm surprised he's getting married. He said he could never trust a woman again.'

I'm feeling as though I'm talking out of turn. After all, Caitlyn's not here to defend herself, so I decide to change the subject. 'We're getting deep here,' I laugh. 'Over the cooking of breakfast. Have you got your outfit sorted for the wedding yet?'

'I'll have something in my wardrobe, I expect.' She butters some toast. 'Or I'll nip out the weekend before and buy something.' She doesn't seem bothered. Not the typical mother of the groom.

'Is breakfast nearly ready, Grandma?' Lucy looks more like her seventeen years with her strawberry-blonde hair loose and a face free of make-up. She's a pretty girl and would be prettier still if she smiled more. She gives me her customary haughty stare.

Karen smiles at Lucy. 'It won't be long, love. Are you all right? You seem grumpy this morning?'

'I'm starving, that's all.'

'Was your room all right?' I say. She might try to ignore me after last night, but I will not let her. 'Did you sleep OK?'

'S'pose so.' She turns on her heel and heads back towards the lounge, making me wonder if it's about last night, or if she heard me and her grandma discussing her mother having 'trapped' her father.

I tilt the blinds in the kitchen so the sunlight streams in. It's one of those sparkly winter days which I love, although I can never get warm at this time of year. I shiver now, even though I'm stood in front of the grill. I remember what my grandma used to say – *It's like someone has walked over my grave.*

'Do you think it's cold in here?' I tug my cardigan from the hook on the back of the kitchen door.

'Cold? You're joking. Wait until you get to my age,' Karen says. 'You'll never be cold.'

'At least we've got the steam room and spa to look forward to this afternoon.' I pull the grill pan out.

I'm relieved to hear laughter and chatter coming from the lounge. I put so much effort into organising this weekend, and just want everyone to enjoy themselves. Especially Caitlyn. I'm sure, on some level, she knows what she's doing. Everything will work out as it's supposed to.

'Breakfast is served, ladies,' I call from the kitchen door. 'Form an orderly queue. Has Caitlyn come back yet?' I ask Michaela who is the first to appear, plate in hand, at the side of me. She's less frosty than last night – probably too hungover to keep up the animosity.

'Come back from where?'

'Her coat's not on the hook,' I say. 'And she wasn't in her room when I called her. I thought she must have gone out for a walk or something.'

'I hope not.' Shelley comes up behind Michaela. 'You know

what her sense of direction is like. She's never been to Dublin before.'

'You're one to talk.' I thrust a plate at Shelley. 'You got lost coming back from the shop.'

As everyone loads their plates up, I reach for my phone. Caitlyn's phone is switched off. 'I'll have a sandwich and then I'll look for her.'

'Has she definitely gone out?' Emma enters the kitchen. 'Has anyone checked her room?'

'Caitlyn!'

'She must have done. Her coat's not there.' I lay some bacon across a slice of bread.

'I don't think we should start breakfast without her.' Emma looks along the line of people waiting. 'It's *her* hen party.'

'Well I'm eating now.' Lucy pushes in front of Emma. 'If Caitlyn can't be arsed getting out of bed or coming back from wherever she's gone, then I'm not waiting.'

I wouldn't expect anything less from Lucy but decide not to react.

'Just make sure you save her some. She is the bride, after all. And she needs to keep her strength up.'

'There's no need to keep giving her special treatment.' Annette picks up a plate. 'My dad's just as bad with her, wrapping her in cotton wool. She's a big girl, and she's better now.'

'I'm glad you're not my sister.' I slam my knife down next to her. 'You're all heart. All I said was save her a bit.'

'We don't want to be eating too much, anyway.' Emma spoons some scrambled egg onto a slice of toast. 'Not if we're going into the spa.'

'I can't wait.' Michaela flicks the kettle switch. 'It might cure my hangover. It's ages since I've been to a spa. Does anyone want a brew?' I look at her. There doesn't seem to be a trace of what she said last night – *I'm going to do everything I can to stop the wedding.*

. . .

'What was that?' We all look at each other as a glass-shattering scream cuts into our bustle and echoes around the apartment. 'Oh my God!' As we all push each other out of the kitchen door, Adele runs from Caitlyn's room. She's as white as a sheet.

'What's the matter, Adele?' I lead the throng rushing towards her. 'Is Caitlyn in there?'

'She's... She's... I'm going to be sick.' Adele darts into the bathroom.

I step towards Caitlyn's door, blood pounding in my ears. I enter the room, which is still in relative darkness, apart from daylight bleeding around the edges of the blind. Shelley and I glance at each other then I walk forwards. Caitlyn is still in bed. Her coat is in a heap on the chair beside her.

'Caitlyn,' Shelley says softly.

I edge closer to her bed. Clothes are strewn all over the floor. Caitlyn's always been the same. Her room was always a tip when we were in our halls of residence. The ensuite door is ajar. It will be the same in there if I know Caitlyn. A mound of make-up and toiletries. I reach for her arm to shake her awake. I'm aware of Shelley right behind me. Caitlyn's arm is cold, wax-like. 'Caitlyn. Caitlyn! Open the blinds, someone!'

Emma is in the room now and dashes straight over to the window to do as instructed, then joins us at Caitlyn's bedside. Now, in the morning sun, there is no colour in Caitlyn's face – just a greying tinge and purply blotches. There are lines of dried blood at the side of her mouth which hangs open as though taking a last gasp.

'How?' Shelley's voice is a whisper. 'She's... She can't be. She's dead.'

FIVE

JEN

Emma's scream is something I'll never forget. She hurtles from the room and the others burst in. The wailing, yelling and weeping ricochets around the walls. I don't know how long it goes on for. *Oh my God, oh my God.* I can't take my eyes off her. I can't wail, yell or weep. All I can do is stare at the shape of her stretched out form beneath the duvet.

I lean against the wall to steady myself and a million questions march through my mind. I was only speaking to her a few hours ago.

Desperate questions echo around the others too. *How has this happened? How the hell can she be dead?*

Though really, the question is 'who?'

'Everybody out of here!' I need to take charge. I don't know how many of us are in here. I can't focus. I certainly can't count. And no one is listening to me.

The wailing doesn't stop. Everyone is touching her. I wonder if any of the neighbouring apartments can hear our commotion. Perhaps one of them has called the police by now. Or maybe one of our lot has.

'Everybody out!' I raise my voice, louder this time. 'Now!' The chaos of the room silences and everyone looks at me, stunned. 'This is a crime scene.' My voice no longer sounds like my own. 'All of us in here. When the police search this room, they'll say it could be any of us that has done this. Our DNA will be all over the place.'

I scan the distraught faces of our 'party'. Emma and Shelley stand at one side of Caitlyn's single bed with Adele and Karen at the other, their presence casting shadows over Caitlyn. Michaela and Lucy are at her feet and Mari is slumped into a crouch near the door. Annette has barely come into the room but stands, like the others, looking at me as though awaiting further instruction.

The words *It could be any of us that has done this* hang in the air. 'Into the lounge. NOW. We need to work out what to do next.'

'We need to ring the police. That's what we need to do next.' Mari hauls herself back to her feet.

"Let's all get out of here and then I'll ring for help.'

'Come here, sis.'

Emma replaces Caitlyn's limp hand back at the side of her and is the first to walk towards the door. She falls into the arms of Annette. After a few minutes, everyone else follows them from the room. It's like a bad dream. It is a bad dream. Any minute now, I'm going to wake from it.

I stare into the ashen face of my friend. It's abundantly clear from the blood and the pressure spots around her face that she hasn't passed away peacefully in her sleep. I can't take my eyes off her. I look at her hands; she only had a manicure the other day and had her nails painted pink. *Spring-like,* she had said. *After all, it'll be spring soon.*

I notice she isn't wearing her engagement ring, which isn't like her. Since Shelley helped Ben choose it, she's barely taken it off. He proposed whilst she was having treatment, so getting engaged gave her a massive lift. *God,* I think to myself. *We're going to have to break this to him.* Who knows how he will react? I remember again what Caitlyn was saying last night. I expect there will be a part of him relieved at not having to go through with the wedding. I hate myself for thinking that. I recall Michaela saying that he's away at a meeting this weekend. I wouldn't be the one who tells him, anyway, thank God.

Sobs and anguished voices continue to reverberate around the apartment. We're going to have to work out how to handle this. As I stride to the door, I can't believe how much my mind is twisting and turning. I look back at her. The police will see for themselves that there's no way she's just died in her sleep. They will know that someone in this apartment has killed her or had a hand in killing her.

The smell of bacon turns my stomach as I return to the kitchen. I try to swallow the rising bile, but the acid taste makes me retch. Before I know it, I'm heaving over the sink with nothing much to throw up apart from the coffee I've drunk. The force of retching makes my eyes water as I grip the edge of the sink. Then I realise I'm crying. Not just crying, but emitting raucous sobs like I've never experienced before, their force shaking my entire body. I feel the weight of hands on my shoulders and I'm turned around into the embrace of Emma. 'Come on.' She strokes my hair. 'Come in here with the rest of us. No one should be on their own.'

'I can't believe it,' I sob, making her shoulder wet. She smells of Caitlyn's perfume.

'None of us can.' Her voice is thick with sorrow.

'We all need to talk. Someone knows *something*.'

'She was in remission.' Emma wipes her own tears with her sleeve. 'She's been through so much in the last year. Who could do this to her?' Her voice changes then, to an almost strangled sound. 'What the hell am I going to say to our dad? It'll kill him too!'

I cast my eyes over the kitchen, remnants of uneaten breakfast strewn everywhere. My stomach heaves and for a moment I think I'm going to be sick again. I fill a pint glass with cold water and gulp it down. If water is going down me, then at least nothing can come up.

I'm astonished to see Lucy finishing a bacon sandwich as I walk across the lounge. She's obviously more heartless than I ever suspected. 'How can you eat at a time like this?'

'I wanted to settle my stomach down.' She rests her plate on her lap, no remorse evident. 'It was churning. Plus, I can't think straight when I'm hungry.'

'What's there to think about?' Mari says. 'That won't change anything.'

'Well, I certainly couldn't eat a thing after what's happened. I've just chucked my guts up.' I look around the room. 'Are we all here?' Only Michaela seems to be missing. She wasn't feeling too well either, but her illness is a self-inflicted hangover, rather than gut-wrenching grief.

'Michaela.' I call her name into the hallway, reminding me of a short time ago when I was calling *Caitlyn* into the same space.

Michaela enters the lounge after a few minutes. 'You called?' I'm struck by how *normal* she seems, to the point of cavalier.

'I'm just ringing the police,' I say to her. Taking my phone from my pocket, I press nine three times. I don't want to do this - somehow ringing the police makes it all the more real. But no one else is rushing to do it. 'I'd like to report a death.'

I go through the rigmarole of questions, as expected.

'Is she definitely not breathing? Can you check for a pulse?'

'She's definitely dead.' My voice is a whisper. 'She looks to have been dead for hours.

'A Gardaí unit will be on its way as soon as possible,' the operator tells me. 'If you could close off the room where she is and all stay exactly where you are until it arrives.'

'How long will it be?'

She hesitates. 'We have several staffing issues today so it could take a few minutes longer than we'd like but certainly within the next thirty minutes. In the meantime, no one is to leave the apartment, or touch anything.'

'Who put you in charge anyway?' The corners of Adele's mouth curl with distaste. I catch her eye and she looks away. She reaches along the wall for the picture she gave to Caitlyn last night. 'Look what I did for her.' She holds it aloft in front of Mari. 'She barely looked at it last night, but we used to be such good friends.'

'While we wait for the police,' I say. 'We can probably save a lot of messing about by finding out who knows what first. The way things are right now, they'll just arrest the lot of us. I, for one, do not want to be locked in a cell.'

'I was asleep,' says Karen. 'I don't know anything, so don't ask me.'

'You were telling me earlier that you don't sleep that great at the moment.' As I notice the expression on her face, I wonder if I've said the wrong thing. 'Because of the menopause,' I quickly add.

'Are you calling me a liar now?'

'Of course not – I didn't mean—'

'I didn't hear a thing either.' Michaela strides across the room and sits back in her seat. 'I was out like a light after all that Prosecco.'

Last night feels like such a long time ago. My thoughts turn back to the last time I saw Caitlyn, here in this room. Thank goodness I gave her a hug. Tears squeeze themselves from my eyes. From what she said, hugs have been scarce for her lately.

'What makes you so sure she died during the night?' Adele asks. 'It could have been this morning.'

'True.' Karen sips from a mug, her hair and make-up still perfect. 'Although she looks like she's been dead for a while. She was stone cold. Did you touch her?' She looks at Lucy.

'Ugh. No I didn't.' Lucy slides her plate under the chair. 'Seeing her was bad enough. It's a sight that will be in my head

THE BRIDAL PARTY

forever. Caitlyn's face, turning black.' She pulls a face. 'We'll have to get her moved soon or she'll rot. She'll have rigor mortis or whatever it's called.'

'Just shut up.' Annette's words are a hiss as we all stare at the girl who would have been Caitlyn's stepdaughter. 'You're probably happy that she's dead. At least you will have your precious daddy all to yourself again now. Anyway, didn't you go to school? It takes longer than that for someone to rot.'

'Come on now,' Karen says. 'Lucy's as much in shock as the rest of us.'

'Surely someone in here can shed light on how she died. There's no point in us all being interrogated when the police get here.' This situation, peculiarly, reminds me of a time when our whole class was held back after school until a particular person owned up for something.

'Who put you in charge?' Michaela's voice bears a trace of a sarcastic snarl. 'Just because you're *chief bridesmaid.*'

'Not any more.' Lucy smiles as the reality of the situation seemingly dawns on her. 'I should let my dad know what's happened.'

'Not yet.' Michaela rests her hand on Lucy's arm. 'He's got a really important meeting this morning. Like, *really* important. It's a make or break meeting. Leave it a bit longer.'

'Do you not think the death of his fiancée is more important right now?' Annette stands and walks to the window.

'No, really.' Karen speaks now. 'We'll have to let him know later. He's got a lot to lose if we disturb him.'

'More to lose than his fiancée?' Mari speaks with a confidence I've only just heard. 'I know he's an insensitive, selfish pillock, but...'

'That's my brother you're slagging off. Shut it.' Michaela glares at her, then looks out of the window. 'Well, there's no sign of any police. Which is a miracle after all the noise we were making.'

I take another gulp of water, feeling its chill slide towards my stomach. Images of Caitlyn's dead body swim back into my mind. They probably always will. I nip the skin on my hand, willing myself to wake up if this is a nasty dream that I'm having. I feel dizzy. Whilst I sit trying to compose myself, the conversation in the room increases. The weeping has subsided and has been replaced with a hum of low voices. I want to rip the balloons and streamers from the walls. God, if only we could turn the clock back twelve hours. To when we were *kind of* enjoying ourselves.

I force my presence back into the moment. 'Someone in this room must have some idea of what's happened to Caitlyn.' I sweep my gaze over the others. 'Why don't we go round, one-by-one and see what we can remember?'

'She's at it again.' Michaela shakes her head. 'The Gestapo.'

'I've already said I was asleep.' There's fury in Karen's face. 'I know nothing. I will not tell you again.'

'Same.' Michaela adds. 'So don't ask me again either.'

'It will be the police asking you all soon.' My voice is trembling. I don't think the enormity of what has happened has sunk in yet. 'If we get to the truth of things ourselves first, we could save ourselves from all being locked up all day – or all weekend.'

'I might have heard some noises.' Everyone looks at Lucy. 'During the night, I mean. But I'm not sure. I never sleep well when I'm away from home. I always hear noises.'

'What sort of noises?' Personally, I think she's attention-seeking. She's that age. And that sort of person. But obviously I don't say anything.

'I don't know. Creaks. Bangs. That sort of thing.'

'They could have been elsewhere in the building,' says Shelley. 'It's an old block and I think people are staying in the apartments below ours.'

'They are.' I rise from my chair and pace up and down at the edge of the room. I can't sit still. 'The police will no doubt want to question all the occupants of the other apartments too. To see if anyone heard or saw anything. What about you, Shelley? Although you were one of the first to bed.'

'I slept like a baby.' She sips from a glass of water. 'I wish I could tell you something that might help, but I can't. Anyway, how can we be sure that someone's actually done it to her? She could have just died in her sleep. She's been ill, hasn't she? And chemotherapy can put a strain on people's hearts.'

'Or there's that sudden death syndrome?' Mari picks up a piece of paper and starts fiddling with it. 'It doesn't just happen to babies, you know. Adults can suddenly die in their sleep too.'

'She hasn't died in her sleep.' I sit back in my seat. 'Didn't you see her face? The burst blood vessels. The trace of blood around her mouth. I think she's been suffocated. Maybe she's had something held over her face.'

'You should ask yourself what *you* know.' Sarcasm drips through Mari's words. 'You seem to know the most about it. "Maybe she's had something held over her face." That seems to suggest something to me.'

'And Jen was the last one to be seen with her last night as well.' Adele gives me a funny look.

'We were talking.' As if they're accusing *me* of anything. 'Does anyone mind if we open a window.' I nod towards Michaela who's nearest to it. It's the end of January but I feel as though I'm burning up in here.

'Yes, your highness.' I don't know why they're all ganging up on me. Caitlyn's gone. So it must be my turn.

'I was up and down all night.' Emma sounds calmer than ten minutes earlier. 'I'm like Lucy – I don't sleep well in strange places. I heard a bit of something on and off, but it sounded as though it was coming from a different apartment. I just can't believe my sister is dead.' She cries again.

'What did you think you heard, Emma?'

'Nothing much. Maybe voices – it could have been a TV though. And a bit of banging.'

'Mari. Adele.' I realise they have added nothing to our discussion so far. 'You were up late last night. You came in here.'

'Yes. We wanted to talk to Caitlyn and got told to do one.' Adele seems unable to disguise her dislike of me. 'After that, I was talking to Mari. And then I lay awake for a while. You upset me. I've been friends with Caitlyn far longer than you.' She points her finger. 'Yet, she wouldn't give me the crumbs off her table last night.'

'We had something we needed to discuss,' I reply. 'And it was private.'

'My sister doesn't keep any secrets from me,' Emma says in a tone I haven't heard before. 'She never has. So what were you talking about?'

'Just how she was feeling about getting married.'

'And what did she say?' Annette looks across the room at me.

'Hasn't she spoken to either of you?' I'm surprised at Annette's sudden interest. 'I thought you'd already know how she was feeling.'

'Well, we don't.' Emma shuffles her chair closer to Annette's as though showing their sisterly solidarity. 'So we're asking you to tell us.'

My voice exudes an evenness I don't feel. Especially in front of Karen, Michaela and Lucy. 'It was nothing major. Normal pre-wedding feelings. She was nervous. Scared.' Maybe I should tell them what I know, but I can't. Caitlyn swore me to secrecy. 'She was just hoping Ben felt as strongly as she did about their relationship.'

'Really?' Everyone turns to Annette, possibly taken aback by the element of surprise in her voice. She changes her tone then. 'She was worried about how Ben *felt*?'

I shrug. 'Yes.'

'When you were speaking to her last night, did you think she seemed depressed, Jen?' Annette looks down at her hands. 'Everyone's considering who could have done this to her, but I'm wondering if she's hurt *herself.*'

'It's impossible to hold something over your own face and smother yourself to death. Your fight or flight response would kick in before you could get that far.'

'I agree with Adele.' Michaela is looking at me, her mouth twisted with dislike. 'You *do* seem to know a lot about it all, Jen.'

'I know how the human body works, that's all.' I frown. 'I'm a physiotherapist, aren't I? Anyway, back to what I was asking you, Annette. About whether you heard anything untoward last night.'

'Not a thing,' Annette replies. 'I always sleep well. Clear conscience, me.'

She's speaking very flippantly for someone whose sister has just died. Like I said to her before, I'm incredibly relieved that she's not my sister. I'd rather be an only child than be related to her. Although, perhaps it hasn't sunk in yet. Grief is a strange thing. 'I'm only running us through what the police will soon be asking us.'

'Jen was just describing herself as a physiotherapist.' Michaela laughs. 'And now she's able to pre-empt how the police might handle this like a proper Miss Marple. Blimey, she's gifted.'

Lucy laughs too.

I stare at the floor. 'You can laugh at me all you want. I can take it. But the police questions will be far worse.'

SIX

JEN

It's bizarre, everyone is sitting in the same seats in a circle around the edge of the room, in the same places as they were last night. At odds with the mood in here is the pink hen-party paraphernalia.

There's a gaping empty chair in front of the fireplace and a half-drunk glass of wine from last night sits on the mantelpiece. So do all the prizes Caitlyn won when we were playing Mr and Mrs. I would give anything for it to be last night again. When what's happened finally kicks in to my psyche, I might fall apart. But right now, I'm numb.

'Do you think you should ring the police back and see if they are on their way?' Annette walks to the window. 'There's no sign of them.'

'Just because I'm Caitlyn's chief bridesmaid, doesn't mean someone else can't ring them. I don't want to be in charge here.'

'You *were* Caitlyn's chief bridesmaid.'

Everyone glares at Lucy who shrinks back into her chair. It's the second time she's said that. She is clearly enjoying the drama. I bite my tongue and swallow my rising temper.

'It was you,' Annette points at me, 'that chucked us all out of the bedroom when we found her. If that's not taking charge then I don't know what is.'

'The bedroom is a crime scene. All of us in there will have contaminated it.'

'There she goes again – PC Jen.'

I roll my head around in a circle, trying to lower my anxiety. My neck cracks with the tension. 'I'm not trying to be PC anyone. It's just that they'll be wanting to search the whole apartment, especially Caitlyn's room.'

'They're not searching through my bloody stuff.' Karen stands. 'I'm going to get it packed up before they get here.'

'Me too.' Michaela also gets to her feet and stretches. 'We can leave the rest of the apartment as it is, but maybe we should all pack up our personal things.'

'I need a drink.' Adele is leaning forward in her seat, looking as though she is trying to hug herself. She looks as stressed as I feel.

'I'm not sure if we should.' Though if I'm honest, I could do with a wine myself.

'I was the one who found her. It'll stay with me for the rest of my life. So if I want a drink, no one's going to stop me, right?' It's the most forceful Adele's been since we got here.

'The police might want to speak to you first.' I ignore the nasty edge to Adele's voice. I'm not coming down to her level. 'It's an image that will never leave any of us.'

'I really can't believe...' Emma wipes her cheeks with the back of her hand. 'That we're sat here, all calm, talking. Meanwhile, my sister is just metres away, dead. What the hell am I going to say to our dad? He'll probably never get over it.'

'Nothing for now.' Annette frowns at her sister and bundles her hair into a ponytail. 'We need to work out what's actually happened first.'

'Won't we all get arrested when the police get here?' Lucy asks. 'I'd better pack my stuff up too.'

'I'm not sure.' My only knowledge of this sort of thing is from reading books and watching crime dramas. It's unthinkable that we're living through one of our own.

Karen returns to the lounge. 'They'll cordon off this whole apartment.' She wraps the scarf she won last night around her neck. 'With our stuff in it unless we move it into the passage outside. They might split us up as well. I don't think we'll get arrested, but we'll all get questioned for sure. It could be a long day.'

'"It could be a long day."' I glare at Karen. 'Is that all you can say? Your son's fiancée is dead through there!'

She opens her mouth as if to retaliate, but then must think better of it.

'It's certainly going to be a very different day to the one we were expecting to have.' Annette stares at the carpet.

'Our sister's body is lying in the next room.' It's Emma's turn to snap. 'And you're going on about the sort of day we're going to have?'

'Us all falling out will not achieve a thing.' There's a calmness in Shelley's voice. 'Personally, like Jen suggested, I think we need to get to the truth *before* the police get here.' Her cheeks flush, probably because everyone is looking at her now. 'I don't think it's fair, us all being held because of the actions of one person.'

At last speaks a voice of reason. Shelley would be bottom of the list in terms of suspects in my mind though. Of course you can never know someone completely, but certainly, on the surface, she's as nice as Caitlyn. So slim and petite, I can't imagine she would have the strength to hurt someone, anyway.

I was in on the engagement ring plan, but it was Shelley who secretly helped Ben choose it and plan the proposal for Caitlyn.

At the time we were all focused on her getting into remission. Shelley loves all things 'wedding' anyway. She's not career driven, her ambition seems to be to get married and have kids. It's inconceivable she could have been involved in Caitlyn's death. *Caitlyn's death.* I can't believe I'm even thinking these words.

I watch Shelley for a few moments. She sits, head in hands, one of the few people not speaking to anyone else, clearly stunned by it all. The room is filled with a low hum of conversation. Lower because Michaela, Karen and Lucy are getting their things packed up.

Emma moves across the room and sits in Caitlyn's chair beside Shelley, taking her hand. I feel detached from everything as I watch my two fellow bridesmaids, comforting each other when really there is no comfort to be had. Emma would also be joint bottom of the list of suspects. With everyone else, perhaps there's a chance – there's a motive of sorts with all of them. I'm trying to sort it all out in my head before I speak to the police – maybe I can give them something to get started with. But really, I can't think straight – I'll just tell them what I know about Caitlyn's relationship with everyone here.

Emma adored her eldest sister. There's several years between them, and Emma has always followed Caitlyn around like a puppy. To the disgust of Annette at times. Emma has confided in me before that she sometimes feels torn between her two sisters who have always seemed to compete for her approval.

Annette has said nothing about not being asked to be a bridesmaid, but I'm sure it must rankle with her. I don't think Caitlyn even considered her for the job. Like she said earlier though, the shock of this news won't do their dad any good, he is already in poor health with his heart. He got worse after their mum died a few years ago. She was the lynchpin that held them all together. Caitlyn and Emma are the only ones who have remained close since she died. They both visit their dad regularly.

Emma, too, whilst we have been sorting bridesmaid dresses and all that, has privately voiced her concerns to me about Caitlyn's forthcoming marriage. 'She doesn't seem happy,' she said, when we went for our last fittings. 'They've apparently had a row, but Caitlyn won't tell me any more than that. They shouldn't be rowing literally weeks before they get married. She's over her illness and should buzz with happiness now – don't you think?'

'I know,' I had whispered back as we were waiting for Caitlyn to call us in for the final verdict on her dress. 'He's probably just being a typical man and scared of losing his freedom. And they have been through a lot as a couple, in a relatively short time.'

I know I've only got Caitlyn's version of whatever was going on between them – Ben would probably give a different outline of events. No one would have understood if he had called off the wedding. Especially so soon after her going into remission.

The only fault I've ever noticed in Caitlyn is her 'neediness'. We've spent increasing amounts of time together throughout her illness and in the run-up to the wedding, and she has been on the phone to me constantly. She sometimes had a way about her that caused me to feel guilty about being unavailable. Ever. But that's her only fault and I suppose we all have a vulnerable or dark side; however, some people's are more obvious than others. As with half the women in this apartment.

Michaela strides back into the room – she's followed Adele's example and has what could be a gin and tonic in her hand. I'm getting a drink too – it might calm me.

'Once the police get here, we probably won't be allowed to speak to each other again.' Shelley glances out of the window. 'We'll get taken off and be questioned. Separately.'

'And it might be all over the news,' Emma adds. 'We don't want our dad finding out yet. Not until he has to be told.'

'And we need to work out when to tell Ben.' Karen looks at

her watch. 'I think he'll still be in his meeting by now. I'm off to get one of those.'

I follow her into the kitchen. 'It doesn't feel quite right that we're pouring gin, does it?' I pull some glasses from the cupboard whilst she pulls the tonic bottle from the fridge. 'Something so normal, when things are far from that now.'

'I think we should do a big round of toast too.' She takes the butter from the fridge. 'Only Lucy has eaten anything. Once the police arrive, we've no idea when we'll next get some food.'

'You're right.' I scrape uneaten breakfast into the bin. 'I think I could just about stomach some toast.' I slide plates into the sink. 'So what do you make of all this?' I ask, without looking at her.

'Who knows what to make of it.' She stares into her glass. 'All I know is that she was larger than life last night, playing Mr and Mrs, and now she's dead. I agree with you though – those purple blotches on her face. There's no way she's passed away peacefully. There's going to be hell to pay when the police get involved. We'd better prepare ourselves and like you said, our DNA is all over the room from before. They'd better not accuse *me* of anything.'

'How do you think Ben will react?' I press more bread into the toaster.

She shrugs. 'He doesn't go in for big displays of emotion. I haven't seen him cry since he was little. He didn't even cry when his grandma died. And he adored her.'

'But he was upset when Caitlyn got diagnosed, wasn't he? And when she was struggling through her treatment?'

'If you ask me, that's what kept them together.' Michaela appears in the doorway with an empty glass. 'If they'd got married, I'm not sure how long it would have lasted.'

'Go easy on that.' Karen points at her glass.

'Yes, Mother.'

'What makes you say that?'

'What?'

'That you're not sure how long it would have lasted.' Poor Caitlyn. And I bet Michaela knows about whatever he's been up to. If she won't tell me, then maybe she'll tell the police. His affair could be the reason behind her death.

'It was obvious. He never even told me he loved her.' She drops ice into her glass with a clink. 'He never said he *didn't*, but he'd make comments like she was "good for his business", or "she'd do, for now". Hardly a good basis to get married, if you ask me.'

'How did you and Caitlyn get along?'

'We were OK, I guess. I felt sorry for her, going through cervical cancer. You wouldn't wish it on your worst enemy, would you? But all of us, Lucy and Mum too, always felt there was *something*, something that we couldn't put our finger on that wasn't quite right.' She fishes through a carrier bag, presumably for tonic water. 'Sorry – I shouldn't be saying all this to you. You're her best friend after all.'

'No, it's fine. I loved Caitlyn, but no one is perfect, are they?' I decide in that moment that Michaela is even less like Ben than Annette is like Emma and Caitlyn. 'So when are you going to let Ben know?'

'Soon. Hopefully. But I'll leave it until we know more about what's happened.'

I take toast out of the toaster and insert more bread.

'You must be dreading telling him.'

This is the most Michaela and I have spoken since we got here.

'He'll be like the rest of us. Shocked. He'll go through the motions of grief, but then he'll get on with his life. That's what he's like. Typical man.' She becomes more animated as she speaks about her brother. Caitlyn was right. She's definitely got him on the tallest of pedestals. And I can't help wondering why when she confesses, 'I once asked him how he'd react if I died. I'm his only sister and you know what his reply was?'

'No.' I have to keep the irritation out of my voice. I've noticed that Michaela always has to bring the conversation around to herself.

'Saddened. *Saddened*, I tell you!'

I'm amazed at her sudden friendliness towards me, but I don't want to talk about Michaela's relationship with Ben. I only want to know what's happened to Caitlyn. 'Who do you think has done this to her?'

She screws the lid off the gin bottle. 'That's for the police to decide. But there's been all kinds of sniping and jealousy going down.'

Karen gives me a strange look as she leans against the kitchen counter. 'Did Caitlyn ever say anything to you about my son and another woman?'

'Yes, but only last night.' I look from her to Michaela. 'Why haven't either of you mentioned this before?' I fold my arms and look at them both. One minute they're a pair of witches, the next they're OK. At least I know where I am with Lucy. She's just a witch through and through.

'It's not the sort of thing you blurt out in front of other people,' Karen continues. 'I think that's at the root of it all. I know he's my son, but he's always been the same. The grass is always greener. Anyway, I'll take this toast to the others.'

They leave me drinking my gin in the kitchen. I've never felt so weird. We've just stood, having a conversation, when as Emma pointed out, Caitlyn is lying metres away, her death still unexplained.

SEVEN

JEN

'Why don't you want your dad to know yet?' I sit by Annette and give her a plate. 'Get this down you. God knows why the police aren't here yet. The woman on the phone said they were short staffed but—'

'I'm surprised you *really* need to ask that – about my dad, I mean. It's something we need to tell him face to face. Not over the phone when there's no one with him.' She accepts a slice of toast. 'I can't imagine how I'm going to get this down me. I feel so sick.' She touches her skinny midriff with a pained expression.

'I think we all do.' I look around the room full of pale faces. We don't know how long she's been dead and we're no nearer to finding out what's happened. 'But we all need to eat something. We don't know what's going to come next.'

'It's giving me the willies thinking of a dead body in the next room.' Annette's ponytail wobbles as she shivers. 'I'd never seen one before today.'

'She's not any dead body. She's your sister.'

'She feared dying.' Annette raises her eyes towards mine. 'She said as much when she had cancer. You don't expect to stare death in the face at twenty-nine, do you?'

There's grief in her face now. It's the first time I've seen it. 'You must have been scared of losing her too.'

'Not really. I always felt she would be OK.'

'You're not very close, are you? As sisters, I mean?' It's a blunt question, but I'm feeling blunt.

Her expression darkens. 'I hope you're not suggesting—'

'I'm not suggesting anything. Just interested. Did you get on when you were younger?'

'I grew up in Caitlyn's shadow. She was the prettiest, the cleverest, the one that got the most attention. Definitely our mum's favourite. God – I can't believe I'm even talking about this. Not after what's happened.'

'But you're adults now. Why would it still matter?'

'Have *you* got brothers or sisters?'

'No. I've often wished I had. I often felt that Caitlyn was like a sister though. I knew her faults, but I still loved her.'

'We all revert to childhood behaviours when we get back together, it's a known fact. I remember covering it in psychology at school.' She nibbles at the edge of her toast. She looks exhausted.

Watching her makes me feel nauseous again. 'Someone has smothered her with a pillow in her sleep, Annette. The question is, who would want to do that, and why?'

'You want to know what I think?' Annette speaks slowly, but then swings her body around and looks at me squarely. 'What I *really* think?'

'No, but I get the impression that you're going to tell me.'

'I think it was *you*, Jen. I agree with Adele and Mari. You're the one getting off on all the drama.'

Every time she says the words *you're* or *you*, she wags a finger at me. 'You're the one going around, accusing everyone else. And I think your so-called dislike towards Ben that I've been hearing about was a smokescreen for something else.'

'What are you talking about?' I wonder then if she somehow

knows that I was seeing Ben when we were teenagers. It's something I never wanted Caitlyn to know about.

'What's up with you two?' At Lucy's words, the room falls silent.

'I was just saying how Jen, here, is being too quick to accuse other people in this room for being capable of smothering my sister to death.'

'Well someone knows something, Annette.' She really isn't a likeable person at all. No wonder she wasn't her parents' favourite.

'You need to take that finger and point it at yourself, Jen.' Adele's voice is full of disdain. 'You were having a pretty full-on conversation about something last night. Maybe you put her out of her misery.'

'You were the one with the grievance with her last night – not me.' Maybe I shouldn't be saying this but she's quick enough to be firing her nasty accusations at me.

'What are you saying?' She stands and walks towards me. For a moment, I think she's going to hit me. I rise from my chair and we face each other. 'Look, I'm sorry, Adele, but you've had a face like the back of a bus since we got here.'

'You and Caitlyn were bloody horrible to Adele last night,' Mari says, her overweight cheeks wobbling with emotion. She's wearing the same clothes as yesterday. I'm not normally this bitchy, but I'm sick of them all ganging up on me. She casts her gaze around the room. 'I'm telling the truth. Adele came back in here for a chat and to give Caitlyn a gift and was literally told to do one.'

'At least you had each other for your pity party when you went back to your room,' Annette snaps. 'Anyway, Mari, according to Caitlyn, you made no secret of the fact that you couldn't stand Ben, and thought her getting married was a mistake. I don't even know what you're doing here.'

Everything is coming out now. This is why I usually prefer

the company of men. Women are such bitches when thrown together. The company of other women, especially lots of them like this, definitely brings out the worst in some people.

'That's not what we're discussing here,' I say. 'What we *are* discussing is who has enough of a grievance against Caitlyn to go into her room whilst she slept and suffocate her.' None of it makes sense.

'The problem is,' says Annette, 'there'll be DNA from all of us in that room. How are the police ever going to prove who it was?'

I tell them I'm going to the loo but instead head towards Caitlyn's room. Her blonde hair is fanned around her pillow and she looks even more dead than she did when I first saw her. I lift her hand. Her mouth is parted as though she's trying to tell me something.

'What is it, Caitlyn?' I whisper in the quiet of the room. Voices rumble from the lounge. They're probably still talking about me. 'If only you could tell me what you know.' I take a jagged breath in and close my eyes against the tears that are stabbing behind them.

As the sirens approach, I head back to the lounge to join the others. I don't tell anyone I've been looking at Caitlyn. I just wanted another moment with her before it all kicks off. Like I said to Michaela, she was almost like a sister to me. As the intercom sounds, everyone is leaning over each other, looking out of the window.

EIGHT

JEN

I open the door to two uniformed police officers.

'I'm Garda Gareth Hughes,' the oldest-looking of the two announces, 'and this is my colleague, Garda Daniel Marchant.'

'We've received a report of a sudden death.' The baby-faced officer peers beyond me into the hallway of our apartment. 'Do you live here?'

'No, we're just here for the weekend. For my friend's hen party.' I lower my voice, hardly believing I am going to say what I'm about to say. 'My friend Caitlyn. Caitlyn Nicholson. We've found her body.'

The others are craning their heads around the doorway of the lounge. 'Where is she?' Marchant ducks under the door frame as he enters the hallway.

I gesture to the bedroom.

'Are you the caller who reported this a short time ago?'

'Yes.' I want to tell them that they took their time getting here but quickly decide against it.

As the two officers head towards Caitlyn's room, Hughes orders the rest of our group back into the lounge. They pause before entering. I watch as one passes gloves to the other. The sound of rubber stretching over skin has always made me cringe.

They don't tell me I've got to wait in the lounge as well, so I hang around. I don't know what to do with myself anyway, and I'd prefer not to be around the others. I'm sick of the lot of them. Other than Emma and Shelley, hopefully I'll never have to see any of them again.

The police will probably need someone to direct their questions to. I linger in the hallway as they circle Caitlyn's bed, like opponents in a boxing ring. Their voices are so low that I can't catch what they're saying as they study her. Eventually Hughes lifts Caitlyn's arm, as though checking for a pulse. Anyone can see that she's dead. Marchant inspects the pillow on the floor beside the bed. He then walks over to the door and closes it. For a moment, I'm unsure what to do. Go back with the others or hover around outside. I can hear the voice of one officer inside the room.

After a few moments, the door swings open. 'We've sent for our forensics services and more senior officers.' Marchant stands before me in the hallway. 'She is definitely deceased.'

I could have told you that myself, I stop myself from saying.

'When did you find her?' Hughes pulls a notebook from his top pocket.

'It's going on for an hour.' My voice is wobbly in the silence of the hallway. There's no sound from the lounge now. They'll be waiting to see what comes next.

'And has anybody any idea of what's happened here?' Marchant asks in a gentler tone to that of his colleague.

'No one here is admitting to knowing anything.'

'Leave the detective work to us from now on, do you understand?' I really don't like this Hughes one. He's looking at me as though I'm something he's stepped in.

. . .

As I go to fill a glass of water, I hear new voices echoing from the hallway.

'This is the lady who called us.' Hughes points at me as I emerge from the kitchen.

'I'm Inspector Tim Retford,' a plain clothes officer informs me, 'and this is my colleague Sergeant David Whinstable. We'll have to speak to everyone separately. How many people are here in total?'

'There were ten of us, including Caitlyn.'

'So nine now?' Inspector Retford barks the words at me.

'We can't take nine women to the station, sir.' Sergeant Whinstable shakes his head and looks thoughtful. 'No way. With the protest and the football match all happening today, we're stretched as it is. They might all have to be taken to different stations.'

Inspector Retford is silent for a few moments, as though thinking it through. 'I'd like to keep them together at this stage.'

He refers to us like we're animals in a zoo and seems to have overlooked the fact that I'm standing here, listening to his deliberations.

He continues. 'We might have to conduct the interviews here if we can get a quiet space. We'll need at least another unit though. A couple of uniformed officers to man the cordons. If you could both stay here?' He gestures to Hughes and Marchant.

'Sir,' one of them says.

'And the forensics team, of course.'

I stand awkwardly, still wondering if I'm even supposed to be here. Then Inspector Retford turns to me.

'Who owns this property?'

'The landlord's details are just there.' I point to a notice next to the door where the landlord's number heads the list of 'useful numbers'.

'I'll get in touch, sir.' Sergeant Whinstable moves towards the notice. 'Are we asking for another apartment to move everyone into?' The round-faced sergeant is definitely more approachable than the miserable inspector, and if it's a choice of which one of them I have to speak with, Retford wouldn't be my choice. The difference in their size makes them look like Laurel and Hardy.

'We'll have to. Sort that first and we'll take it from there. Right.' Inspector Retford turns his attention back to me. 'I need to get some details. Firstly, of the deceased.'

The deceased. Oh my God. He's talking about Caitlyn. My stomach churns again.

'Her full name, please?'

'Caitlyn Elizabeth Nicholson.'

'Do you know her date of birth?'

'Erm. She's twenty-nine.' I reel it off.

He then takes her address and the names of everyone in our party, reiterating the need to speak to everyone in turn. Throughout our conversation, his expression is grim and unyielding. I guess that's his job. He'd have certainly made a good traffic warden.

'The landlord's on his way, sir.' Sergeant Whinstable tucks his phone into his pocket. 'He says we can move to the opposite apartment.'

'Give us a minute please, will you?' The inspector looks at me, then jerks his head towards the lounge door. 'Wait with the rest of your group. We'll be there in a moment to tell you what will happen next.'

'What's going on?' Michaela hisses at me as I take the seat in the lounge nearest the door.

'We're getting moved out of here.'

'Where to?' Eight expectant pairs of eyes look at me.

'To another apartment, I think.' My attention is diverted to the door as I notice Inspector Retford opening and closing doors and looking in all the rooms. I can hear the low voice of the other officer, presumably on the phone again.

'I need the loo.' Lucy stands, youthful uncertainty in her expression. 'Am I allowed?'

'Well, they can hardly stop you.' Michaela cocks her head in the direction of the door. 'Go on.'

Not a word passes between us for a few minutes as we sit, looking at one another, waiting.

Finally, the two officers enter the lounge. Lucy slips around the side of them and retakes her seat.

'Right, everyone. We're going to move you into another apartment. The longer you're in here, the more contamination of evidence is likely.' Inspector Retford looks from me to the cases which have been piled up in the corner. 'You are to leave all your personal possessions in here until the forensic investigation has taken place.' He shakes his head. 'You shouldn't have moved *anything*, let alone packed your things.'

'But I need my stuff.' Lucy sounds like a petulant child. She might as well stick her pet lip out.

'An unexplained death has taken place in this apartment.' It's Lucy's turn to receive Inspector Retford's hostile stare. 'We need to go through *everything* and that includes your mobile phones please.'

'Why?' Annette wraps her fingers around hers in an almost protective gesture.

Good luck with prising that off her, I think to myself.

'My colleague here' – he gestures to Sergeant Whinstable without answering Annette's question – 'will come around you, one by one, for your mobile phones and their passwords. He will then seal your phone in an evidence bag. You must then make your way into the flat opposite,' he points as he speaks, 'and take a seat in the lounge there. Leave the rest of your belongings here, whether or not you have packed them away. We'll then let you know what will happen next.'

'What happens if we *don't* give up our phones?' Lucy again.

She's got more guts than I've given her credit for. 'Or our passwords?'

'You would be formally cautioned and taken to the station,' Inspector Retford begins. 'Our forensic team will still be able to access your device although not only would it take longer to return them to you, there is also the risk of damage being caused.'

'Also,' Sergeant Whinstable begins, 'Because we've got staff issues today, you'd likely be in for a long wait before being interviewed. It is in your interest to let us look at the phones all together and this can take place whilst we speak to you all. It's your choice.'

I look at Lucy, wondering whether she will argue this further. Personally, I would rather get the whole thing over and done with here than be stuck for hours at a police station. They would probably put us in a cell too. No thank you.

'There's another unit on the way, sir.' Sergeant Whinstable starts with Shelley as he makes his way around our group, taking our phones. She doesn't look well at all. I wonder if she's remembered to take her antibiotic. The infection she's got must be getting on top of her. As well as what's happened. Then he moves to me.

I'm the first to leave the room. I pass Caitlyn's door, which is now closed. I shudder when I think of how she looks on the other side. The sight of her lifeless body is something that will live on in my head forever. I walk towards the foyer outside our apartment where a man with a bunch of keys points to a door. He must be the landlord.

'The lounge is at the end of the hallway if you'd like to wait in there.' A uniformed officer, standing beside him, waves his hand towards the open door.

I'm gradually joined by the others. Lucy is clearly very disgruntled at having to give up her phone.

'Someone needs to let Ben know what's happened.' Shelley looks pointedly at Michaela.

'Well, we've no way now of telling anyone anything,' I say.

'*We* need to be the ones to tell him.' Michaela nods in the direction of Karen and Lucy. 'His family. As soon as we know more of what's happened.'

'He's got a right to know *now*.' Shelley's voice rises a notch.

'Are we talking about the fiancé of the deceased here?' Inspector Retford appears in the doorway. We've already got his contact details from your friend here and will inform him shortly. Is there anyone else who needs to know?'

'Our dad.' Emma gestures towards Annette, fresh tears appearing to well up. 'We're Caitlyn's sisters. But he can't be told over the phone. He's got a heart condition.'

'The shock would kill him.' Annette shifts her chair towards her sister and hooks an arm around her shoulder. It's the first time I've ever seen any affection between them. 'It's not even sunk in with us yet.'

From the radios in the hallway, it sounds like more officers have arrived. The apartment is exactly like the one we have just vacated apart from it is back to front and not decked out with hen party balloons and banners. The blinds have got the same ghastly leaf pattern. I feel numb. This time, twenty-four hours ago, we were at Leeds Bradford airport.

'My colleagues are just setting up two of the rooms to speak to each of you,' Sergeant Whinstable tells us.

'Are we being arrested?' Lucy's voice sounds almost childlike. It's a fair question though.

'At this stage, you're helping us with our enquiries; we will not be making arrests until you've all been spoken to.' He appears to look closer at her then. 'You will be interviewed under caution. How old are you?'

'Seventeen,' Lucy replies. Without her big hair and make-up, she looks younger today than her seventeen years.

'In that case, you'll be required to have an appropriate adult sitting in with you,' Sergeant Whinstable tells her.

'I've got my grandma and my auntie here.' Lucy gestures to Karen and Michaela.

'I'll come in with you.' Karen reaches across and rests her hand on Lucy's shoulder.

'We'll start with you then.' He nods at Lucy.

Inspector Retford clears his throat. 'If you could all listen, please. Like I just said, we're setting up two rooms.' He casts his gaze over us all. 'We're moving beds out into the largest room, and the two smaller rooms are being set up with table and chairs. No one is under arrest at this stage, but as mentioned, we will interview you under caution.' He glares at Lucy who is whispering something to Michaela. They look up like naughty schoolgirls caught talking in class.

'We would normally conduct these enquiries at the station but our cell capacity is severely compromised today, therefore we have decided to record our conversations here, using portable digital recorders. In each case, two officers will be present – one asking questions and the other taking notes.'

'What about Caitlyn? Will she be moved?'

'The forensics team has just arrived.' Sergeant Whinstable looks towards the door, then back to us. 'Hopefully their investigations can be concluded in the time it takes for us to speak to all of you, and then we will have more idea of how things will proceed. Whilst these interviews are taking place, Garda Sellars will remain just outside in the hallway.' He gestures towards a weaselly-looking man who looks as though he's barely left school.

'Why?'

'He will be available should any of you have questions. He's also there to prevent any of you re-entering the scene of the investigation.' He then directs Hughes and Marchant to where he wants them. One in the passageway between the two apartments and one at the main entrance downstairs.

'What if we need to eat or drink?' Lucy again. She must be getting on their nerves. She is certainly getting on mine.

'You can't go back into your original apartment, but we will try to get this done as quickly as possible.'

'Do we need a solicitor?' Adele speaks now. Michaela sniggers, but again, it's a perfectly valid question.

'I was just coming to that,' Inspector Retford begins. 'You are not, at this point, being detained. You are free to leave if you wish. However, it may be necessary, if you were to take that course of action, to formally arrest you as this would be seen as perverting the course of justice. We do need to speak to *all* of you. If anyone wishes to have a solicitor present, let us know now; though, of course, we would then have to wait for their arrival.'

'Can we just get on with it?' Mari looks on the verge of tears now.

'Right, well, if you could all be thinking whether you would like to access independent legal advice at this stage. We will check this again at the start of each interview. Does anybody have any further questions?'

A surprising hush falls over us.

'If we could start with the lady who found Caitlyn, please?'

Adele stands, looking even more anxious than usual.

'It'll be fine,' Mari mouths at her.

'If you'd like to follow my colleagues into the room on the left. It's ready for you now. And if you...' Sergeant Whinstable points at Lucy, 'would like to follow myself and Inspector Hobbs...' he gestures to another, much younger, female officer who has just entered the lounge, 'to the room we've set up on the right.'

'I said it was going to be a hell of a day.' Karen rises from her seat and follows Lucy towards the door.

NINE

ADELE

I follow the officer into a room. As we enter, a policewoman is already sitting at a table. The room is decorated exactly like the bedroom I shared with Mari last night, except there are no beds and a table has been brought in, presumably from the kitchen. The policewoman gestures for me to sit. I've never been interviewed by the police before, and I can feel my heart thudding inside my chest.

'Can I take your name, please?' Her pen is poised over a notebook.

'Adele Cater.' My voice is echoey in the large room. Inspector Retford sits next to the woman. He reminds me of an uncle I used to be terrified of. It's not only the pointed nose, it's the booming voice. I wonder what questions they're going to ask me.

'Thank you. Right, I'm going to start the recording. If you're not aware, we have to record everything that is said between us.' She presses a button. 'OK, Adele. I'm going to begin by reading you your rights – you do not have to say anything, but it may harm your defence if you do not mention, when questioned, something which you later rely on in court. Anything you do say may be given in evidence.'

'I thought we weren't being arrested.' If my heart rate gets any faster, I'll be having a heart attack.

'You're not. You're being interviewed under caution, so you are free to leave at any time. You can also stop the interview at any point and request the attendance of a solicitor.'

'I'll just get on with it if you don't mind. I don't want to wait for a solicitor.' I stare at the sky through the window. We would have been at the spa by now. I've never been to a spa with Caitlyn. Being around these glamorous women this weekend has made me realise I've got to start making an effort with myself.

'Adele Cater. Is that your full name?'

'Adele Louise Cater.'

'If you could speak up, please. What's your date of birth and address?'

My mother always used to accuse me of mumbling. 'I'm the same age as Caitlyn.' I give them my date of birth. 'Flat Two, Main Street, Bramwell, Leeds.'

'Thank you. My name is Sergeant Polly Arthington and you've already met my colleague, Inspector Tim Retford. He will remain present as I conduct this interview.'

'Yes.'

'Do you understand why we're questioning you?'

'Yes, I do.'

'Adele. Is it correct that it was you that found the body of your friend Caitlyn Elizabeth Nicholson, earlier this morning?'

'Yes. I'll never get it out of my head.' It's true. I'm sure that every time I close my eyes, I'll see her, lying there.

'And what time was this?'

Without my phone, I have no idea what time it is now. 'A couple of hours ago, I think.'

Sergeant Arthington looks at her watch. 'So, around ten thirty-five this morning?'

'About then. Yes. Maybe slightly later. I've lost all track of time today.'

'And did you know she was dead straight away? As soon as you saw her?'

'Yes, I think so. I mean, she was a strange colour and there was blood on her face and her eyes were glassy-looking. I thought of giving her CPR, but obviously there wasn't any point.'

'It must have been a shock for you. How did you think she had died at that point?'

'I didn't really think about it. I was just terrified. And shocked. I haven't seen a dead person before.'

'So what did you do?'

'I just screamed and everyone else came running in. It was awful.'

'How long have you known Caitlyn?'

'Since we were eleven. We went through high school as friends together.' I think back to the days of making our own school skirts and wearing braces on our teeth. Caitlyn was one of the most popular girls at school – especially with the boys. I was so plain and used to wonder if she hung around with me to make herself look good. But I knew she was truly grateful to me when I'd looked after her on her first day. She'd started six months after the rest of us and had a nosebleed. Everyone just stared at her as though she was an alien, and were jumping away, shouting 'ugh.' She'd been really embarrassed, and I'd helped her mop herself up and taken her to first aid.

Some other friends she'd made were weird though. There was the group of bitches in school who were nice to me in front of Caitlyn and awful if I was on my own. I was terrified of them. Once, when Caitlyn was away on holiday, they'd waited for me at the school gates.

Then there was the odd girl with a short fringe who seemed to pay Caitlyn to do her homework, and also an older guy in her street. Apparently, he'd done bad things. But she seemed to adore him. She was like that – always on the side of the underdog. At least, she used to be. She's changed.

Caitlyn stuck by me right through high school, so it had been a huge wrench when we'd gone our separate ways at sixteen. I got a boring job with a boring company, whilst she did A levels and went to uni. She seemed to have a ball, whereas I was stuck in a customer services department, hiring out workwear and janitorial equipment. I'd needed a job, any job, after Mum died. Caitlyn was cool and blossomed into someone everyone wanted to date, whereas I stayed small, uninteresting and mousy.

'Are you and Caitlyn still as close as adults as you were as school friends?'

Sergeant Arthington's question brings me back into this chilly room, where I'm being blinded by the rays of the low winter sun bouncing from the mirror straight into my eyes. 'Not quite. We saw little of each other when I left school. But we keep in touch by messaging and on social media.'

A night out I had with her and Shelley floods into my mind. It was Caitlyn's eighteenth birthday, and I soon realised she had invited me out of pity and obligation, rather than her wanting my company.

'Adele, this is my friend Shelley, from college.' Caitlyn's eyes had shone as she introduced us.

She had really changed in the year since I'd last seen her. Her hair was cut above her shoulders, she had a new way of dressing and a different air about her.

'Shelley, this is Adele, a girl I knew at school.' The lack of the word *friend* stung and immediately made me go into myself.

I spent all evening listening to their in-jokes about college and watched as they made eyes at some boys on the next table.

'So what A levels did you say you were doing, Shelley?'

She didn't answer my boring question but hissed, 'They're coming over, mine's the dark-haired one.'

They had giggled as the two boys sat down. It was clear I was surplus to requirements. I watched as they took selfies with them and befriended them on Facebook. I didn't have a smartphone at the time.

'Let's go to The Dark Room,' one boy suggested. 'You've got ID, haven't you?'

'Of course,' Shelley replied. 'Great idea. I do fancy a club. What about you, Caitlyn?'

'As long as someone will dance with me.' She peered at the blond one from behind her fringe.

'You won't be able to come with us, Adele.' Shelley looked me up and down. 'They don't allow jeans and trainers.'

I was secretly glad, although then peeved that Caitlyn didn't seem bothered about making sure I got home OK, nor did she check afterwards that I had. They simply parted company with me as we left the pub. They went towards The Dark Room, whilst I headed for the taxi rank feeling as insignificant as it is possible to feel.

'And what about lately?' The voice of Sergeant Arthington slices into my miserable memories.

'We've obviously stayed friends but have become really different people. Caitlyn seems to prefer people like Jen nowadays.'

Inspector Retford must notice that I spit Jen's name out as though it's something nasty in my mouth. I didn't mean to. 'Do you not like Jen?' He raises an eyebrow.

'Not especially. But I don't really know her enough to make a proper judgement, to be honest.'

I got invited out again for Caitlyn's twenty-first, which both Shelley and Jen were attending, so that time I made my excuses. Besides, I was expecting Louisa.

'But you know Jen enough, by the sounds of it.'

'Enough for what?'

'To decide you don't like her. Why is that?'

'Look, it'll sound petty, but I couldn't believe it when Caitlyn asked Jen to be her chief bridesmaid. They've only known each other since the start of university. I've known her since we were eleven. We've been through thick and thin together.'

'Such as?'

'Her mum dying, my mum dying, me getting bullied, her endless nosebleeds at school, boy trouble, friend trouble, you know – teenage stuff.'

I don't add that I couldn't bring myself to speak to Caitlyn for a couple of months after I found out that she wasn't going to ask me to be her bridesmaid. I thought she might even have asked Louisa to be her flower girl – that would have been wonderful and, in some ways, I would have preferred Louisa to be asked over me, but in the end, neither of us were.

It was only when I found out she had cervical cancer that I got back in touch with her. When we met up, she didn't even mention that we'd lost touch for ages. She probably hadn't even noticed – too busy with all her cooler friends. She looked terrible when I saw her, but still ten times better than me. I'm small and wiry with short hair – in fact, I've been told I look like a boy. Now we're older, I'm more aware of how much I'm not in Caitlyn's league. And coming here on this hen party has really zapped my confidence. Not only have they forced me into a room with fat, bitchy Mari, I feel like shit amongst everyone else. With their expensive smartphones, handbags and made-up faces, I feel even more shabby and plain than usual. I glance down at my jeans and trainers.

'When did you last see Caitlyn? Before you found her this morning, I mean?'

'Last night. We were all together – all evening.' I think back. My cheeks had been aching from forcing a smile for so long.

'What were you doing?'

'Playing hen party games. Drinking. Having a laugh.' I don't tell her that it wasn't a laugh at all. There was an undercurrent of animosity, and Caitlyn hardly spoke to me. Nobody did really.

'Until what time?'

'Um, around eleven, I think.'

'That's quite early for a hen party.' I look at Sergeant Arthington's ring finger. 'Did everyone go to bed at the same time?' She's married, so she would probably know about hen parties. Louisa's dad didn't want to marry me and didn't even want to know when I was pregnant. It had been a one-off between us and he had blamed drink. But I've forced him into a corner with the Child Support Agency. Made him pay. But I can't force him to see Louisa. To be honest, she's better off without him.

'No. I was one of the first ones to go to bed. I could hear others going just after me, but I could still hear Caitlyn talking in the lounge. I'd barely had a chance to speak to her all night on our own, so I got back up. I had a picture to give her as well.'

'What picture?'

'It was a collage. Of times we'd spent together at school.' The hours it took me to find and print the photos, then arrange it for her. And she had barely looked at it. There'd been all sorts in there. Sports days, school trips, discos, the time she came on holiday with us...

Sergeant Arthington's voice makes me jump. 'Then what?'

'She was talking to Jen – having what they called a "private conversation", anyway, they tried to send me packing.'

'Do you know what they were talking about?'

I feel pissed off thinking about it. Even if she is dead. I recall a thought that popped into my head when I found her earlier. One word, 'karma'. Then I felt as guilty as hell for it. I suppose we can't help what goes through our minds. 'Caitlyn doesn't tell me *anything* anymore. We've grown apart, especially in the last few years. So no, I don't know what she and Jen were talking about.'

'It's a shame, but it happens.' Sergeant Arthington nods. What would she know? She doesn't seem like someone that everyone would sideline. Unlike me. 'So what happened next?'

'Mari heard us all having words. I felt really left out. Caitlyn and Jen made me feel worthless. I haven't got a lot of confidence. Mari came in and stuck up for me.'

'Which one's Mari?'

'I don't really know her – we've never met before but were forced to share a room together.' I try to keep the bitterness out of my voice, but it's hard. I *am* bitter.

'So, you weren't asked to be Caitlyn's bridesmaid, she wasn't paying you any attention yesterday, you were made to share a room with someone you don't know, and then told to go away when you tried to join a conversation. It doesn't sound like you were having much fun this weekend.'

'No. I wasn't.' And put like that, it sounds terrible. But I hope I haven't said too much. The word *karma* returns to me. I had to call a big favour in order to even get here this weekend. Caitlyn doesn't know that. Nor could I really afford it.

'So what was said between you all? After Mari joined in last night's discussion?'

'It turned into more of an argument than a discussion. Eventually I couldn't be bothered with it anymore and went back to my room.'

'What was said in the argument?'

'Jen was really awful. Calling me names. Like I'm not withdrawn enough as it is.'

'What sort of names?'

'Just "pathetic" and telling me to grow up. That sort of thing.'

'So did you return to your bedroom with your roommate?' She turns to look at a previous page she has written on. 'Erm, Mari?'

'That's right.'

'Leaving Jen and Caitlyn still in the lounge?'

'Yes.' Something comes over me. It'll serve her right for calling me *pathetic* and telling me to grow up. 'Jen and Caitlyn seemed like they were arguing over something themselves. I'd listened for a bit before I went in.'

'Really? About what?'

'I couldn't be sure. It was just, you know, the tone of their voices and the look on their faces when I interrupted them. It looked pretty serious. I heard Caitlyn saying something about Ben, that's who she was supposed to be marrying, seeing another woman.'

I look from Inspector Retford who isn't saying a word, to Sergeant Arthington who seems really interested. 'Go on.'

'My money would be on Jen. For the other woman, I mean. From what I've heard from Mari, she's well known for only being interested in men who are in long-term relationships. It's probably the thrill of the chase.' Oh God, my mouth is really running away with me now.

'If we could stick to facts rather than speculation.' Inspector Retford finally speaks.

Sergeant Arthington's tone is gentler. 'Did you actually hear Caitlyn accuse Jen of having illicit relations with her husband-to-be when they were speaking last night?'

'I think so. I wasn't in the room with them, but it sounded like that's what was being said. They were definitely arguing.'

'And you didn't see Caitlyn again until this morning?'

'No. I poured a glass of wine on my way back to bed. I was watching a film on my phone to take my mind off things. So with my headphones on, I didn't hear any more. Sorry.'

'How well do you know Ben, Caitlyn's fiancé?'

'I don't. We've never been introduced.' Another bone of contention.

'Really?' Sergeant Arthington's voice rises. 'Even though you're one of her oldest friends?' I bet she's very happily married. It must be wonderful to belong to someone. To know you're special in another's life.

'That's probably why she didn't introduce me. I'm not cool

enough for her anymore. She's changed. I feel like she only invited me here because she had to. She forgot about inviting Mari though – until the last minute. But I'm the best friend she's ever had – I'd have done anything for her – she just forgot that.' I squeeze my shoulder blades together. I'm aching like I've never ached before. I don't know if it's down to last night's uncomfortable bed or the stress.

'OK, Adele. We'll leave it there for now. If you'd like to rejoin the group until we've spoken to everyone.'

'How long's it going to take?'

'As long as it takes.' Inspector Retford surveys me over the top of his glasses as though I'm an insect.

I only asked, I want to say, lowering my gaze to the floor. Maybe if I stuck up for myself a bit more, people might treat me better. If this weekend has taught me anything, it's that it's time to sort myself out.

'A young woman is dead.'

Like I need reminding.

He continues. 'No one is getting out of here until we've found out what has happened.'

TEN

LUCY

This would be more exciting at a police station rather than in this stuffy bedroom. The heating must be on full blast.

'Can we open a window, please?' Grandma unwraps the scarf she won last night. She's been moaning for as long as I can remember about hot flushes or something like that.

Sergeant Whinstable, or whatever his name is, opens the window – so slightly that I wonder why he's bothered, then sits next to a policewoman, facing me and Grandma. 'Right, Lucy, I'm going to press go on this machine so that everything that's said between us can be recorded.'

'OK.' I try to control my leg which I have been swinging rhythmically without even realising. I hope they don't notice me trembling, they might think I've done something wrong if they do. I wonder what they're going to ask and just hope I'll be able to speak without clamming up. I glance at Grandma. She reaches across and squeezes my hand, which reassures me.

A long beep sounds from the machine. 'My name is Sergeant David Whinstable, and this is my colleague, Inspector Tina Hobbs of Bridewell Gardaí Constabulary, Ireland's National Police and Security Service.' He says the last bit as though explaining it. 'Have you ever been interviewed by the police, Lucy?'

I shake my head. 'Never.' I'm glad Grandma is here with me. This is well scary. I feel like a criminal or something. Mum's told me several times that I always look guilty when asked about things, even when they're nothing to do with me.

'I need your full name, Lucy, and that of your appropriate adult, please?'

'Lucy Jane Mortimer.' I look again at Grandma. Gosh, if I'd been a year older, I'd be having to do this on my own.

'Karen Anne Mortimer.' She looks nervous too, and red in the face – redder than normal. She winds her scarf around her fingers.

'And you're Lucy's grandmother, is that correct?'

'Yes.' Grandma's voice sounds shaky too. 'I'm her father's mum.'

I feel sick. I have done since I woke up. It's partly hangover and partly all this. I've never seen anyone dead before, and this is the weirdest situation I have ever found myself in.

With a wobbly voice, I give my address and date of birth when they ask for it, then listen as some words which I've only ever heard on the TV are read out to me. My rights. This really will be something to tell all my friends about, but it's all so creepy. Caitlyn being dead is certainly not something I'll be shouting all over Instagram about, although everyone will want to know at college.

I tell them I don't want a solicitor – I've got Grandma with me, anyway. She'll look after me. I'm her only grandchild, so she always has done. I'd hate to share her with anyone else. Before Caitlyn had cancer, I'd threatened Dad that if he ever had a kid with her, I would never want to see him again. A conversation I had with Dad a couple of months ago comes drifting back.

. . .

'It looks like they've got Caitlyn into remission.' I'd gone into his office to ask him for some going-out money. He had slid his phone into the top pocket of his shirt when I walked in.

'What does that mean?' I threw myself onto the sofa. No doubt my workmates would bitch about me skiving, but only because they're jealous of me having the boss as my dad. 'Remission?'

'It means that the dangerous cancer cells are no longer being produced. She'll have regular checks to make sure they don't come back.' His expression was hard to read. I would have expected him to look happier than he did. Maybe he didn't want to show it in front of me.

'So she's not going to die?'

'No. She never was.'

'Everyone has to die one day.'

'The age of twenty-nine is too young though, don't you think, Lucy?'

I shrugged. 'So you're going to get married, have lots of babies and live happily ever after.' My voice was full of scorn, but I didn't care.

'Listen, Lucy. If I tell you something, do you promise that you'll keep it to yourself?'

'Depends what it is.'

'Caitlyn's had cancer of the cervix. She knew when she started treatment that she would be unlikely to have children after it. They gave her the chance to have her eggs taken and frozen.'

'And did she?' Anxiety rose in me like smoke.

'No, but I'm not going to go into that. All you need to know is that Caitlyn and I won't be having children together.'

I know it's wrong to be pleased that someone has been left infertile by cancer treatment. Which is why I haven't told anyone. It would make me sound like a right cow. But it's been bad enough having to share Dad with Caitlyn, without another kid coming along too. Especially when they might muscle in on all the money that should come to *me* one day. Caitlyn has her own job but has wheedled her way into Dad's company. She knew what she was doing all along. It has belonged to our family for years, and should be nothing to do with Caitlyn.

Dad never asked me what I thought about him getting married – he just went and got engaged to her, without ever saying a word to me. It was like I didn't matter. When I had a go about how much he was affecting my life, all he could say was that I would be grown up and leading my own life before long. It took me weeks to calm down. I ignored all his calls and would tell anyone who would listen how Dad had treated me. I think Mum quite enjoyed it. She doesn't like me being too close to him.

'So, Lucy.'

I jump as the policewoman speaks. 'I was miles away.'

'Can you tell me in your own words, what's happened since you arrived in Dublin yesterday?'

Her strong Irish accent takes me by surprise. I haven't really spoken to anyone local since we got here. The green man we had the photo taken with didn't really say anything, and the waitress in the restaurant was Italian. We didn't speak to the taxi driver; there was a screen between us.

'I wasn't even going to come to this stupid hen party,' I begin. It's true. I really wasn't, although it was probably rotten of me to come out and tell Caitlyn that. 'If it wasn't for my grandma and auntie being here, then no way would I have come. Dad paid for my place in the end. But probably only because Mum's away with her new boyfriend, and Dad knew he had to go to London for some business meeting. They won't leave me on my own as I had a big party last time.'

Inspector Hobbs smiles which helps me to relax slightly. She only looks a few years older than me.

'How did you get on with Caitlyn, Lucy?'

I notice she's talking about her in the past tense – she uses the word 'did'. I feel a flicker of excitement in my belly. I squash it down with the palm of my hand and shrug. 'She was OK, I suppose. I didn't spend much time with her.'

'Did you want to?'

There's no point lying. 'Not really.'

'She would have been your stepmum, wouldn't she?'

'I suppose.'

Wicked stepmother, as I called her when talking about her to my friends or to Michaela. She always looked at me as though she wanted me out of the way and Dad all to herself. Who knows how she'd have been with me after they were married? I hated Dad for choosing her over me. That's how I saw it, although he insisted otherwise.

'You must have thought *something* of her to come to her hen party?'

'It was something to do. Maybe I was being nosy as well.'

'What do you do, Lucy?'

'What do you mean?'

'I mean, do you work? Are you still at school? Who do you live with?'

I don't know why she wants my life story. She's supposed to be finding out who killed Caitlyn. 'I'm doing A levels at sixth form college. And I live with my mum. Unfortunately. I wanted to live with my dad, but he's always away. At least I used to want to live with him until he moved in with Caitlyn. I do a bit of work for him at weekends – that's the only time I've been seeing him – at work, I mean. Really, I want to work there all the time, but my mum's making me do A levels.'

'Your mum sounds like a wise lady.'

Are all policewomen as nice as this one? Or maybe it's

because I'm only seventeen. If she really thought I could do something to Caitlyn, surely she would be awful to me?

'So would you have wanted to live with your dad after he'd got married to Caitlyn?'

'No, not at all. I'm older now though.' It would have been a nightmare living with Caitlyn. She would have been trying to boss me about. She already acted like she owned the place whenever I was there. Which wasn't very often in the end.

'Why wouldn't you have wanted to live with Caitlyn?'

'I dunno. I guess, well, me and my dad were doing fine. Then she came along and I had no say in anything. She came between us.' Grandma's not speaking. I'm not sure if she's allowed to, or whether she has just got to sit here. I suppose they'll be speaking to her on her own. This is all seriously weird.

'Has my dad been told yet?' I can't imagine how he will react to this, or if he will cry. I have never seen Dad cry. Would he cry if I died? 'About what's happened to Caitlyn, I mean?'

'Let us ask the questions for now, Lucy.' The policeman's voice is sterner now, but his eyes are still friendly. He's probably being OK with me because I'm the youngest out of all of us.

Inspector Hobbs continues. 'What time did you arrive here in Dublin?'

'About three-ish. It only took an hour on the plane.'

'You're all from Yorkshire, aren't you? So you flew from Leeds Bradford airport?'

I nod.

'Lucy, for the benefit of the tape, you need to answer our questions out loud – not just make gestures.'

'Yes. I don't live far from there and Dad only lives around the corner from the airport.' My face is burning. It's like an oven in here, as Mum would say. Who cares anyway, what airport we've come from? What's that got to do with anything?

'Then what did you do?'

'We went for a meal. It was OK.' Then I remember awful Adele, having a go at me for drinking an alcoholic drink.

'I've got ID,' I had hissed at her. 'Anyway, I'm allowed to drink with a meal. It's legal. Google it if you don't believe me.' I don't know who she thought she was.

'You shouldn't even be here,' she had snarled back at me, her lip curling. 'You don't even like Caitlyn – don't worry, I've heard all about you.'

'I've heard all about you too,' I had said, flashing a false smile. I hadn't really, but the look on her face said it had got her thinking.

Michaela and Grandma had been deep in conversation with each other, so I'd turned my chair around and joined in with them. I don't know how I'd ended up sitting next to Adele and not sure why Caitlyn would want to be friends with her. I'm not sure why *anyone* would want to be friends with her. She has a look about her that reminds me of a rat. I felt *really* pissed off with Caitlyn though and wondered what she had been saying about me. I bet she'd slag me off to anyone who would listen.

'Was everyone getting along at the meal?' Inspector Hobbs asks. 'As far as you could see?'

'I guess so. Not everyone knew each other, so it was awkward. Shelley and Emma weren't there – after we landed they came to the apartment to get it decorated. For the hen party, I mean.'

'Shelley and Emma?'

'They were to be Caitlyn's bridesmaids – along with Jen. Shelley and Jen were her friends and Emma was Caitlyn's sister.' I'm talking in past tense now. It's not as if I'm grieving, not like some of the others. How could I be? I didn't even like her.

'Were *you* not going to be a bridesmaid?'

I've lost count of how many people have asked me that. 'No. I got asked, but I didn't want to be.'

'Really? At your own dad's wedding?' Everyone has said that

too. What they don't understand is that I would feel as though I was betraying Mum if I'd said yes.

'It was the stepmum thing. It was happening too fast. I just didn't want it.'

'Want what?' Inspector Hobbs raises her eyes from the notepad and I notice they're green. She's wearing a big green engagement ring that's a similar colour. I wonder if she'll get to her wedding day without getting murdered in her bed.

'To be a bridesmaid. For them to get married. For him to have ever met her. Any of it.' My fists bunch in my lap and Grandma is looking at me with a look that says, *Cool it*. She dabs at the back of her neck with her scarf.

'So what happened after your meal? Did you come back here, to the apartment?'

God all these questions. I thought Mum was bad. 'Yes. We went to a shop first, then came here in two taxis?'

'Were you in the taxi that Caitlyn was in?'

'No.' What I don't say is that I'd gone to great lengths to avoid being in Caitlyn's car. Luckily Adele went in the taxi with her as well. I wouldn't have wanted to sit next to *her*.

'How did you spend last night? Did you stay in... go back out?'

'We stayed in. We all got into our pyjamas and were playing daft games. Talking. Drinking. It was strange really.' There are certainly other things I would rather have been doing on a Friday night.

'Why was it strange?'

'Everyone pretending to love Caitlyn, even though I had heard a few people saying nasty things about her behind her back, and everyone was mostly only pretending to enjoy themselves. Half the people there hardly knew anyone else. I bet lots of us secretly didn't want to even be there. I certainly didn't – it was my dad who wanted me to come.'

'It sounds awkward.'

'Yeah. I was glad when it got to a time when I could go to bed.'

I decide not to say anything about being the last one to be sitting with Jen and Caitlyn. And I certainly don't want them to know we had argued. They might think I've done something. 'I just wanted to get on Snapchat and send my friend Ella the goofy pictures I'd been secretly taking of them all throughout the evening.'

'Did you hear anything? After you went to bed?'

'I was talking to my Auntie Michaela then we heard a load of carrying on.' Shit. I'm going to have to make sure Auntie Michaela says the same thing as me and doesn't mention our argument. It's too late to say anything now. Besides, it wasn't a big argument, anyway. Just a few cross words.

'Oh? What was that about?'

'Adele. She and Caitlyn were having a right go at each other.'

'Do you know why?' She fans her hand in front of her face. 'Gosh, it's so warm in here. There must be something wrong with the heating. The other room we are using is freezing.'

'Me and Michaela stayed in our room. We didn't want to get involved, but it sounded like Adele was crying.'

'Are you sure it was Adele?'

'Yes. I put my head out of the door and saw her in the doorway of the lounge.'

'Do you know if anyone else was there?'

'Jen probably.'

'OK. What about after that?'

'I had my earpods in, like I always do. I didn't hear a thing all night after that. The row didn't last very long.'

'Lucy always sleeps like a log.' Grandma smiles.

No one answers her. I really don't think she's supposed to say anything. Just sit and be an appropriate adult. I'll laugh with her about that label when this is all over. Grandma – appropriate? Yeah, right. Right now, no one's laughing at anything.

'What about this morning?'

'What do you mean?'

'What did you do?'

'I got up for some breakfast, like I normally would. Hardly anyone was talking to each other. I heard Adele saying awful things about Caitlyn to Mari whilst we were in the lounge, waiting for Jen and Grandma to sort breakfast.' She's going to get it, Adele is – I'll make sure she does.

'Can you elaborate on that, please? The conversation between Adele and Mari?'

'I don't want to cause any trouble.' This is all getting heavy. Maybe I should have kept my mouth shut.

'Lucy. A young woman is dead through there. We need to find out who has done this to her. Whether or not you liked her.'

'I never said I didn't like her, just that their relationship had got between me and my dad. I was worried too in case she took over the business which me and Michaela should have a share of.' I'm rambling. I need to change the subject. 'Has she definitely been *murdered*? She hasn't just died in her sleep?'

'We can't talk about that at the moment. I just need to know what you think you overheard between the two ladies you mentioned.'

'I *did* overhear. Adele was telling Mari that she was thinking of getting an early flight home. She said things had gone too far.'

'Did she say what things?' Inspector Hobbs is writing this down, I don't even know what this other guy is doing in here. He looks bored, if anything.

I shake my head, then remember I've got to speak out loud. 'No. But I also heard Mari asking her to see if there were two seats on the plane when she was looking at flights.'

'Do you remember anything else?'

'I couldn't hear exactly, but I could tell by their faces and their tone of voice that they weren't saying kind things. You just know, don't you? They realised I was listening and started whispering then.'

'Was it Adele who found Caitlyn?'

'Yes, she was screaming her head off. I suppose I would have been too. That's when we all found out she was dead. It was awful.'

'How do *you* feel about it all, Lucy?'

'About what?'

'What's happened to Caitlyn.'

'It's never mattered before, how I feel. I just have to put up and shut up. It's always been the same. I've been pushed and pulled between the homes of my mum and dad for years.'

She's nodding like she understands, so I continue.

'I'm shocked. I'm not sad. I know I should be, but I think Caitlyn was only pretending to like me. For my dad's sake. We weren't close or anything.'

'Right. We'll leave it there for now. We'll probably need to speak to you again at some point though.'

'When can I have my phone back?' I don't care about my suitcase, but I need my phone. I can't just sit in that awful room, doing nothing. I'll go mad. This has got to be the crappiest day of my life. I want to go home.

'As soon as we have checked them all.' Inspector Hobbs closes her notebook and tucks a stray hair behind her ear.

'Why are they being checked? I've done nothing wrong.'

'We're not saying you have, but we have to look at messages, calls and GPS.'

'What's GPS?' If I had my phone, I would Google it.

'We're making sure that no one's phone left the building. GPS allows us to track the movement of phones which could tell us if anyone left the building during the night.'

'Will you be looking at CCTV as well?' Grandma speaks again. 'In case anybody got into the apartment whilst we were all asleep?'

'Yes, of course.' Inspector Hobbs nods towards Sergeant Whinstable, who announces the end of the interview and stops the tape. He's got a huge belly. I bet he goes home on a night and just drinks beer and eats.

'We'll speak to you next whilst you're here,' Sergeant Whinstable says to Grandma. 'Lucy, if you'd like to take a seat back in the lounge with the others.'

'How long will it all take? When can we leave here?'

He gives me a funny look and I regret allowing my voice to sound so whiny.

'Not until we've spoken to everyone. Then we'll take it from there.'

Adele comes out of the other room at the same time as me. She looks the other way as she heads towards the bathroom. Dad reckons I've got a scowl on me, but bloody hell. She looks even worse than she did yesterday. Her hair's stuck out all over the place and her legs look like sticks in the skinny jeans she's wearing. Hopefully, I've given them something to think about with what I've said about Adele.

I'm taken aback by the policeman standing next to this flat's partially open front door. I pause, pretending to adjust my shoe. I want to know what's going on. A man in a white suit comes out of our apartment, holding a couple of bags. From the shows I've watched on TV, they must find things in there that they want to look at more closely. I can't believe she's dead, but in a warped way, it's all very exciting.

'You need to get yourself back in there.' The policeman looks at me with cold eyes as he jerks his head towards the lounge door.

I stride past him and once in the lounge throw myself on the chair next to Auntie Michaela. The room is silent and everyone's eyes are on me. I don't know why. It's not as though I'll be allowed to say anything. Not with that stupid policeman standing at the door.

'How was it?' Michaela whispers without looking at me.

'OK,' I whisper back. 'They didn't ask me that much, really. They're speaking to Grandma now. I didn't tell them about the argument we had with Caitlyn last night though.'

The policeman puts his head around the door. 'You're not to speak to each other. This is a murder investigation.'

'So we're supposed to just sit here?' Jen stands and walks towards him. 'You can't expect us just to sit here and not to speak for hours on end. This really isn't on.' She always has to have her say.

'You'll have plenty of chance to speak after we have interviewed everyone.' He puffs his chest out as though he's really important. 'Anyone who can't comply with that will have to be interviewed at the station. I promise you it's a nicer wait here than it is in a cell.'

ELEVEN

KAREN

I look at the young police officer in front of me, fresh-faced with a blond ponytail – probably just out of training. 'Can I be the one who tells my son what's happened?'

'It's all in hand,' she replies. 'In fact, someone will have possibly let him know what's happened by now. We should be able to confirm that for definite when we've finished speaking to you all.'

'As if he hasn't got enough going on already. Not to mention what he's already had to contend with.'

'Can I ask you to hold that comment please? We need to have everything you say on record.' She reaches forward and presses the button on a machine, her beautiful ring catching in the light. Because it's the only one she wears, it's striking. I look down at my own ageing hands where I have got at least one ring on every finger. I'd give anything to be young again. Boobs and Botox only go so far. Coming on this hen party has made me feel even older. The next one down in age from me is forty-two. And she's my daughter.

I listen as the same spiel that was recently given to Lucy is read to me. If anyone had told me this is where I would be sitting on the second day of Caitlyn's hen party, I would have said they were mad.

'The time is 1.27 p.m. on Saturday, the twenty-fifth of January. My name is Sergeant David Whinstable and my colleague is...' he nods towards her.

'Inspector Tina Hobbs.'

'...who will take notes throughout this interview. We are speaking to...' He nods at me now. 'Can you state your full name, please?'

'Er, Karen Anne Mortimer.' Every time I say my surname out loud, I am aware I should change it. Rick has remarried now — there is a new Mrs Mortimer. I'm pathetic, hanging on to his name.

'You're the mother of Benjamin Mortimer, meaning you would have been Caitlyn Elizabeth Nicholson's mother-in-law?'

'That is correct.' I didn't actually know her middle name was Elizabeth. If the truth be known, I didn't actually know all that much about her.

'Could I ask you to confirm your address and date of birth?'

I give him what he asks for then wait for what comes next.

'Thank you, Karen. We've got the recording of you acting as the appropriate adult just now for your granddaughter, Lucy Mortimer. Do you agree with her account of the order of events from yesterday, from you all landing at Dublin airport?'

'Yes. I was with Lucy the whole time, and my daughter, Michaela. The only difference is that I went to bed slightly before Lucy.'

'Can you say what time that was?'

'Probably half an hour ahead of everyone else. I was like Lucy — waiting for an acceptable time to make my excuses. There really was an atmosphere.'

I recall my own hen party, forty-four years ago, when I'd been dressed in a net curtain and L-plates. It had been such a laugh, with people who were happy for me and Rick. Lots of the women here seem to have grievances of one kind or another with Caitlyn. Maybe Ben's had a lucky escape.

'Can you elaborate on that?'

'Well, both my daughter, Michaela, and my granddaughter, Lucy, have had their issues with Caitlyn over the time she and Ben have been together. Things have improved since she's been ill though – obviously they have felt a great amount of sympathy for her.'

'What sort of issues?'

'It's as though they're all competing with one another. For Ben's attention mainly. I suppose girls can be like that though. But I also know there have been concerns over inheritances and who will end up with the company. We've all got stakes in it. So it's that sort of thing, really.' I don't add that I was also concerned. Not that I'm uncomfortable in life. Not only do I get a generous share of Rick's pension, I am also paid a healthy dividend from the company – well, for now I am. It's all in the balance at the moment. I just hope Ben gets through his meeting before the police contact him.

'Do you think the jealousy would have been the case with *any* partner your son took, not specifically Caitlyn?'

'I suppose so.'

'You mentioned, though, that relations have improved recently?'

'Yes. Like I said, I think they both felt sorry for her. No one wants to hear of someone fighting cancer, do they?' I'm not going to tell them the truth – that the treatment was likely to have left Caitlyn unable to conceive. Therefore the threat of competition for Ben's time and money from a new addition had been eliminated.

'How did *you* get on with Caitlyn?' Beads of sweat are dotted across Sergeant Whinstable's forehead. It's that warm in here, it's easy to forget it's January. Another hot flush snakes over me; at the moment I'm getting a dozen an hour. Apparently I go red when

I'm having them too, which isn't to my advantage whilst being questioned about a murder. The windows only open a fraction – probably a health and safety thing because we're so far up. Health and safety didn't do Caitlyn much good though.

'I keep Ben's girlfriends at arm's length. They rarely stick around for long. He gets bored. There's been no real point in getting to know them.' It's true. Other than Deborah, Lucy's mum, who was forced on me. But she was only around longer because she trapped Ben into parenthood; every other woman he's ever 'entertained' has never lasted more than a matter of months. Michaela doesn't bother meeting them at all. It surprised us to be introduced to Caitlyn. And she seemed so 'nice'. I would have expected a woman who gained Ben's interest to have had more sass about her.

I remember Michaela's fortieth birthday party. Rick was there with his younger model and looked as though he thought the sun shone out of Caitlyn's backside. She schmoozed him in the same way she apparently schmoozes all of Ben's male business associates. Rick probably fancied her for himself. I decided within the first hour of the party that I didn't much like her.

'But Caitlyn was about to *marry* your son.' Sergeant Whinstable's voice interrupts my thinking. 'Which surely changed her status from being merely your son's "girlfriend".'

I pause for a moment. *Should I tell them the truth?* Yes, I think I should. 'To be honest, I suspected Ben was having cold feet. I met him the day before yesterday for a coffee. I'm not convinced the wedding would have gone ahead.'

'What makes you say that?' He sits up straighter in the chair. He doesn't look very comfortable – in fact, he's spilling over the sides of it. He needs to go on a serious diet. He's here, investigating a death, when he's a heart attack waiting to happen himself. I do like his Irish accent though.

'He actually wanted to break up with Caitlyn before she got diagnosed with cancer. But obviously, he'd have looked like a complete rotter if he'd ended things between them whilst she had that to face.'

'So he stayed with her out of *pity?*'

'I know it sounds bad, but yes, I believe he did. And besides that, she was great for his business and worked for him, alongside her own job.' I'll say that about Caitlyn. She was a grafter, not like some other hangers-on he was good at attracting. 'Ben and Caitlyn would give dinner parties for clients and investors – they all thought Caitlyn was wonderful.' It had been like history repeating – I recall the parties I had to give when I was married to his bloody father.

'Judging from your expression though – you didn't.'

'What?'

'Think Caitlyn was wonderful.'

I've always been told that my face gives me away. God knows what they must think of me. 'I thought she was OK. I know all mothers probably say this – I just thought Ben could do better for himself. I thought he might be happier with someone else, and that's all you want for your kids. He and Caitlyn never seemed well suited.'

The problem with Ben is, not only is he a philanderer like his father, he has also inherited his father's chiselled features and piercing blue eyes. Now that his father has moved on to pastures new, Ben's also taken over the business, meaning that, at face value, he is an attractive proposition. But I am one of the few people that knows the once-thriving business is teetering on the edge and needs some serious investment to pull it back. And this has been something that Caitlyn proved herself to be competent at securing. God knows what he is going to do now.

'When was Caitlyn diagnosed with cancer?'

'Oh, about a year ago.' There's the scratch of pen against notepad as Inspector Hobbs writes this down.

'What sort of cancer was it?' Sympathy is etched across her face. I hope it's not directed at me. I don't deserve it.

'Cervical.' I hope they will not go too much into this. I know that as her partner's mother, I probably should have been there more for her. Or there for her at all – particularly with her own mother having passed away. Still, she had her friends and her sisters. I've never been good around illness or weakness. Nor do I ever say the right things. All I could do was support my son with his side of it all. Be there to listen to him – whatever has happened.

'Were she and your son engaged to be married *then*? When she was diagnosed, I mean?'

'No. In fact, it all came as rather a shock. One minute he was on about ending things, the next he was planning to marry her. Caitlyn was in the middle of her treatment when news of their engagement came up on Facebook. He'd secretly planned it. I've never understood this, because he'd wanted to break up with her only months before. Her friend had helped him shop for the engagement ring so I can only assume that he had been persuaded to do it.'

'Was the engagement celebrated? As a family, I mean?'

'Well, Michaela, my daughter, went mad with him but I think that was because she was the last to know. It was Lucy who he really had to pacify.'

With a new car. She was making threats not to see him again and all sorts. I don't think she meant it though – she just felt left out. After that, we had to force smiles at the dinner party they put on to celebrate.

'We didn't do anything too elaborate. They invited us to dinner at their house along with Caitlyn's family, but it was a stilted affair.'

I can recall the atmosphere that night – it wasn't exactly celebratory. It suddenly dawns on me that I didn't even send them a congratulations card. Rick was there, this time without his wife, and spent the evening ingratiating himself with Caitlyn – *if she needed this... if she wanted that...* It was sickening.

'Let's go back to the other day. What did Ben say that made you think he was having cold feet?' Whinstable tilts his head to one side, like a pet awaiting a treat, as he waits for my answer.

'It was when I was telling him about the hen party arrangements. I could tell by his face there was something amiss.'

'Did he actually talk about it?'

I can hardly tell them I know for a fact he's been seeing someone else. He's not told me directly, not yet anyway. Same old Ben. Just like his father. He nearly always confides in me eventually though. I'm his mother and would never betray his confidence, and he knows that. Not to the police, Caitlyn, or anybody.

'No. But I'm his mum. I know him. I could just tell that his heart wasn't in his forthcoming wedding. Not like it should have been. It was written all over him.'

'I'm sorry to press you on this, I know it's a really difficult time.' Sergeant Whinstable pushes his glasses back up as they have slid down his sweaty nose. 'But we need to get a full picture of Caitlyn's life in the months, weeks, and especially the days leading up to her death. You saw your son two days ago. *How* could you tell that his heart wasn't in it? He must have said *something.*'

'There were a few reasons.' I'm sure I'm not speaking too much out of turn here. 'He had nothing planned for a stag party himself, and there was no excitement about the wedding from him. He looked more like he was going to the gallows.'

'Maybe it was just nerves?' But Sergeant Whinstable's face bears a faint smile as though he can identify with this.

'You'd have to ask him that. Anyway, can you find out if he's been told yet?'

'Like I said, once we've spoken to you all, and when we've finished with the forensics side of the investigation, we'll be in a much better position to give you some more information.'

'We can't discuss too much with you,' Inspector Hobbs adds, 'obviously, as it's an ongoing inquiry and we need to tie everything together.'

'I only want to know if my son has been informed of his fiancée's death.'

'So, merely by being his mother and judging by his actions and his mood, you *suspected* he was having cold feet?' He completely ignores my last comment.

'Yes, I just hoped he'd work through things on his own.' I can't tell them he would definitely have gone through with it no matter what he was feeling – he had to for the sake of his business.

I've no idea which woman he's been carrying on with – I expect he'll tell me at some point. All I know is that she's saved in his phone as a love heart and I saw a message flash up on his home screen whilst he was at the café counter,

Please get this sorted B – it's me you should marry, especially now.

A look had crossed his face when he glanced at his phone on his return. He had quickly slipped it into his pocket and started talking about the upcoming business trip to London. I refrained from quizzing him about the message, figuring he'd tell me soon enough.

'If you don't mind me saying, Karen, you seem to be taking all this very much in your stride.' There's an almost accusatory edge to the sergeant's voice. I wonder what he's getting at.

'You mean Caitlyn's death? I've never been one for the dramatics. We just need to stay calm and find out what's happened.'

'You'd be forgiven for being dramatic. It's not every day you stumble across a body in your apartment. Particularly of the woman due to marry your son. Are you sure you're OK?'

'Yes.' I allow my eyes to meet his. They look to be full of fake concern. 'I've already told you, Caitlyn and I weren't close. Of course, her death is a tragic waste of a young life, but I've had enough drama and loss in my life already. That's why I'm equipped to take things "in my stride", as you put it.'

'I wasn't implying any—'

'If you want to see who really is taking it all "in her stride", speak to Caitlyn's sister next. Cool as a cucumber, that one – you wouldn't think her sister's body had just been discovered. All she cares about is having her phone taken off her.' I don't say which sister I'm talking about. I'm sure they'll work that out for themselves. On the couple of occasions they have forced me into Annette's company, I've never liked her. And I wouldn't trust her as far as I could throw her. I thought Caitlyn set my teeth on edge, but Annette takes this to another level.

'We'll be talking to everyone.' Sergeant Whinstable looks at me over the top of his glasses.

'Have you finished with *me*?'

'For now. If you've nothing else you'd like to tell us about? We'll come back to you if we have any more questions.'

I get to my feet and pick up my scarf. I feel grotty. I haven't even had a shower yet today, and in my current post-menopausal state, I need one. 'What happens now?'

'You can join the others until we've seen everyone.'

'Then what?' God, what a weekend. I'll never forget it, and for all the wrong reasons. We should be in the spa by now – gosh that would be wonderful.

'We can't say what will happen next, but I promise that we'll keep you all in the loop as much as we're able to.'

'I'm allowed to the loo, aren't I?' I'm aware there's a note of sarcasm in my voice as I look pointedly at the police officer standing guard by the lounge door. The sweep of his arm towards the bathroom door suggests that it's permitted. He can hardly stop me, can he?

Sitting on the loo, I sigh deeply and drop my head into my hands, relishing the momentary peace whilst trying to stop my mind from spinning. I study the dreadful bathroom décor, wishing I was anywhere but here. God knows how much longer we're going to have to sit in that oppressive lounge, just looking at one another.

TWELVE

EMMA

I stare at my hands, twirling my thumbs around and around each other, trying to quell the nausea that won't subside. My sister is dead. I glance at Annette, trying to read what is going through her head. She and Caitlyn weren't as close as we were, in fact I sometimes wondered if they even loved each other. They were always fighting over something – especially me. Still, they were sisters. Annette must be struggling in her own way.

The police officer steps into the room to make way for Karen to return. She smiles at Michaela and Lucy as she sits down. Cow. What the hell is there to smile about? Caitlyn seems to have been right about Karen – she really is a cold fish. She's never bothered to get to know any of us and it's not as if her family are a cut above ours – all three of us have been to university, none of her kids have. Just because they've got more money… I hate that – it's not what life should boil down to. The police officer lingers in the room this time, rather than standing in the hallway like he has been doing. I wish he'd go away.

It's ridiculous but being around the police evokes feelings of guilt within me. I think it's something to do with the time when Annette and I were arrested for shoplifting when I was about twelve. We were let off with a caution at the station and my parents naturally went mental. Caitlyn, who'd have been nineteen, blamed Annette. I could do no wrong in Caitlyn's eyes.

After Mum died, Caitlyn became my second mother. She always saw the best in me, and in everyone else for that matter. She had a friend on our street who lived with his nan and stayed on there after she died – Jim. He was seriously weird and no one would give him the time of day. But Caitlyn did. She volunteered at the local food bank and also shopped for an elderly lady. She's the first person I run to in a crisis, apart from recently with all she has been going through. At first, she let me look after her when she started going through her treatment – when I was around, anyway. But over the last couple of months, she hasn't let me in – she's kind of shut herself off. I felt like she was keeping something from me, which wasn't like her. She would have normally told me everything. I absolutely can't believe I'm never going to see her again.

'Emma Nicholson?'

I jerk my head up, taken by surprise at the tears that are dripping from my chin onto my hands. I didn't even realise I was crying. *Oh God. It's my turn.* And I'm in a right state with it all. I feel wheezy as well. My asthma inhaler is zipped inside my case. Surely they'll allow me to get at it. My breathing always plays up when I'm stressed.

Annette shoots me a look. 'You OK?' she mouths.

I shrug my shoulders in response as I get to my feet and walk towards the waiting police officer, trying to breathe deeply into my abdomen. The last thing everyone needs is me having an asthma attack.

'If you'd like to follow me, please.'

It looks like I've got the more horrible police officer. 'I really need my asthma inhaler.' I point towards the main door. 'It's in the other apartment.'

He ignores me. 'Take a seat, please.' As he opens a door, he gestures towards a table which has a woman police officer waiting at it.

'I really need my asthma inhaler,' I say to her this time. Maybe she'll be more approachable than he is. 'It's in a purple case in one of the bedrooms in the other apartment.'

'Is it desperate?'

'Not yet, but I'll need it soon.'

'What colour is it? The inhaler I mean?'

'Blue. I was in the bedroom right at the end of the apartment.'

'The forensics team are doing their work in there right now, but we'll have a word with the officer on the door, and it'll be brought to you as soon as possible.'

'Thank you.' My breathing feels steadier just knowing that my inhaler is on its way.

The two officers look at each other as if silently debating which one of them is going to sort it out. Finally, the man stands and strides to the door.

'Are you sure you're OK?' I see concern in the woman's face as she looks at me. I'm grateful for it. I'm feeling too wobbly for anyone to be harsh with me at the moment.

I nod. 'As long as I know my inhaler's coming.'

'It will be.'

We sit in silence for a few moments. I keep brushing the tears away. I can't seem to stop them, and I don't really know why I'm trying to. Caitlyn was my big sister, when all is said and done. If I weren't crying, there'd be something wrong with me. There's a lump in my throat the size of a grapefruit. The female police officer, who is about the same age as Caitlyn, watches me, her expression loaded with sympathy. I wish she wouldn't look at me like that. Sympathy makes me cry more. I absently twiddle my locket between my fingers. It's where my hands are always drawn towards. It was Mum's, and she left me it after she died. It had a photo of her parents inside. I cut Mum's face from a photograph and placed her over the top of Grandad. Now I'll have to find one of Caitlyn to put in the other side. Keep her close to me. As if all I'm going to have left of my beloved sister is her face in my locket. I blow my nose and jump as the man returns to the room.

'Someone will bring it in a few minutes.' He hitches his trousers up as he lowers himself onto the chair facing me. The creases in his trousers are pristine and his shirt is crisp and white. It's crazy what you notice, especially when your sister has just been found dead. He slides tissues towards me that he must have picked up on his way back. 'Are you sure you're up to answering our questions?' Maybe he has a heart after all.

'I'm Caitlyn's sister.' My shoulders shake with the force of what I'm feeling. 'So I'm just in a bit of a state with it all. I'll be fine to answer your questions though.'

'I thought you must be sisters – obviously with the same surname. You look similar as well.' I hardly think that's an appropriate observation from the policewoman, given the fact that Caitlyn's dead. I wonder if she's just seen her as she is now, in that room, or whether she's looked at her ID or a picture of her online.

'I don't think I can tell you much, but I'll do my best.' My words pump out in gasps, because of the tears or the asthma.

'Do you want to take care of the questions?' The man looks at his colleague, his voice far gentler than it was at the start. He's finally realised the state I'm in.

'Yes. OK, Emma, we need to get through this with you, but we'll make it as quick and as painless as we can.'

'Thanks.' I try to steady my breathing. In for two. Out for two. I watch as she presses a button on a machine. The loud beep startles me.

'My name is Sergeant Polly Arthington of Bridewell Gardaí Constabulary in Dublin. I am conducting this interview with... can you state your full name, date of birth and address, please?' She points from me to the recording machine.

I give them what they want and then wait for what comes next. I just want to get this over with.

'Thank you, Emma. Also present is...' She gestures to the man.

'Inspector Tim Retford, also of Bridewell Gardaí Constabulary.'

'Emma. I'm going to read you your rights and then we'll get straight on with it.'

'OK.'

'You are here to help us with an ongoing investigation into the death of Caitlyn Elizabeth Nicholson.'

My heart plummets at the sound of her full name. Being the eldest, she got Elizabeth, after our mum. I wonder if they've found each other wherever we end up after death. Mum will be surprised to see her already. I can almost hear her voice: 'What on earth are you doing here?' Caitlyn will probably come out with some smart reply about not being 'on earth' anymore. But she shouldn't be there. It wasn't her time. She was in remission. She had beaten cancer. Tears are still cascading down my face. *Get a grip, girl.* I brush the tissue across both cheeks.

'You do not have to say anything, but it may harm your defence if you do not mention, when questioned, something which you later rely on in court. Anything you do say may be given in evidence. Do you understand your rights, or do you need them explained to you?' The stark words stop the flow of tears. This is unbelievable.

'No. It's fine. I understand them.' I press my fingernails into the flesh of my hands. Panic is threatening to overwhelm me. I really need my inhaler. Then, as if by telepathy, there's a knock at the door. Inspector Retford answers it and returns to the table with my inhaler.

'Excuse me one moment.' I gratefully breathe the vapour into my lungs, taking four puffs, just to make sure. I glance at Inspector Retford who looks slightly impatient.

'Is that feeling better?' At least his female colleague is more humane.

'Yes, thank you.' I'm feeling calmer. The lump still engulfs my throat, but the tears have subsided – for the moment, anyway.

'Before we go any further, I will remind you of your right to legal representation whilst we speak to you. Is this something you would like to request?'

'No. Thank you.' What would I need legal representation for? Surely they can't think that I would have gone into my sister's bedroom during the night and held a pillow over her face until she died. I can't believe she would have allowed it. Caitlyn, I mean. She and Annette used to fight like cat and dog, and Caitlyn always had the upper hand. She was as fit as a fiddle until she got cancer. Being a physio, she respected her body and never smoked, hardly drank and used to cycle everywhere. She must have been out of it last night, not to have fought back. I know she was much weaker than normal, but I don't understand her just caving in and allowing herself to be suffocated.

'So you're Caitlyn's sister – you're younger than her presumably?'

I swallow. I don't know how I'm going to get through these questions. I've never felt so bad in my entire life. This feels much worse than when Mum died. At least they prepared us for that. 'Yes. Then Annette is in the middle.' I suddenly recall Caitlyn's delight when people used to ask who was the oldest out of her and Annette – that is until last year. Her illness seemed to age her – I think it was because of the weight loss. Her hair was thinner and her eyes large in her sunken face.

'I understand from Adele that you came back here with Shelley, the other bridesmaid, to decorate the apartment whilst everyone else went for a meal?'

It feels like a lifetime ago. I'd give anything to turn the clock back. 'That's right. We were here for nearly three hours before the others arrived. Caitlyn got a pizza delivered for us from the restaurant they went to.'

'It sounds as though she looked after you.' There's an unexpected softness in Sergeant Arthington's eyes as she makes the comment. Something about her makes me think she's probably got sisters too.

'Yes. Our mum died six years ago and Caitlyn, being the eldest, took over somewhat. Our dad isn't well either.'

'Oh. What's the matter with him?'

'He's got a heart problem. He's waiting for an operation to have stents. That's why he needs to be told about what's happened to Caitlyn gently. And face to face. Really, I need to get back to Yorkshire so I can be with him. He can't hear about this any other way.'

'We can discuss that later, Emma. It sounds like you've really been through it as a family already. And I understand Caitlyn has been ill as well?'

'It's been horrendous. And just when she's gone into remission and should be looking forward to her wedding, this...' Tears are sliding down my face again. Inspector Retford still has that impatient expression on his face. Maybe it's his natural look.

'So the rest of the ladies arrived approximately three hours after you and Shelley...' Sergeant Arthington continues. 'What was the mood like when they arrived?'

'Fine, as far as I could see.' I look down at my hands again, clasped on the table in front of me. 'Apart from Ben's family who seemed to prefer keeping themselves to themselves from the moment we got off the plane. That didn't surprise me though.'

'You mean his sister, mother and daughter?'

'Yes. Michaela, Karen and Lucy. Caitlyn's often said that they don't like her.'

'Do you think that's true?'

'I saw it for myself at the meal Caitlyn and Ben invited us

around for – to celebrate their engagement. God, what a night that was. Caitlyn was a couple of months into her treatment and Ben's proposal had perked her up. But I watched everyone really closely throughout the evening. Caitlyn was trying so hard, it was painful to watch. And it was obvious they didn't want to know her.'

It's all flooding back now. Over that evening, I saw Caitlyn's smile steadily decline. I wanted to pull her to one side and say, *Stop trying to make them like you* as I listened in to her attempts at trying to break into the inner circle that was Lucy, Karen and Michaela.

'We'll have to go for a coffee sometime,' she'd said to Michaela. 'It would be good to get to know my sister-in-law better.'

'Yeah, but she's not, is she?' Lucy chipped in. 'Your sister-in-law. You and my dad have to be married for that.'

'That's if he makes it that far.' Michaela had nudged Karen. 'Eh, Mum. We all know that Ben's not exactly the marrying kind. You might find that out for yourself, Caitlyn.'

I'd watched her face fall, but she wasn't deterred. 'We'll have to think about dresses, Lucy, won't we? With it being a Valentine's wedding, I was thinking red.'

'Red,' Lucy snorted. 'Can you imagine me in *red*, Auntie Michaela? Can't I just wear my jeans and a hoodie?' They all laughed.

'You want to be my bridesmaid, don't you?'

Lucy didn't answer her but hollered something across the table to Ben. He'd been telling *our* dad that Lucy was nearly seventeen, so she'd chipped in about wanting a car for her birthday.

'How about you, Karen? Do you fancy a coffee sometime? Or we could all even have a spa day. To get to know each other.'

'I thought that's what we were doing tonight. Getting to know each other better. That's why you've invited us, isn't it?'

'I'd love to go to a spa with you, sis.' I'd winked at her, struggling to watch her putting in so much effort with these women who were clearly not interested. None of them had even asked about her treatment. Ben sat at the other end of the table, between Shelley and his dad, talking animatedly about business. At his engagement celebration.

Annette and Dad kept each other company and Jen sat with me – I got a sense she was sympathetic to my observations. She was watching, listening and occasionally nudged me. Eventually Dad broke the mood.

'Right, if I could have your attention, please.' He tapped the side of his glass with a spoon. 'I am a very proud father of three wonderful daughters,' he began, smiling individually at us, 'and although their mum, Elizabeth, God rest her soul, and I have always loved our girls equally, the eldest always has the edge. I will not talk too much this evening about the dignity and bravery Caitlyn is showing in the face of her recent diagnosis – that's a conversation for another day. We're here tonight to celebrate her engagement to Ben here.'

Finally, Ben stopped talking and turned his attention to Dad.

'I can see that you've made my daughter happy, Ben, and that's all I could ever want for her. So please look after her – well, if you don't, you'll have me to deal with.'

Everyone laughed then. Dad's so frail he couldn't fight his way out of a wet paper bag.

'And I'm sure everyone will join me in raising their glasses in congratulations to Caitlyn and Ben.'

I watched Lucy, Karen and Michaela and there was a marked lack of enthusiasm in joining in with the toast.

Then Ben's dad got to his feet. Like Karen, he didn't look old enough to have children either side of forty. 'Caitlyn. Well, what can I say? If I was only twenty years younger.'

That didn't raise many laughs.

'I'd like to say a massive welcome to the family. From what I've heard, you're a huge asset to the business I built up, you've been the one who puts up with my son, and you're clever and beautiful as well. I know what you're facing and if there's ever anything – and I mean *anything* – I can do to support you, please let me know. You'll get through this and then you and Ben can have a happy future together. And I'll await Grandad news.'

That didn't raise any laughs at all. Nor did his toast invite much celebratory cheer either.

'So the two families had a meal which wasn't a huge success in bringing everyone together. Then what happened beyond that?' Sergeant Arthington's voice brings me back into the present. 'I imagine Caitlyn had some gruelling treatment to face.'

'She did, and it shocked me, to be honest, and my sister, Annette, how little Ben's family bothered with her whilst she was ill. She spent a right stretch in hospital when she was having the worst of the chemo, and there wasn't a visit from them, or even a get-well card – nothing. I can't imagine why they wouldn't have wanted to support her. It surprised me to hear they were all coming to her hen party.'

'Why do you think they came?'

I shrug. 'Nosiness. Something to do. Or maybe Ben made them. I don't know. All I know is that I'll never forgive them for not bothering with her when she needed all the support she could get last year. If the shoe had been on the other foot, Caitlyn would have done all she could.'

I think of how much I've worried about my sister over the last year, whilst stuck over in Liverpool, trying to keep my head in my veterinary degree. If Caitlyn had been diagnosed in the summer, I'd have taken a year out.

'But you went back to Liverpool?'

'By then, it was the end of September and Caitlyn seemed over the worst of it, and at least it wasn't too far away for me to get back every two or three weeks and I rang her nearly every day. Some days, she sounded terrible though.'

'She would have had your other sister to help take care of her, wouldn't she?'

I pause. I don't want to speak out of turn, but I don't want to lie either. 'I love Annette to bits, but she can be funny. She's a workaholic and doesn't seem to get the concept of illness. Nor does she have much time or sympathy for it. But she would have been the same if I was ill.'

'What about your dad? Does she help to look after him?'

'She visits every weekend but stays as short a time as she can get away with. She reckons he compares her unfavourably to us, but that's not true.'

'How would you describe your sister's relationship with her fiancé?'

'I don't know. He was all over her one minute and then taking off the next – really hot and cold. As far as I could see, she seemed to be on some kind of emotional roller-coaster. I never knew how up or down she would be when I saw her. It was like she had given him full control and she'd changed. She never used to be like that.'

'You've mentioned that they seemed happy after they'd got engaged?'

'It gave her a lift, and I was grateful to him for a short time. But things seemed to have gone downhill again.'

'Did she confide in you about this?'

'Once, she would have done. But I'd say for about the last two or three months, she's stopped talking to me.'

'Have you any idea why that is?'

'I just thought it must have something to do with the wedding coming up. Maybe she felt like she was betraying Ben by talking about him behind his back and confiding in me.'

'How was Caitlyn's relationship with your dad?'

Oh God. I wish they'd stop mentioning Dad. I don't see how

this is going to move things on for them. I just hope this doesn't kill him. 'Caitlyn always said I was his favourite, but I think *she* was, really. She doted on him. She visited him at least twice a week. She had a couple of friends on our street too who she caught up with.'

'Is your dad still in the home you all grew up in?'

'Yes.' I've got to say something. My sister is dead and they're trying to take me down memory lane. 'Look, I hope I don't sound rude here, but I'm struggling to see what all this has to do with finding out who has killed my sister.' Saying the words *killed my sister* is surreal. I keep expecting to wake up any moment and be able to ring Caitlyn and say, *Bloody hell, sis, I had an awful dream about you last night.* When we were kids, I always used to creep into her bed when I'd had a bad dream. A tear plops on the table next to my hands.

'I'm sorry, Emma. We're just trying to get a full picture of Caitlyn's life and everyone in it.'

I blow my nose. 'I just want you to find out who's done this to her.'

'So do we. And don't you worry, we will.' Sergeant Arthington glances at some notes she has made. 'So we've established that relations with her prospective in-laws were strained.'

'Caitlyn told me they thought she wasn't good enough to join their family. Not enough money, you see?'

'What job did she do?'

'Well, she was still on sick leave after her illness. I'd been surprised when she didn't go back to work in the new year, but she'd told me she was waiting until after the wedding. She did work for Ben's company but mainly she is, was, a physiotherapist.' I've just used the word *was*. The tears are sliding thick and fast again. I want to go to sleep and never wake up. I just want to be with my sister.

'And what about Caitlyn's other two bridesmaids – Jen and Shelley, is it? Was everything OK there?'

I dab at my eyes with a tissue. We must be nearly done here. I must be nearly through it. 'They're great friends. Not as a "three" though. Caitlyn had a separate friendship with each of them. She did her physio degree with Jen, and I think she was at sixth form college with Shelley so had known her longer.'

I remember how quiet Shelley was at the 'celebration' meal last year. 'Shelley was miffed at first at not getting to be *chief* bridesmaid, from what I can gather, particularly when it was her who got Ben organised with the ring and the proposal. She'd got over that though and seemed OK yesterday when we were getting the apartment ready.' I gesture in the apartment's direction. I can't bear the thought of my sister lying cold and lifeless in there.

'There are another two ladies with you, aren't there?'

'Yes. Adele is an old friend of Caitlyn's from school, and Mari's her neighbour.' I think back to their acidic expressions last night. 'Though I don't think they've been enjoying themselves all that much since we got here.'

'What makes you say that?'

'They've never met each other before, yet we put them in a bedroom together. I'd no idea it would cause so much offence. Plus, according to Jen, there was an argument last night.'

'Between who?'

'Jen and Caitlyn, and Adele and Mari. I don't know too much about it. I'd already gone to bed – I was sharing a room with Annette.'

'Why was Caitlyn in a bedroom on her own? Didn't you want to share with her?'

'I wanted to give her the best room. It was the only one with an ensuite. The main reason though was Caitlyn had said she wanted her own room. She still wasn't a hundred per cent after the treatment. She said she wasn't sleeping well and didn't want to be disturbing anyone. And my other sister Annette would have got the hump if Caitlyn and I had shared.' I gather we all must sound pathetic. Ten females together, sniping, backstabbing and all jealous of one another. Well, I wasn't. But the rest of them were.

'Did you hear anything of the argument last night?'

'I was out like a light. I'd been on the shots – I'm not that used to drinking, and it had been a long day.'

'Can you recall hearing *anything* during the night?'

'Not a thing. Then this morning, we all thought Caitlyn must have gone out for a walk. When she didn't get up with the rest of us. Nobody thought to check on her. To think she was laid in there... dead.' I choke on a sob. 'I'm her sister. I should have known something was wrong.'

'Have you any thoughts on who could have done this, Emma?' Sergeant Arthington has a soft voice. She seems too nice to be a police officer – dealing with God knows who for God knows what. 'You sound like you were one of the closest people to your sister.' Both officers are staring at me. I wish I knew something.

Another wave of nausea washes over me as I contemplate who could have smothered Caitlyn in her sleep. I wheeze with the force of it. 'I need some water,' I reply. 'I don't know. All I know is that she wouldn't hurt a fly. I'm sorry. I still don't feel so good.'

'OK, that's all for now. This interview is terminated at 1.44 p.m. We'll come back to you if we need anything else.' Sergeant Arthington reaches towards the recording machine.

'If you'd like to have a seat with the others.' Inspector Retford closes his notebook. 'We shouldn't be too much longer now.'

'I think we're nearly halfway with the interviews.' Sergeant Arthington stands and walks me to the door.

I'm glad things are moving. But after all this, then what? Life has changed beyond all recognition, and I don't know how to carry on living without my sister. As I enter the hallway, I am thankful for the fresh air coming from the foyer beyond the front door. 'I need some water,' I mutter at the stern-faced officer as I walk towards the kitchen, silently challenging him to try and stop me.

I gasp as I firstly splash water onto my face, then fill a glass and gulp it down. I really am wheezing again. I grip the side of the kitchen counter and take two more blasts of my inhaler. I'm not supposed to take over eight puffs in one go without getting medical help. This is so not the time for an asthma attack.

I hear some movement from the hallway between our two apartments. Curling my head around the kitchen door, I immediately recoil at what I see. A trolley, with the body of my sister covered in a sheet, ready to be taken God knows where. Nobody has even told me she's being moved.

'No!' I lurch towards the door. 'I don't want you to take her.'

'Go back inside.' The patrolling officer steps towards me.

'That's my sister! I need to see her. I'm never going to again.' I rush towards the trolley and the officer catches me by the arm. 'You can't be out here. I'm really sorry. You'll get the chance to see her after the post-mortem.'

'I want my sister.' My broken voice echoes around the hallway. 'Please. Let me see her!' As I reach for my inhaler again, I feel strong arms come around me from behind and turn into the embrace of my other sister.

'Breathe, Emma, for God's sake. Calm down. You're making yourself ill.'

I sob into her shoulder, pretending all the time that she's really Caitlyn. I'm never going to get over this.

THIRTEEN
MARI

Despite all that's going on, I'm starving. Some people lose their appetite when confronted with a stressful situation but I'm definitely one of the comfort eaters brigade. I didn't get any breakfast, apart from a slice of toast, and I've never gone this long without something proper to eat. Some might say I could do with skipping a meal. Or four. Jen certainly insinuated this when she allocated me the aisle seat on the plane with a smirk yesterday.

I glance down at my size eighteen frame as I wait for the questions to start. They've read me my rights and I've refused a solicitor. Why would I need a solicitor? My money's on Jen or Shelley for this, or possibly Annette, but who would kill their own sister?

'How long have you and Caitlyn been neighbours?'

'About six years.'

'How much time did you and Caitlyn spend together?' The police officer, Sergeant Whinstable, is overweight as well, not like his colleague, Inspector Hobbs. She looks like she could do with a good meal inside her. Though she is really pretty. She is at least ten years younger than me with blonde hair, green eyes and a great big rock of a ring on her finger. She's got everything I've ever wanted. There's only been once in my life that anyone has shown an interest in me – it gutted me when he dumped me – I'd spent a fortune on him too.

Caitlyn, too, had everything I ever wanted, or so I had thought. A beautiful home, a stake in a successful business, a good-looking man, even if he is a bit of a prat – and the possibility of marriage and children. On the face of it, she had everything to look forward to, once she'd made it into remission. I never told her and I'll never admit to it out loud, but it terrified me that she wouldn't need me so much once she wasn't ill anymore and had married Ben. It was nice to be needed and I liked to be around her. Which was why I had a plan up my sleeve.

'I haven't seen Caitlyn as much over the last couple of months.' I twiddle one of my plaits around my fingers as I speak. 'She told me she'd gone into remission. I became worried about her after that as I hardly saw her after she'd told me, and that was unusual.'

'"Worried". Why were you worried?'

'Her husband-to-be isn't always as supportive as he could be.' I could mention now about the amount of times I've seen Shelley going in and out of their house when Caitlyn wasn't there, but that's my trump card and I'm saving it for later. 'He works away all the time and puts a lot on her. She was supposed to be looking after herself. Or better still, have someone looking after her.' I press my hand down onto my rumbling stomach. I hope they can't hear it – it's so quiet in this room.

'Even whilst Caitlyn was ill, Ben would leave her a long list of instructions. She was like his personal assistant, unpaid too. Sometimes I'd help her out with orders or social media.' *Not that I ever got any thanks for it from Ben*, I nearly add, but stop myself. Caitlyn seemed grateful though.

'It sounds as though you felt a certain amount of responsibility towards her.'

'That's normal, with a friend, isn't it?' They were long days when spent on my own. I suppose I'll have that all the time, now Caitlyn's gone. I'll have to make a new friend. I despair at the prospect. I used to wait and watch for her coming home when Ben was away. I don't think she ever realised how dependent I was on her.

'So when you spent time together, was it at your house, or hers?'

'A bit of both, really. Although I only went to her house when Ben wasn't around.'

'Why was that?'

'A couple of times when I was there, he came back before Caitlyn was expecting him. He didn't make me feel very welcome. I don't know if he was like that with everybody or just me.' I don't tell them I loved being at Caitlyn's house and would pretend it was mine when I was there. My house is shabby and old-fashioned in comparison. Black and grey, like most of my clothes. Although I felt safest in my home, I enjoyed living out the fantasy when I was at Caitlyn's.

'Oh? In what way didn't Ben make you feel welcome?' The police officer leans forward in his seat.

I slump even more at the memory. 'He would completely ignore me. Then he would speak to Caitlyn in a way that suggested he had thought she would be on her own. I hate that – I'd rather people would tell me straight.' Ben had made me feel like nothing, a nobody. The only person who has made me shrink under their condescending gaze in the way he did was Jen, yesterday on the plane. They'll get what's coming to them.

'That must have been upsetting for you.' He removes his glasses and mops his brow with a grotty-looking hanky. I know how he feels. When you're as overweight as we are, stress and a warm room are not a good mix. I probably whiff a bit too. I didn't get a chance for a shower or even a squirt of deodorant this morning. I was going to get one after breakfast. If I'd have got some breakfast. I hate myself for this. My poor friend is dead and I'm thinking about my stupid fat stomach.

'It was upsetting. Especially when I helped to look after her when he'd not been there. He should have been saying thanks instead of telling me to shove off. It was nearly every day when he was working, and he was always working away. I didn't mind though – it's what you do for friends, isn't it? I just didn't expect *him* to be so rude.'

'In what ways did you look after her?'

'I'd make sure she got some dinner and when she was really struggling, I'd tidy around, do some ironing, that sort of thing. Some days she couldn't even get out of bed. It's awful stuff, that chemotherapy. I hated seeing her like that.'

'Do you think Caitlyn was happy with Ben?'

I secretly like the questions I'm being asked. Sergeant Whinstable is definitely regarding me as a close friend of Caitlyn's, not just some lonely, nuisance neighbour without a life of my own. Sometimes I felt a little 'used' for my services, particularly when I was sent packing by Ben, and initially I felt jealous of what Caitlyn had. Not the illness, of course, but the life. On the surface, Ben's a good-looking, charismatic and successful man, but she was definitely on course to be badly hurt by him and as her friend, I had a duty to protect her.

I certainly didn't feel like a friend of Caitlyn's last night though. I look at the police officer, watching me. I'm wasting time getting carried away with my thinking and he's waiting for my reply.

'I would say their relationship was up and down. It was up after they got engaged but then, like I say, I've hardly seen her for a couple of months.' I remember when she first showed me her beautiful diamond solitaire. I tried to act congratulatory, but when

I left her, I came home and stuffed my face to console myself. Firstly, because an engagement ring was what I wanted for myself, and secondly because I was worried about the risk of our friendship changing.

'Were you not involved in all the hen party preparations?'

Here we go. The bit that really, really upset me. I don't even want to talk about it, but I'll have to tell them the truth in case it comes out via one of the others. And Jen is such a cow that she's bound to say something. 'I didn't know about her hen party until last weekend.' I bite my lip.

'Oh? Was it a last-minute thing?'

'Well, no. Just nobody had thought to invite me. I was so upset with Caitlyn and I felt really left out.'

'That must have hurt.' He frowns. 'Particularly when you've been such a good friend to her.'

'It really did. Caitlyn said she'd not put me on the list because she didn't think I'd come. I don't really have nights out, but it would be nice to have been invited.'

It was one thing when we were just spending time in each other's houses, but clearly I'm not the coolest person – I don't fit in anywhere and Caitlyn was embarrassed about me. Having said that, she'd invited Adele, and she's not what you'd describe as *cool* either.

'Do you know anyone other than Caitlyn – out of the people who are here?'

'Not really. I've seen Jen and Emma in passing, when they've been visiting Caitlyn. I was there once at the same time as Emma. She's nice, like Caitlyn. I've got medical issues, so I'm nearly always at home. It's not that I'm nosy, but my chair is right next to the window that faces onto her house.'

'Did you see much of Ben's family going around?'

'Hardly ever. His daughter, Lucy, stayed there from time to time, but less so recently. It surprised me at their lack of visiting whilst Caitlyn was ill, especially when she was really struggling.'

This would be an appropriate time to mention Shelley, but something stops me. I was going to speak to her this weekend and was planning to get her on her own. I would have liked to witness her expression when telling her who I'd seen her with. I'd rehearsed my line so many times – *You've got until the end of the day to tell Caitlyn... or I will.* I've never had such power, and I was hanging onto it for a bit longer – at least until I knew what to do with it. Clearly, everything has changed now though perhaps there could still be something in it for me when I let on to Shelley and Ben what I know.

'If you don't go out too often, it was quite brave of you, then, to have attended this hen party, only really knowing the bride-to-be.'

I'm not sure whether he's asking a question here or making an observation. *Am I brave?* I know I haven't been. 'I probably shouldn't have come.' I'm really sweating in this oppressive room. It's like a furnace in here. I long for the coolness of the lounge, no matter how slowly the time is passing, just sat there. 'Caitlyn had barely spent time with me since we arrived here yesterday.'

I was so miffed when she chose Jen over me to sit with on the plane, especially with me not knowing anyone else. It wouldn't have been so bad if I could have chatted with her across the aisle but Jen had her hemmed in next to the window and there was someone we didn't know at the end of our row as well.

'So who have you been spending time with so far? Surely you've not been sitting alone?'

'They lumped me in with Adele.' I know I sound pathetic. I'm a grown woman of thirty-eight and I'm whining about who I'm having to share a room with. 'I'd never met her before, but we just had to make the best of it.'

'How were you getting on with the others? Did they make you feel welcome – part of the group?'

I almost laugh at his question. 'Not in the slightest. Most of them ignored me. Jen made a few quips about my weight and apart from that, never spoke to me. Other than when we had an argument last night.'

'Oh. What was that about?'

He likes saying *oh* – like I've surprised him. It's irritating. 'I'd heard Adele arguing with Jen and Caitlyn in the lounge. This was after everyone else had gone to bed. So I'd gone in to see what was going on. I couldn't understand why they'd be arguing. It was supposed to be a party.'

'And what was going on?'

'Adele, like me, didn't know anyone else and was also feeling left out and ignored. She'd been quiet all night. Both of us – me and Adele – had to scrape the money together for this, and pluck up courage to come, so we weren't feeling thrilled at how we were being treated, mainly by Caitlyn, but by everyone else too.'

'Go on.'

'I shouldn't have been surprised really.' I try to keep the bitterness out of my voice. 'I'm used to Caitlyn snubbing me whenever Ben returns home, but it really hurt when she literally turfed Adele and I out of the room.'

'Why did she do that?'

'She was apparently having a *private* conversation with Jen.'

'Did you find out what that was about?'

'No, but it sounded heated. Have you spoken to Jen yet? She'll obviously be able to tell you. It sounded as though it continued after they'd got rid of us.'

'I can't comment on that – but we're getting around everyone as quickly as we can. Along with the other two officers in the opposite room. Why?'

'If you haven't, you should question Jen. Like I said, their conversation sounded quite heated, and she was, of course, the last person to see her alive as far as I know.' I'm glad to be able to make the point that Jen was the last to see her. I don't expect a reply to that, and I don't get one.

'Who got up first this morning?' Inspector Hobbs asks.

'Jen and Shelley. I heard them crashing about and one of them calling from the hallway to the other. I didn't want to face anyone until I had to – not after last night. Nor did I really want to go to the spa which is what they had planned for today.' I pause and think of the hideous swimming costume I bought myself yesterday. I'd have been a laughing stock in front of the rest of them. Apart from Adele. I reckon she's got the same level of self-confidence as I have. 'I honestly should never have come here. And what a weekend it's turned out to be.'

I look around at the chintzy wallpaper. It's worse than mine at home, but at least there's a bit of colour involved. I could get my house decorated exactly like Caitlyn had hers, now that she's not around to witness me copying what she had. I'll have to get saving. Perhaps there could be something in it for me from Shelley and Ben when I let on what I know.

'Why didn't you want to go to the spa?' Inspector Hobbs looks surprised, but then she wouldn't look like ten-ton-Tessa in a cozzie.

'Have you seen the size of me? I reckon that's why Caitlyn didn't invite me in the first place. I'm an obese embarrassment.'

'I'm sure that's not the case.' The woman police officer speaks again, even though Sergeant Whinstable has asked most of the questions so far. I suppose it would be improper for him to comment on whether I am, in fact, *an obese embarrassment*. But looking at him, he probably understands how I feel.

He glances down at his notebook – he seems to note his questions before he asks them of me. 'So you were one of the last people to get up this morning?'

'That's right. Like I said, I wanted to keep myself to myself.'

'And it was your roommate, Adele, who found Caitlyn, wasn't it?'

'Yes. Poor thing. It was a huge shock for all of us, but to have been the one who found her...' Her violent scream will probably echo in my mind for the rest of my life.

'Did *you* hear anything during the night, Mari?'

'Not a thing. I sleep really heavily. I'm sorry – I wish I could tell you something that could help. I thought the world of Caitlyn, I really did, despite things going awry lately. I just put it down to her getting over cancer and all the pre-wedding stuff. Things would have gone back to normal between us.' *Especially when I'd stopped the wedding,* I think to myself.

'Thank you, Mari. You can rejoin the others now.' He says it like it's something I want to do. Really, I'd rather sit somewhere on my own; be alone and make sense of my jumbled thoughts.

'I could really do with getting some lunch.' My belly growls as I stand. 'I'm on tablets that have to be taken with food, you see.'

'We've only got four more people to see.' Sergeant Whinstable closes his notebook and stands. 'I don't think we'll be looking at more than another hour.' He's got big sweat patches under his arms. I probably have too. It's a good job I'm wearing black.

'That also depends on what's happening in the other apartment,' adds Inspector Hobbs. 'But after we've spoken to the last four ladies, we'll give you all a full update on what will happen next.'

Everyone looks up as I return to the lounge. I notice Michaela is missing; she must have been called whilst I was in. Everyone else is sitting, waiting in silence. I wish they had allowed me to bring my holdall in with me from the other apartment. There's some chocolate and crisps in there.

I retake my place beside Adele who weakly smiles at me. She's the only ally I've got here. It's like it was when I was at school. All the way through high school, I sat next to Catherine Jessop who was about as uncool and unpopular as I was. I need to shed this person I've always been. Suddenly, I feel a fire in my belly that has never been there before. Caitlyn's death has triggered something within me and things are going to change.

'They've taken Caitlyn away,' she whispers. 'Whilst you were in there. Her body, she's gone.'

Jen looks across the room at me, her expression a cross between grief and condemnation. I don't like her one bit. She jerks her head up as they call her name. I look around at the others, noticing that there's only Shelley and Annette left after Jen and Michaela come back.

If they've taken Caitlyn away, they must be getting close to finishing whatever they're doing in the other apartment. I wonder where she's gone. I can hardly bear to think of her on some cold metal trolley, being sliced and diced for evidence.

I need some food. I need my meds. My anxiety rises at the realisation I've not taken any of my tablets today. No wonder I can't think straight. I roll my neck around in a circle to release the ache of tension whilst I pray they won't be longer than another hour. It's like waiting to be hung, drawn and quartered. I hate myself for thinking these impatient thoughts. Caitlyn would probably have done anything to be here with us, even if sitting, watching the time and staring at a wall. She wasn't even thirty. What a waste of a life. I'm going to really miss her.

FOURTEEN
MICHAELA

As I follow the policewoman past the closed door, I hear Mari's voice behind it. She even *sounds* fat. God, I've become so bitchy since I got into my forties – I must be perimenopausal or something. I see the worst in everyone. Especially my now departed sister-in-law-to-be. At least I'm going to get my brother back now.

'We're just in here.' The woman pushes the already ajar door open.

The skinnier of the two police detectives is screwing a lid back onto a bottle of water. There's no warmth in his face as he gestures for me to sit.

'I'm Inspector Retford,' he says, like I care. 'This is Sergeant Arthington.'

I nod at them. After all, this is no time to be exchanging pleasantries.

'Let's get started.' Sergeant Arthington reaches across the table and presses a button. 'Because we're not in a usual police interview room, we're using the portable recording equipment, just so everything that is discussed between us is on record.'

I nod again. A long beep signals that recording has begun. She reads me my rights and then asks whether I require legal representation whilst they ask me some questions. 'No. I've nothing to hide. Ask away.' I realise I probably sound glib for someone who's in this situation. Someone whose potential sister-in-law has just been found dead. I should probably tone it down a bit. I don't want them to suspect that I'm glad she's out of the way.

'So. You're Michaela Mortimer,' Sergeant Arthington begins. There's a weariness to her voice which suggests she'll be glad to get to the end of these interviews. 'Do you have a middle name?'

'Ann,' I reply. I've always hated my middle name. It's the same as my mother's – boring.

She takes my date of birth and address, then surveys me with a serious expression. 'We'd like to ask you some questions in relation to the death of Caitlyn Elizabeth Nicholson. I understand you're Ben's sister, so had she lived, Caitlyn would have become your sister-in-law?'

'That's right.' I try to load a sadness I do not feel into my voice. In all honesty, Caitlyn marrying my brother would have complicated everything. She had enough clout in my brother's life and our family company as it was. If they'd married, Caitlyn would have got her hands well and truly on the business then. The business that *my* dad built from the ground up. Ben bought him out when he took early retirement.

If Ben were to die, or they were to divorce, Caitlyn would have been entitled to some sort of settlement. Mum and Lucy were worried about that too. Especially Lucy. Mum did nicely when Dad left her. In fact, she took him to the cleaners. Lucy, well, it's her inheritance. It should be her company one day, and I know she'll always see me right. I couldn't have said the same about Caitlyn.

'There must have been some sort of relationship between Caitlyn and yourself. Just for you... for you to be here, as part of her hen party.' Sergeant Arthington taps her pen against her chin as she speaks.

I suppose it would look like that at face value. But it's a long way from the truth. I look the policewoman straight in the eye.

'To be honest, it surprised me when I got invited. Caitlyn and I have always kept some distance between us. I figured that by inviting me, she wanted to get to know me better before the wedding, who knows?' There's no point in me lying. I'll only trip myself up. 'Plus my mum and niece, Lucy, said they'd go as long as I did, so it was a chance to spend time with them as well.'

My voice sounds hollow in this room. Probably because they've removed all the furniture. I don't think any of us would have gone without the other two. Caitlyn's OK, but Ben could do much better. He was only going through with this wedding, in my opinion, because he feels sorry for her. They only got engaged after she'd been diagnosed with cancer. But I don't tell the police this.

I also don't add that without us three, there'd have been a paltry seven people. And two of them would have been Adele and Mari! What a hen party! I'd like to think that if I ever get married, it would be better than what I've seen here. I'd want to go abroad and have clubs, strippers, get dressed up, the works. It would have to be all about me. I've always been outgoing and love to be the centre of attention. This has been more like a wake than a hen party. Literally.

I must admit, I felt sorry for Emma before. She's probably the best out of the three sisters. It must have been horrendous, seeing Caitlyn's body carted out like that. I do have a heart, despite what people say, and I can imagine what it must be like to lose a sibling.

Dad had another kid with the woman he ran off with, but I don't much care for my half-sister. I can't see that ever changing either. *She's* got my dad whilst Ben and I rarely see him these days.

If anything was to happen to Ben though, I don't think I could cope. We've always been close. He's my rock. I'm aware I rely on him far more than I should. He's always looked after me. Our dad provided for us in a physical sense, but he was never there when we were growing up. Ben was the one I went to when I needed help or support. We were both gutted when Dad left, Ben especially. After years of trying to get Dad's attention, he chose another woman and thought allowing Ben to buy him out of the company at a cheaper price made up for the fact that he was moving away and leaving us.

'What do you mean when you say you and Caitlyn kept one another at a distance?'

The night Ben told me he was leaving our flat enters my head. We'd lived together for three years and it was a great arrangement. Ben had plied me with gin before telling me. If he'd been deeply in love with some woman, maybe I'd have taken it better.

'I've been with Caitlyn for a year, Michaela,' he'd said.

'That's nothing. Aren't you happy with things as they are? Me, you and Lucy, when she stays here?' I'd glanced around at our fabulous kitchen as I spoke. Filled with gadgets and usually lots of laughter.

'Of course.' He had put his arm around me then. 'But we always knew it was only going to be a temporary arrangement, didn't we? Until one of us met someone.'

'I'd hardly call Caitlyn "meeting someone".'

'Why not? What's up with her?'

This was my chance to speak up. To try to stop him. 'Just an observation, Ben. You've always seemed very matter-of-fact about her. And...' I sniffed, 'you could do a hell of a lot better.'

'Look. You're right to a point. I like her and we get on well.'

'You like her and you get on well!'

'It's not purely a personal decision.'

'What do you mean?'

'Well – on a practical level, we've found a place by the airport.'

'You've already found a place? Without telling me! Great.' I couldn't imagine life without him being here. Lucy would probably stop coming to stay as much too.

'Nothing will change for you, Michaela. I own this flat outright. You don't have to pay a thing. You'll stay on the payroll, as always. And we'll have a spare room at the new house anytime you want to stay.'

'I think I'll pass on that, thanks. I'll leave it for Lucy. That's if she still stays with you. She's not enamoured with the Caitlyn situation either.'

'What do you mean – "the Caitlyn situation"?'

'Don't think we haven't noticed. She's only been around for a year and she's sticking her beak into the family business.'

'She's an asset, Michaela. She's got an eye for the designs and she's brilliant with the clients. And I only give her access to certain things. Don't worry, I've got total control. But the business side is another reason I'm moving in with her.'

'I don't get it.' My eyes had fallen on a photo of me, him and Lucy from the year before last. Before *she* had turned up and made herself an *asset*.

'The house will be great for giving dinner parties. It's what we need to move things along. Investment. Clients. Schmoozing. It's what Mum and Dad had to do. Remember?'

'I've not heard you use the word "love" once in all this.'

'Michaela?' Sergeant Arthington is staring at me, presumably still waiting for me to answer.

'Sorry, I was miles away. Can you repeat the question please?' I wish I was miles away. Back at home. Away from all this.

'What did you mean when you said that you and Caitlyn kept a distance from one another?'

'When we saw each other, we got on fine. Though we only really had Ben in common. We never became friendly.'

'How did you feel about their relationship?'

I reply without hesitating. 'I was surprised when they got engaged – he wasn't the marrying type and preferred playing the field. I could never keep up with him. I hope I'm not speaking out of turn here, but I think Ben proposed to Caitlyn because he felt sorry for her. You probably know she was really ill last year?'

'Yes. Everyone we've spoken to has mentioned it.' Sergeant Arthington looks down at her notes. 'But I'm sure that even though you weren't close, it was still good news when you were told she'd gone into remission.'

Is that a question or an observation? There's only one way I can answer it, isn't there? 'Yeah, I guess so. I can't remember who told me about it.' I actually remember exactly who had told me. It had been Lucy, moaning and groaning about how the *royal wedding*, as we had dubbed it, would now go ahead. A full day of watching Caitlyn gloating in the spotlight. Trying to smile all day would have cracked my face. Especially as I knew Ben didn't really love her.

'Did your brother seem excited about getting married?' She asks as though she's a mind reader.

'My brother doesn't do getting excited.' I half smile, then a cloud crosses my thoughts. 'Has he even been told yet? He'll be out of his meeting by now so his phone should be back on.'

'I can't answer that question just now. I'm sorry.' There's a look of regret on her face. Her colleague sits next to her, still as a rock. I know there needs to be two of them, but he's not exactly doing a lot.

'Why? I only want to know if my brother has been told. He's got a right to know what's happened.'

'I know it must be frustrating for you all.' Oh! He speaks. The officer, Retford or whatever his name is, says, 'But I'm sure you can see the importance of speaking to you all before you can confer any further with one another, or with anyone else,' Sergeant Arthington adds. 'And that includes your brother for now.'

I want to challenge her on what she is insinuating with the word *confer* but decide to leave it. 'When will we get our phones back?' I ask instead. I know it sounds crass, given the circumstances, but I'm lost without my phone. And Ben will need me when he finds out what's happened. It will be nice to have him leaning on me for a change. I've no way of getting hold of him in London. Not so long as they've taken our phones and they're keeping us holed up in here. I don't even know exactly where his meeting is to ring the hotel direct. Mum or Lucy might know.

'Your phones will be returned to you as soon as possible.' The sympathetic expression Sergeant Arthington seemed to be displaying when I first entered this room has changed, and now looks to be one of judgement, not in a good way. But that might just be my imagination. I guess every one of us is a suspect at the moment.

She glances down at her notepad. She's got immaculate handwriting. 'I'll continue with our questions by asking whether you heard anything throughout the night? Any comings or goings, noises or voices, anything at all?'

'Just Caitlyn and Jen arguing. For ages.' I add the last bit for effect. It's true. I heard them; Mari and Adele too but I won't bother mentioning them. I want the finger pointing firmly towards high and mighty Jen.

I don't mention that Lucy and I had words with her too. It was only brief and I don't want to complicate things. Besides, from what I can gather, Lucy didn't mention it either.

'Caitlyn and Jen were close friends, weren't they? Why were they arguing? Do you know?'

'No idea. You'll have to ask Jen about that. The only thing I know that might help you is that many moons ago, when they were teenagers, Jen was going out with my brother.'

'Oh?' The tone of her voice and the look on her face shows more interest than in the whole of the conversation so far. 'So you've known Jen for a while then?'

'No. I only met her once at some family do. It was years ago.'

'What occasion was that?'

'A wedding. I used to make fun of him. *Jen and Ben!* It soon fizzled out though.'

She looks to be stifling a smile. Not really appropriate at a time like this. 'Did Caitlyn know about this, erm, relationship?'

'Again. You'll have to ask Jen that.' I'd love to be a fly on the wall in this room when they get her in. I reckon we might wait some time for them to interview her.

'Did you hear anyone or anything else during the night?'

'Now you come to mention it, perhaps there was a bit of banging. I was half asleep, so I didn't bother seeing what was going on. It was a long day yesterday, and I was tired.'

'Banging?'

'Yes, doors or windows maybe.' An obtrusive thought enters my mind. The money I could make selling this story to the press. *Chief bridesmaid smothers bride-to-be to death as she sleeps.* 'Jen and Caitlyn were the last people to go to bed. Probably no one saw her alive after Jen.' It's like something out of Cluedo. Whodunnit. We'd even dubbed our lounge *the drawing room*.

'After you went to bed, you stayed there, in your room, all night? You didn't get up for the bathroom or anything?'

'I did but everything was dark. I didn't see or hear anything during the night apart from a bit of banging, like I said. God, maybe Caitlyn was lying dead *all* night. If it was Jen who killed her at the start of the night, that is.' I watch their faces for a reaction, but there isn't one. 'She looked as though she'd been dead for a while when we saw her this morning.' The image of Caitlyn's face returns to my mind. Pale, bruised and bloodied, she reminded me of the princess in the fairy tale who was asleep for a hundred years, with her blonde hair fanned around her. My brother never could resist blonde hair. She was lucky not to lose it with her treatment, but according to Mum, she risked her fertility instead. They had apparently given her a newer type of chemotherapy, which doesn't cause hair loss. I'd rather temporarily lose my hair than my fertility. Me and Lucy have talked about that and she was beyond relief when she found out there was little chance of her ever having to compete with a younger half-brother or -sister for Ben's attention or money. And I also would have done anything necessary to protect my lifestyle.

'So,' Sergeant Arthington says, making me jump. 'The first you knew of what had happened to Caitlyn was when Adele raised the alarm earlier this morning?'

'That's right. We were just waiting to have our breakfast, and she was yelling the place down. It was awful. We were going to eat, get ready, then go to the spa this afternoon. It's where we should be now, in fact.' I loop my shoulders around. I could have right done with being there. This must be the longest day I've ever known.

'How are *you* feeling, Michaela?' Sergeant Arthington brushes her fringe back as she peers at me, as though I'm a specimen under her microscope. 'All this must have come as a shock for you.'

'It has. Of course it has.' I lower my voice. 'I'm sorry I'm not weeping all over the place. I'm not like that, and I guess it hasn't sunk in yet. And like I said, my family and I hadn't got to know Caitlyn all that well. Until I get out of here and see my brother, it probably won't sink in. I'll have to support him then.'

'We should be in more of a position soon to let you, and everyone else, know what's going to happen next.'

Her tone is dismissive. Thank God. It looks like I'm out of here. One step closer.

'Is that it? Can I go?'

'For now. But we might need to ask you some more questions, Michaela.'

'Well, you know where to find me.' I don't like the condescending use of my name. I get to my feet and walk to the door. Retford is there before me and opens it. *Aren't you the gentleman?* I resist saying.

As I pass the end of the hallway, I see two people in white suits brushing the front door of our apartment, presumably for fingerprints. Maybe, unlike how Jen has insinuated, they're thinking that it wasn't one of us – that someone came in from the outside. Or it could be a combination of both. I guess we'll find out soon enough.

'You were quick,' Mum mouths at me as I retake my place in the room that's become our prison cell today. It's a relief to be sitting back next to her. At least that's over with.

'I couldn't really tell them a great deal, could I? I was fast asleep all night. And it's not as if Caitlyn and I were great mates, is it?'

'No talking,' barks the officer at the door. Jumped up twerp. He's only one of those community officers getting off on ordering us about. I shoot him a look that hopefully conveys what I think of him.

FIFTEEN

JEN

I pass the two policewomen, muttering to one another in a corner of the hallway.

A blast of heat hits me as I enter the room they've directed me to. It's decorated like the one I slept in last night – one wall is a headache-inducing geometric pattern, so I'm glad that the seat I am directed to faces the plain magnolia wall. Though, instead of the faint smell of Shelley's perfume and my body spray, it reeks of body odour in here. 'Is it possible to open a window?' I say to Sergeant Whinstable. I don't know how his colleague stands it. I'd be sick, spending all day breathing in his stench. No wonder she's in the hallway.

He pushes the window as far as it will go, which isn't far at all, and the curtains suck themselves into the gap that has been created, eliminating any chance of extra air. The policewoman enters the room, glances at me, then presses a button on a machine at the side of us.

'I'm Inspector Tina Hobbs,' she announces after a long tone sounds from their recording machine. She positions herself directly in line with me. 'I will conduct this interview and Sergeant David Whinstable will take notes.' She takes my full name and address before continuing. 'Do you want us to call you Jen or Jennifer?'

'Jennifer please. Only friends call me Jen.'

She appears to raise an eyebrow before continuing. 'As we've explained before, Jennifer, we'd normally conduct this sort of inquiry at the station. However, because of the number of you that we're having these preliminary conversations with, we'll only move you on to the station should it become necessary.'

'Why would it become necessary?'

'If we decide to arrest anyone after these meetings, or if any evidence comes to light from the apartment.'

Something tightens in my stomach at the word 'arrest'. 'How long will it be before we know? What happens next, I mean?'

'I can't say at this stage. I'm sorry.'

She doesn't look sorry at all. 'You can't keep us locked in that room all day.' I gesture towards the door. 'We've only had water to drink. People are getting hungry as well. If we were at the police station, you'd have to bring us lunch. We haven't had a proper breakfast after what has happened. We're talking basic human rights here.'

'I'm sorry for the loss of your friend.' Inspector Hobbs looks pointedly at me, the slap of her words stopping me in my tracks, as if to say, *Focus on what's important, you selfish cow.* 'You were to be her chief bridesmaid, weren't you?'

'Yes.' I think of the beautiful deep-red bridesmaid dress I would have worn alongside Caitlyn's lace and silk gown. Sadness gnaws at me.

'How long have you known each other?' Her tone seems softer now that I've stopped moaning about basic human rights and the rest of it. We're bound to be touchy though. This has been going on for hours. Someone had to say something. Whilst they won't let us know what is going on, or even speak to each other, we cannot even begin to process what has happened to Caitlyn.

'Since I was about nineteen. We did our physiotherapy

training at university together.' I recall Caitlyn when we were teenagers, before she became ground down with the loss of her mother, then her father's illness – then her own. We had such a laugh at uni. Our rooms were side by side in the halls of residence. By the end of freshers' week, I felt as if I'd known her all my life. I realise I'm smiling as I'm thinking of her. Inspector Hobbs is staring at me.

'Sorry. I was just remembering when we were in our halls together. We had some good times.' I don't want them thinking even worse of me for smiling. It's not exactly a day to smile. I haven't cried a great deal yet, though I think once we're over this formal bit, it will hit me like a train.

'So did you get to know Caitlyn before or after your relationship with Ben?' Inspector Hobbs's face bears a strange expression, like they've got the upper hand.

'How do you know about that?'

'It doesn't matter.'

'Was it Karen?' I hope no one else knows. It's been my best-kept secret for years. I look at her. She's waiting for an answer and evidently not going to tell me where she's got the details from. 'It was before. I was only seventeen. And it was nothing. We just went out a bit.'

What I'm saying isn't strictly true. I was upset when he dumped me after six months, saying we were getting too serious. Then I saw him out in town a week later with someone else. He was the first boyfriend who I ever let get close enough to hurt me.

'How did Caitlyn feel about the two of you having… history?'

'She never knew. It was years later when they got together and there didn't seem to be any point in telling her about it.'

The truth is, we both, me *and* Ben, let the opportunity go by, well, Ben did anyway.

. . .

'This is Ben,' she announced, looking from him to me. 'Ben, this is my best friend Jen. That's hilarious – your names rhyme – imagine if the two of you had got together instead – Jen and Ben!'

She didn't know how near the knuckle she was. And I had nearly fallen through the floor when I saw him. Though eight years had passed, he'd barely altered. I waited for him to acknowledge me, but he had held his hand out and said, 'Pleased to meet you, Jen.' The chance to tell Caitlyn that we had once been together passed. And to be honest, as soon as I saw him, old feelings came flooding back – I didn't want to risk her finding out. There was nothing to be gained, and I didn't want her to know that I still liked him.

'OK, we may come back to that. I gather from speaking to the others that Caitlyn has been poorly recently?'

Thank God she's moved on. I didn't expect my historic relationship to be mentioned. 'Yes. She's really been through it. She lost her mother to the same disease. I've been in awe of what a fighter she's been over the last year.' I stare at the table. 'She's only been in remission for a couple of months. I can't understand who the hell would do this to her.'

'That's what we intend to find out.' The police officer brushes her fringe from her eyes. 'Was it you who organised her hen party?' She sweeps her eyes across the room we inhabit as she speaks. She's probably thinking I could have chosen somewhere somewhat more salubrious for the hen party of my best friend.

'Yes. It took a fair bit of sorting. People dropped out who should have been coming, and others, like Mari and Lucy, didn't decide they were coming until the last minute. Karen and Michaela were late in the day too with their acceptances.' I take a breath. 'At one point, I had been wondering whether the whole thing would have to be cancelled. We needed a minimum of eight for the apartment, plus what fun is a hen party with only four or five people there?'

'Who dropped out?'

'A couple of university friends and Ben's cousin. Oh, and a cousin of Caitlyn's.'

'We'll need to take their details from you, if that's OK?'

I don't see why they would need to speak to people who haven't even come this weekend, but they must have their reasons. I don't ask. The sooner I get out of here, the better. 'Well, I'd need my phone to get at them. I'd set up a hen party group online to get everyone together. Without Caitlyn in it, of course. It was all to be a surprise. She didn't know where we were going until we got to the airport.'

'What made you decide to come to Dublin?'

'Caitlyn didn't want to go too far and would have happily stayed in Yorkshire. Her dad isn't well, and she was still getting her strength back after her illness.' Her face swims into my mind again. Though she had regained little weight, her face was looking less gaunt than it had since she had gone into remission, and she had been looking *slightly* better.

When we had our dress fittings a couple of days ago, the seamstress had said she would have to nip the dress in at the waist and pad out the bust. Caitlyn had looked sad when trying it on. She didn't fill it like she originally had, but still looked beautiful. I could picture how she would have appeared, walking down the aisle at the church they had booked, her cathedral veil cascading behind her.

'What can you tell me about an argument in your apartment late last night?' Inspector Hobbs looks me straight in the eye. I feel as though I am being accused of something.

I inhale the sharp smell of body odour as I'm about to open my mouth to respond. I don't know how she bears working with her colleague if he always smells like this. I'd have to say something to him. 'Well, it wasn't me and Caitlyn arguing with each other, if that's what you're asking. We were friends for ten years without a cross word. No, we were discussing something privately, then Adele came in, wanting to have a chat with Caitlyn, clearly expecting us to shut up, and for me to leave her and Caitlyn to it.'

'So, it was Adele that was arguing with Caitlyn?' She writes something down and I get the impression that someone has told her otherwise.

'She was arguing with both of us. I know it sounds like schoolgirl stuff, but Caitlyn and me were in the middle of talking about something important. Caitlyn couldn't just switch off from it and give Adele her undivided attention. She promised she'd spend some time with her tomorrow – well, today now.'

'Was Adele OK with this?'

'Not at all. She was already peeved at not being asked to be a bridesmaid, as they're old school friends, and was upset at having to share a room with Mari, who she'd never met. But we didn't have enough rooms to give them a room each.'

'What happened next?'

'Mari must have heard the raised voices, so she came into the lounge too. She was sticking up for Adele. It was the last thing Caitlyn needed. And she'd had such a good day up to that point. I'd made sure of it.' Sergeant Whinstable's pen scratches against his notebook. He appears to be making notes of key points, and I hope that doesn't mean that some of us will have to answer extra questions relating to what someone else has said.

'So four of you were arguing then? Didn't anyone else in the apartment get up to see what was going on between you? You must have been making a fair amount of noise.'

'No. Everyone had had quite a lot to drink. That's what I put it down to with Adele. Her reaction to us was totally over the top.'

'But you can definitely confirm that there was no argument between you and Caitlyn?'

'No argument whatsoever. However, she'd also had words with Lucy prior to that. Lucy had been the last one to go to bed.'

'Oh, what was that about?'

'Just Lucy being snarky. She's never taken to Caitlyn.'

'Why's that?'

'It was all jealousy, if you ask me. Typical stepfamily stuff. Caitlyn usually handled it well.'

'And did she last night?'

'To a point. Until Michaela came in and put her oar in. She reckoned to be sticking up for her niece but she was awful.'

'What do you mean?' Inspector Hobbs has sat up straighter in her seat, clearly interested.

'There wasn't that much said between them, but Michaela had the last word by saying that she would do everything in her power to ensure the wedding didn't go ahead.'

Inspector Hobbs nods slowly then glances at Sergeant Whinstable who is writing something down. I feel a short sense of power at possibly incriminating Michaela.

'What was it you and Caitlyn were talking about after everyone else had returned to their rooms? You've mentioned it was private, and important.'

I don't know whether I should say anything. I could really open up a can of worms. There's a big enough one opened up already with the revelation that I used to go out with Ben. Would Caitlyn have even been friends with me if she'd known? Who knows? I can't imagine she'd have confided in me much. Is the fact that Caitlyn thought Ben was having an affair relevant to anything? My hesitation doesn't go unnoticed by Inspector Hobbs.

'We need to know *everything*, Jennifer. This is an investigation into a suspected murder. In order for us to catch whoever has done this to your friend, we must know whatever you can tell us.'

'OK. I'll tell you. Caitlyn became *really* upset. I think Lucy and Michaela, then Adele and Mari, tipped her over. She told me she'd barely been holding it together all day. I'd never have guessed until we spoke. She'd hidden it well. She was quieter than she usually would be, but she seemed to be having a good time, especially in the evening.'

'Why was she upset?' Sergeant Whinstable's pen is poised over his notebook again.

'It was the first time she'd said anything to me, which I'm surprised about. She would normally confide in me, especially about something like this. She'd found out that Ben was having an affair and said she had known about it for a couple of months. I can't believe she kept something like that to herself for so long.'

'Was she certain?'

'That's what I said to her, and she said she was.'

'How did she find out?' I see a note of sympathy in Inspector Hobbs's eyes.

'He'd been acting weird for a while, apparently. She said he had become really distant with her and was working away from home all the time. She found out for sure when she overheard him speaking on the phone with the woman he's been carrying on with.'

'Did Caitlyn tell you what she'd overheard?'

'Yes, he'd said something like, "You're like a drug to me." She didn't tell me much more. Adele interrupted that bit of our conversation, like I said.'

'Did she say *how* Ben was acting weird?'

'She said he was acting kind of indifferently towards her – I think you can sense these things, can't you?'

Neither of them replies, so I continue. 'The more she tried to bring him back to her, the more he pulled away, so she said.'

'But they were getting married in, what...' Inspector Hobbs looks at her watch, presumably for the date, 'three weeks. Ben might have been nervous. Marriage is a big step for anyone.'

'That's another thing.' I slide my cardigan off. We didn't need to go to a sauna today. I'm getting boiled alive in here. 'They'd had a row – Caitlyn and Ben. He'd told her he didn't want to get married to her anymore, then he said he felt trapped and was being forced into things.'

'Trapped. Why?'

'Caitlyn had only just gone into remission. He'd have looked terrible, calling their wedding off with only three weeks to go.'

'It's better than marrying someone if you're not sure about it.'

'I agree. But Caitlyn was devastated. And she'd apparently threatened to ruin Ben if he called it off.'

'How?'

'She hasn't been as active recently, but she was the energy in that company he has. Ben doesn't know how to speak to people. He's abrupt – a real narcissist, if you ask me. I can see I had a lucky escape when I was younger. If it wasn't for Caitlyn, they'd never have had the investment, or the contracts she'd secured for them. She had warned him that she would damage his reputation if he carried on treating her so badly.' When she had told me this, I felt proud of her – no matter what she had been through, and was going through, she still had some fire in her belly.

'But these are *business* people?' Sergeant Whinstable leans back in his seat, which creaks under his weight. 'Surely they wouldn't just pull their contract, or revoke on an investment because of some marital hiccup between the people they're doing business with?'

'Caitlyn has got to know some of them really well, especially the women – she and Ben have given dinner parties in their own home. What she also could have been planning to tell their investors and customers was how much trouble the business was in.' Another can of worms. 'I don't know the ins and outs of it all as Caitlyn only mentioned it last night, and like I say, the conversation was interrupted. I was more interested in how he had been treating her than the problems with his company. But you'll be speaking to Ben, won't you?'

'Yes, of course. Do you know whether his family knew about any problems the company has been having?'

'I've no idea. They keep banging on about some important meeting Ben's at today though.'

'Do you know whether Caitlyn had life insurance, or any substantial savings?'

That's an interesting question. I'd like to know why they're asking it. 'I know she had life insurance and maybe some sort of mortgage cover as I witnessed both documents for her. She also put a hell of an amount of the money she inherited after her mother's death into Ben's business.'

'Do you know how much?'

'I don't – sorry – but I'm sure there will be a record of it somewhere.'

'What about savings?'

'I'm not sure, other than the savings for their wedding. She mentioned on the journey over that all the balances were due to be paid. The venue was the main one.'

'Was it to be a fairly big wedding then?'

'Big enough. Family and friends, obviously, but like I said before, Caitlyn knew many of their investors and larger customers on a personal level – I know some of them had been invited. To the evening reception at least.'

I'd joked to her when she told me about the business attendees, that lots of people meet their future spouses at someone else's wedding. I reminded her to make sure she kept her chief bridesmaid in mind and be sure to invite plenty of eligible bachelors. I'm smiling again as I think this. Inspector Hobbs's serious expression drags me back into the here and now.

'What I don't understand,' she says slowly, 'is why she was even considering going through with a wedding if she seriously suspected her future husband was having an affair, especially if he'd also told her, plain as day, that *he* didn't want to go through with the wedding?'

'I completely agree with you, but her self-esteem was on the floor.' Caitlyn's face enters my mind again, all its sparkle having faded away. 'I guess she thought she needed him. She admitted herself that she had become clingy and needy. Things used to be great between them, so she was probably chasing to get that back again.'

'So last night.' Inspector Hobbs glances at her watch again. 'The four of you are all having words about who is, or isn't, speaking to who, and who should have been a bridesmaid, or not – then what?'

'Mari and Adele eventually went back to their room. They were still in a foul mood with me this morning though. Before all... this.' I wave my hand as though that covers it.

'And what about yourself and Caitlyn?'

'I gave her a hug and told her to get some sleep. She looked done in. I said we'd talk more at the spa today and I'd help her get it all sorted. One way or another.'

'So who went to bed first – yourself, or Caitlyn?'

'Me. I was sharing with Shelley, one of the other bridesmaids. I left Caitlyn in the kitchen. I think she was getting herself some water to take to bed. She had her own room – the one with the ensuite.'

'Why was she in her own room? I'd have thought it more usual for a bride-to-be to share with their chief bridesmaid.'

'Again, I agree, but she'd asked for her own room when I was making all the arrangements – I don't think she was sleeping too well.'

'OK. So who locked up and turned everything off?'

'There were only the lights. I think it was me who turned the light off in the lounge. Caitlyn must have turned off in the kitchen and hallway.'

'What about locking the door?'

'Well, that's the really strange thing. I'm meticulous about locking the door at home, and even though I'd had a few glasses of wine last night, I'm absolutely certain I locked the main door.' I've gone over and over this in my head this morning and can visualise myself locking that door last night. 'However, when Shelley went to the shop this morning, she said the door had been unlocked all night.' I remember some joke she had made now about how *we could all have been murdered in our beds*. I didn't know how ironic that comment would be.

'And you're definitely sure you locked it?'

'Well, I think so, but you know what it's like when you doubt yourself. And I'd had a few drinks too, like I said.'

She nods, with a hint of a smile. 'So as far as you know, you were the last person to see Caitlyn before she went to bed?'

'Yes.' I hope they're not suspecting me of anything. Surely not.

'Who got up first this morning?'

'Shelley and me. Like I said, we were sharing a room so woke each other up. I was tidying the apartment and Shelley went to the shop to get some bits and pieces so I could cook breakfast for everyone.'

'You were cooking breakfast on your own? For ten people? Wasn't anyone helping?'

'Karen did eventually, after they'd got up. Mari and Adele still weren't speaking to me. I tried to talk to Karen whilst it was just her and me in the kitchen. To see if she knew anything about Ben – she is his mum, after all. I gather from what Caitlyn's said that they're fairly close. I got little from Karen though.' It's hard to believe this was just a few hours ago – it feels like much longer.

'At that point, did you not think to wake Caitlyn? Especially given the fact something had upset her the night before?'

'I thought I'd let her sleep. God knows she needed her rest after what she'd been through. But then Shelley noticed her coat had gone, so we assumed that she'd gone for a walk. Which also explained the door having been unlocked at that point. It was only when we started to serve breakfast that Adele went into Caitlyn's room.'

'So what *did* you do, in the time between finding Caitlyn and us arriving at the scene?'

'Obviously, I was in a complete state of shock. We all were. After we had heard Adele screaming, we were all in the room with her... just panicking, crying.'

'How long were you all in the room?'

'I'm not sure. Maybe about five minutes. Everyone was in a right state.'

'Then what?'

'I realised that we were contaminating a crime scene, so I got everyone into the lounge. I asked everyone what they knew, or thought could have happened before you got here. I wanted to have all the information for when you got here. Then I sat with Caitlyn for a few moments. I knew it might be my last chance to be on my own with her.' Tears fill my eyes as reality hits me again. It's a peculiar feeling that keeps coming and going.

Her eyes narrow. 'You sat with her even though you'd already asked everyone else to vacate the room – being that it was a crime scene, as you rightly said?'

'I'd already been in there, so I didn't think going in again would make much difference. Besides, I touched nothing.'

She lets a long breath out. 'Do you know whether anyone in your party has informed anyone else, outside your group here, of what has happened? Obviously, people still had access to their phones.'

I really could be in trouble here. 'I don't know. I don't think so. Everyone was in total shock. Shelley suggested contacting Ben, but Michaela, Ben's sister, said we shouldn't. All she was bothered about was him not being interrupted at some "important" meeting he was in, like that would be more urgent than news of his fiancée's body being found. She said his phone would be switched off, anyway.'

Sergeant Whinstable pokes his fingers beneath his glasses and rubs the corners of his eyes. 'There will be officers checking everyone's mobile phone logs so we'll be able to clarify any external contact soon.'

Inspector Hobbs hovers a finger over the button of the recording equipment. 'I think that's probably all we need to ask for now, Jennifer, unless you've anything else you'd like to ask, Sarge?' She glances towards her colleague.

'No. Have *you* anything else you'd like to tell us, Jennifer?' I'm sure I detect an accusatory edge to his voice.

'The only thing is that I really think you should be speaking to Ben.'

As I return to the lounge, I notice across the passageway that our apartment door has been closed. There's no longer an officer guarding it, and I can't see or hear anything going on over there, so maybe they've finished their search. I know they've taken Caitlyn away. As if poor Emma had to witness that. She'll probably need counselling after what she's been through today. And what she's still got to go through. Obviously, what's happened has yet to come to light.

Everyone watches me as I sit down. Nobody speaks. The presence of the officer in the lounge doorway ensures that. Once they release us, I think the pub is in order. I need a gin. It will be interesting to know what questions everyone else has been asked. I imagine the questions are quite similar at this stage. That will change if any one of us is interviewed for a second time.

Annette isn't here – she must be in the other makeshift interview room. I look around the group. Now they've finished with me, they'll be in any minute for Shelley, and after that we should be told what is going to happen next. They will have spoken to all of us. I drop my aching head into my hands and feel someone's hand on my shoulder. What an absolute mess.

SIXTEEN
ANNETTE

I don't like leaving Emma on her own but haven't exactly got a lot of choice. She's barely stopped crying since she returned from being interviewed. At least she has got on top of her asthma. I just feel numb. I might not have shown it, but I loved Caitlyn – as sisters, we've always clashed and people might have thought we didn't like each other but when push came to shove... I just haven't cried yet. Maybe I will when I'm forced to talk about what's happened.

I silently follow a policewoman towards one of the rooms, the soles of my flip-flops sticking to the carpet. 'This shouldn't take long,' she tells me. 'We're just asking some preliminary questions – fact-finding at this stage.'

'Have you any idea what happened to my sister yet?' I sit where she points to. 'I can't bear to think someone in that room knows something.'

'We've nearly finished speaking to everyone.' She takes a seat opposite me.

I'm surprised how cold it is in here. One or two of our group have come back sweating. They must have gone into the other room. I wrap my arms around myself. To be honest, I could do with a hug.

She continues speaking. 'Once that's been tied in with the findings of the forensics team, we should all know more. We'll speak to you then.'

'Where's Caitlyn been taken?' Not that it changes anything to know this. She's never coming back. Then I realise there'll be a funeral to arrange. I'll have to know where she is. Although I know I'll want to view her body again. Seeing her dead in her bed this morning will haunt me forever. But Dad won't be up to arranging anything, that's for sure. It will be up to me.

Now that Caitlyn's gone, I'm the eldest. After a lifetime of living in her shadow, this feels strange. I've now got one sister, not two. Maybe it will be me that Emma looks up to now, rather than Caitlyn. And perhaps Dad will appreciate me more than he has. Whenever I visit him, which is far less often than it should be, he only seems interested in talking about Caitlyn or Emma. He's always on about what they're up to or asking whether I've heard from them. One of these days he'll say, *And how are you, Annette?* No sooner have these thoughts intruded into my thinking, they've made me hate myself more than I usually do. My poor sister is dead and I'm still competing with her.

'I promise I'll find out where she's been taken. Just bear with us.' The policewoman is kind and I'm grateful. I hope they were gentle with Emma as well. 'Right, I'm going to switch the recording machine on and then you'll be interviewed under caution.'

'OK.' I just want to get this over with and get back to Emma. Eventually, when Dad goes, we'll only have each other. I was always jealous of the relationship Emma had with Caitlyn, but now, she'll have to come to me more. The thought warms me slightly. It pops into my head that the family 'estate', if that's what we can call it, will only be split two ways, rather than three. Another intrusive thought. I wish I could stop thinking like this.

'The time is 2.46 p.m. on Saturday, the twenty-fifth of January. This interview is taking place at Roundhill House Apartments in Dublin. My name is Sergeant Polly Arthington of Bridewell Gardaí Constabulary, and I am conducting this interview with...'

'Inspector Tim Retford, also of Bridewell Gardaí Constabulary in Dublin.'

'You are here to answer some questions involving the death of Caitlyn Elizabeth Nicholson. You do not have to say anything, but it may harm your defence if you do not mention, when questioned, something which you later rely on in court. Anything you do say may be given in evidence. Do you understand your rights, or do you need them explained to you?'

'I understand them.' I've heard them before. I wonder if they know anything about my shoplifting caution from when I was younger. I'll never forget Dad's face when he arrived at the station to act as Emma's appropriate adult. It was disbelief combined with disappointment – far worse than his angry face. It was a moment of madness, stealing expensive make-up, especially dragging my little sister into it. Emma, luckily, had no action taken against her, not even a caution. It was nearly a fortnight before Mum could bring herself to speak to me. Caitlyn tried to peacemake but I despised her for that.

It feels like I'm dreaming though, having the rights read out to me. The whole thing is like a bad dream. And it's only just started. We've got to tell Dad yet. We've got to tell everybody. Neighbours, colleagues, extended family, friends, wedding guests. Oh my God, wedding guests. I wonder if Ben knows yet.

'I have to check whether you would like any legal representation with you whilst you answer our questions?'

'No. I'll be fine, thank you.'

'Could I get you to confirm your full name, date of birth and address for the recording?'

'Yes.' I reel off the information.

'So that makes you younger than your sister?'

'That's right.'

'I've heard mention of your dad whilst we've been speaking to everyone. Is your mother still around?'

'No, she died six years ago. Cervical cancer. Like Caitlyn had.' I close my eyes against the memory. My brave mum fought the disease for nearly two years until she stopped treatment and admitted defeat. Dad already had heart problems but has really gone downhill since we lost her. I've heard of people dying of a broken heart, and I think this is what's happening to him.

'I'm so sorry.' I see genuine sympathy in Sergeant Arthington's eyes and for a moment I'm reminded of how much Emma and I are at risk from cervical cancer too. I'll just let them take my womb. It's not as if I'm ever likely to have children anyway. Out of the three of us, I'm the ugly duckling and probably destined to spend my life on my own. I've always been on the outskirts, even of my family. Caitlyn was Mum's favourite and Emma has always been Dad's. I'm merely the middle child, the unnoticed. Not that I'm a child anymore – I've got to snap out of this way of thinking. My thoughts won't stop swirling around one another – I feel like I'm going mad. I just want them to stop. It's ridiculous being jealous of my prettier, cleverer sisters at my age, particularly when one of them has just died.

'Right, we understand this is a horrendous time for you right now, so we'll keep our questions to a minimum.'

Focus, Annette. Focus. 'Thank you.' I wonder if she's been as nice as this to everyone. Or if it is because I am Caitlyn's sister. I can't imagine I'd be a suspect, anyway. If the police have asked any of the others about me and Caitlyn as sisters, they might have heard we could be spiky with one another, but surely no one would accuse me of being capable of killing her.

'I would like you to talk me through from when you arrived at Dublin yesterday, to when you were alerted to what had happened to your sister this morning.'

A vision of her mottled face flashes into my mind, blood crusted around her mouth. After fighting so hard to stay alive last year, it—

'Annette?'

'Sorry. I'm just not with it today.'

'I know. It's no wonder. But if you could just talk us through.'

As I recount the journey, to the meal, to the arrival at the apartment and the games, Sergeant Arthington continually interrupts me, apologising each time as she seeks to establish relations and hostilities between everyone in our party. We're certainly a complicated group, all thrown together, some here because they wanted to be, some because they felt as though they had to be.

I'm drawn to elaborate on the relationship between Caitlyn and Michaela. 'I was surprised to see her here, at Caitlyn's hen party,' I begin. 'She never seemed happy about the engagement. I heard her bitching in a corner with Lucy on an evening when both families were invited for a meal to celebrate. "If she thinks I'll be her bridesmaid, she can think again," Lucy was saying. "I'll be turning up in jeans and a hoodie if I'm forced to go to their stupid wedding." They shut up sharpish when they realised I was listening. Caitlyn never confided in me about anything, but I'd found out from Emma that she always felt on the edge of Ben's family.'

'Go on.' Inspector Retford speaks for the first time.

'Apparently Michaela was *always* hostile to Caitlyn and openly criticised their wedding plans. According to Emma, Michaela lives in Ben's old flat and gets a monthly salary from the clothing company. Emma reckons she does nothing to earn anything. Unless, of course, you count having your nails done.'

That was a bitchy thing to say, but I don't care. I'm on a roll now. I tell the police of all the snide remarks I know about, and the fact that Michaela, along with Lucy and Karen, barely visited Caitlyn when she was ill last year.

What I don't mention is that I didn't either. I do feel guilty about this, especially now, and wish I could turn the clock back. Sometimes you don't realise about the important stuff until it's too late. In my defence, though, I'm never too good at being around ill people. Being around Dad is bad enough, but at least he doesn't moan and groan like Caitlyn did. I obviously cared about what she was going through, and Emma would give me updates.

'Did you go to bed at the same time as Emma last night?'

'Yes. I haven't been to many hen parties, but this one was so divided. Not much fun at all. I was glad to get to bed.'

'What do you mean?'

'You've probably gathered this for yourselves, but Lucy, Michaela and Karen were one little group, then Adele and Mari. Shelley and Emma stuck together – they came here first to get the apartment ready and Caitlyn stuck with Jen.'

'So where did that leave you?'

'I wasn't bothered. I'm too old to be fussed about feeling left out. If I'd have been able to, I wouldn't have come this weekend, but Emma persuaded me I had to.'

Sergeant Arthington lets a long breath out. 'Did you hear any arguing going on last night?'

'Yes. Emma and I stuck our heads out of our bedroom. It didn't sound like it was anything serious and didn't go on for too long. I can't believe it might have led to what happened to my sister.'

'Did you hear anything during the night?'

'Not a thing, but then our room was the room furthest away from Caitlyn's. I heard people getting up and going to the bathroom once or twice, but that was it.'

'And what about this morning?'

'I wasn't surprised when I heard Caitlyn had gone for a walk. She enjoyed walking. I remember thinking to myself that at least she was escaping the atmosphere in the apartment. You could have cut it with a knife this morning. Then when she'd been found, everything changed.'

'In what way?'

'It was strange. There was a divide between those who were crying and wailing and those who didn't seem to care. I was just numb, in the middle of it all. I still can't believe she's dead – it hasn't hit me yet. Then Jen started blaming everyone.'

'Can I ask more about this divide, who would you say was on either side?'

'Emma, Mari, Adele and Shelley seemed really upset. Ben's family weren't. I was numb and like I say Jen was busy firing questions about.'

'And what about you?'

'I think I went into some sort of shock. Normally I'm quite anxious and can't stop thinking, but this morning, it was as though time had stopped.'

'I understand your father will need to be informed of what has happened gently. Is this something you would like us to attend to?'

'No, definitely not. Emma and I need to tell him, in person. He can't be left alone when he's been told.'

As soon as we get back to Leeds, we're going to have to break the news. We should probably pour him a brandy first and make sure we've got his heart medication to hand. If it was me who'd died, he probably wouldn't be bothered.

We'll probably have to tell Junkie Jim, too. I know our weirdo neighbour isn't into drugs anymore, but that's what I've always called him inside my head. But Caitlyn, for some strange reason, was really good friends with him. I might leave it to Emma though. He was a right pillock to me when we were younger. I suppose I started it – I went up to them and said, 'Ugh! What are you talking to *him* for?' He was only ever going to be nasty back.

But I can't imagine why she was such good friends with him. He was as dodgy as they come.

I'll also have to tell the other next-door-but-one neighbour, who Caitlyn used to shop for. They were pretty close too. There are so many people we're going to have to tell. I need to check that it will not be on the English news before we get back. Dad can only hear this from us.

I feel smug as I retake my seat in front of Michaela. *Hopefully, I've raised some suspicion about you,* I think to myself. She's probably been in there, pointing the finger at me as well. Emma reaches for my hand. She, along with Dad and my work, are all that matter to me now.

SEVENTEEN

SHELLEY

I'm crying again before I've even sat down. This has got to be one of the worst days of my life. And it feels as though it will never end. Nothing is ever going to be the same again.

'You were one of the first to get up this morning,' Inspector Hobbs begins after reading me my rights, asking me to confirm my details, and also if I want a solicitor, which I've declined. 'Along with Jennifer, is that right?'

'Yes.'

'Talk me through what you did when you got up.' She reaches towards a box on the windowsill and passes me a tissue.

'Nothing much. I helped Jen tidy up for a few minutes and then I went to the shop for some breakfast things.'

'And how did you find the door when you left your apartment – locked or unlocked?'

'Unlocked. It must have been like that all night.'

'Are you absolutely certain it was unlocked?' She taps her pen against her notebook as she speaks.

'Yes. I even made a joke to Jen that we could have all been

murdered in our beds. Obviously I didn't realise what I was saying.' Looking back, it's not one of the most sensitive things I've ever said. 'But then we thought Caitlyn must have gone for a walk.'

'You were to be one of her bridesmaids? Is that right?'

'Yes.' I think of two days earlier when we went for our final dress fittings. It feels like a different life now. There was so much I should have said to her whilst I had the chance, but equally, I'm glad I didn't.

'Was everybody happy about the wedding going ahead?'

God, what sort of question is that? 'Like who?'

'You? Everybody?'

'I don't know. You'd have to ask them that.' If she's wanting me to get into finger-pointing, she can think again. My gaze falls on a stain on the carpet under the window. I'm lucky really that I got out of this building to get some fresh air this morning – I'm the only one who did.

'How did you feel about the wedding?'

I avoid her eye. 'It's what Caitlyn wanted, wasn't it? And I'd agreed to be her bridesmaid.' I want to move away from this line of questioning. Well away.

'How long have you known Caitlyn?'

'We met at sixteen at sixth form college – and we worked together as well. We were chambermaids together at a hotel.' I think back to how easy life was then. We had such a laugh together. We'd get there at six thirty in the morning for croissants and coffee, then serve the breakfasts. Caitlyn was always spilling things – once on a customer. Then we'd move onto servicing and cleaning the rooms and would have the music blasting out whilst we worked. We'd enjoy having a nosy at the possessions the guests who were out for the day had unpacked, trying to imagine who they were and what sort of lives they led.

'I understand you were the friend involved in the cloak and dagger operations that led to Caitlyn and Ben becoming engaged.'

'That's right.' Despite her almost casual reference to this, something plummets within me. 'It was just a couple of months after her cancer diagnosis. It gave her some extra fight.'

'Getting engaged did?'

'Yes. She'd been so down after they diagnosed her. Especially with it being the same cancer her mum had died from. I was with her when she got the news. I'll never forget it. She'd put it off though and left things longer than she should have as she was so frightened.' Fresh tears heat my eyes. 'It was about this time last year. She had told no one apart from me that she'd had a succession of abnormal smear tests along with a range of other symptoms. She was like that – she never wanted to worry people. But when the doctor had messaged to request a face-to-face appointment, she knew it was something she couldn't face alone. I was glad to be there to support her.'

But that was before other areas of my life changed forever. 'We'd left the surgery with her saying, "This time in a year, I might be dead." It's extraordinary to know that it wasn't cancer that took her, but...'

'It sounds as though she was lucky to have a friend like you by her side.'

'Erm, yes. Well, you can't receive news like that on your own, can you? Although she suspected the result before we got there.' As soon as she got the message, she knew. I'd gone on and on at her to stay positive, but she couldn't after what had happened to her mum. A wave of sickness crashes over me. I don't want to think back to when Caitlyn was at her lowest ebb. God, this is all so... I just can't believe...

'Are you OK, Shelley?'

'I could do with some water.'

'You've gone very pale.'

'I'm, erm.' I'm going to have to say something. I need some breakfast. It feels like my blood sugar has dropped. Only food will stop me from being sick, or fainting. I haven't really told anyone yet, but I'm going to have to tell the truth. 'I'm ten weeks pregnant.' There's a shake in my voice as I say the words out loud. It still doesn't feel real. 'But the others don't know. They think I wasn't drinking last night because I'm on antibiotics.'

'I see. Do you want to get yourself some water?'

I lurch towards the door and rush along the hallway, praying that no one is in the bathroom. I had heard how awful morning sickness can be, but never thought it would make me feel this rough – it's a miserable affliction, not knowing when it's going to end either. As I retch over the toilet bowl, with nothing to come up but yellow bile, my eyes water with the force and once there's nothing left, the tears continue. *What an absolute mess.* I splash cold water onto my face and rinse a plastic beaker out. I feel the cold water slide straight into my belly, but feel slightly better for allowing myself to be sick. It's as though it released something else as well. I sit on the edge of the bath for a moment, hoping nobody's heard me in here with it being so quiet in the lounge. If they have, hopefully they'll just put it down to the stress we're all under.

'You don't look too good.' There's genuine concern in Sergeant Whinstable's expression as I return to the room. 'We'll wrap this up as quickly as possible. As far as I know, we've just about spoken to you all.'

'I'd appreciate that. This room isn't helping – it's so hot in here.'

'I think there's a problem with the thermostat.'

'As far as I know, Inspector Retford is going to have a word with you all together and then you'll be able to get something to eat,' he says. 'Are you OK to continue?'

I nod, resisting the urge to let him know that judging by the smell in here, there's something wrong with his own thermostat.

The sooner I get this over with, the sooner we'll all get out of here. I might even tell Jen, and perhaps Emma, of my predicament. All this has made me feel fragile, and I could do with them looking out for me. I don't feel as nauseous now – just a bit dizzy. The room suddenly lights up as though the sun has come back out. I feel a huge need to be out there.

Inspector Hobbs presses a button on their recording device. 'Interview with Shelley Watts resumed at 3.12 p.m. So, Shelley, we've had an account of what everyone did from arriving here in Dublin yesterday afternoon. We've been given insights into some relationships that existed between Caitlyn and the other members of the hen party. Is there anything that you would like to tell us, anything else that may interest us?'

'No. Nothing. You've probably heard about the argument that went on last night and the hostility with her in-laws, and if you have, there's nothing much I can add to that. Just please don't mention my pregnancy in front of the others. I don't want anyone else to know yet. I might tell one or two of them, but I want it to come from me when I'm ready.' I'll never forget the moment I realised the test was positive. Part of me was terrified, part of me elated. Being a mother is what I've always wanted – but I didn't expect the circumstances to be like they are.

I remember Caitlyn confiding in me about the warning she had been given in her follow-up appointment. Ben went with her for that. The treatment she would need was likely to leave her infertile. She'd been invited to have eggs harvested but apparently Ben had said, there and then, that he didn't want that. Already the father of a then sixteen-year-old, he wasn't interested in starting over with parenthood. Caitlyn seemed OK with that, admitting that children can be a big thing in a relationship and sap all the energy from it. I wondered if she knew something when she said, *When a man feels like he isn't getting enough attention, and it's all going to the children, that's when he looks elsewhere.* But I would have still felt dreadful breaking the news of my pregnancy to her. With or without the full story behind it.

'Don't worry. We won't tell anyone. All we're concerned with at the moment is getting to the truth of what's happened to Caitlyn.'

'Aren't we all?' How can someone be here, larger than life, the centre of attention one minute, then the next they're gone? I can still see her face. I can still hear her voice and her laughter. I can almost feel her presence. I wish we were sixteen again, with everything to look forward to, and nothing, or no one, to get in our way.

EIGHTEEN

JEN

Inspector Retford looks at us all over the top of his glasses. 'Thank you for your cooperation so far today.' It's the middle of the afternoon and if I don't get out of here soon, I'm going to scream. Shelley looks dreadful – she must sense my concerned glance and smiles weakly at me.

'We're investigating two possibilities,' he continues. One is that Caitlyn was killed in her sleep by one or more people already in the apartment.' He sweeps another, more severe, gaze over us this time. I squirm beneath it – I always do when I feel as though I'm being accused of something – I've always been the same. He rocks from one foot to another as he speaks – it's quite irritating.

'The other is that someone came in from outside, being that the door was possibly left unlocked overnight. There could, of course, be a combination of these two factors. We are still examining your mobile phones and studying CCTV in and around the area. This will ascertain whether anyone gained entry during the night. So, as these enquiries continue...' He stops as someone taps him on the arm from behind. As he turns, I see the thinning hair on the top of his head. 'Bear with me one moment, please.'

We all look at each other as he leaves the room, stooping under the doorway. I strain to catch what they are saying as low voices echo from the hallway. Maybe we won't get out of here after all. They're going to have to let us get some food though. None of us has eaten since the toast earlier. I just hope it's not down at the police station. As if we haven't been through enough today. After an agonising few moments, he returns.

'OK.' His voice carries more authority and affirmation than before. 'The investigation is moving forward. We're going to release you to get yourselves some food. We need to know exactly where you'll be, so we can release your phones back to you as soon as we have finished with them, and clearly, there might be further questions.'

'Is there a pub or a café nearby?' I ask, hoping the answer is a pub. My stomach is grinding into itself, but it's still a gin I need. A double.

'If you leave this building and turn right, there's a large pub on the corner, the Dublin Tavern,' Sergeant Whinstable offers. Something about his sweaty red face tells me he's a regular in there.

'We really need our phones,' I say. 'We should plan whether we're going to get a flight back or be able to stay here again tonight.'

'There'll be no flying back tonight, I'm afraid.' Sergeant Whinstable shakes his head.

'I don't want to stay *here*,' Emma says. 'Not in this building where my sister died.'

'Me neither,' says Lucy.

'We'll sort it out soon.' Half of the room is staring at me. Maybe I should just concentrate on where *I'm* going to stay. Let the rest of them sort it out for themselves.

'For all but one of you, you can have your belongings back. We've finished examining them.' I can hear a bustle in the hallway which sounds like our bags being brought in from the other apartment.

For all but one of us! Shit – what does that mean? I stare at him, waiting for more.

'What about our phones?' Michaela speaks now. 'And which one of us? Why?'

'Your phones are still being analysed at the station, but that should be concluded soon.' Inspector Retford seems less fierce than he did when they first arrived this morning, but I'm worried. 'We're getting logs of calls and messages, and your GPS information – then they will be returned to you. Are you going to be where Sergeant Whinstable suggested?'

'Yes.' Mari stands. 'If I don't get some food, I'm going to pass out, and I need my medication.'

'You must wait there, at the Dublin Tavern, until we come back to you,' he adds. 'We will arrest anyone trying to leave.'

'I wouldn't go anywhere without my phone.' Lucy and her bloody phone. It's all she keeps bleating on about.

'As you collect your bags, you must all surrender your passports and photo ID. These will be bagged separately, we will give you a receipt. We will return them either with your phone or shortly afterwards.'

'I didn't travel on a passport,' I say. Evidently, none of us are going anywhere yet. 'I used my driving licence as photo ID at the airport as my passport has run out. It's classed as an internal flight from Leeds to here.'

'Just surrender your driving licence then.'

I'm reassured slightly. He wouldn't be telling me to surrender my driving licence if I was about to get arrested. They'd take that off me at the station.

'If you could all be making your way into the hallway, Inspector Hobbs will allow you to retrieve your belongings.' Inspector Retford sweeps his arm towards the doorway as though directing traffic. 'Sergeant Arthington and Sergeant Whinstable will give you a receipt for your documents as you leave.' He nods towards his colleagues. 'Make your way straight out of the building, please.'

My heart is thudding. *Which one of us can't go?* Come on, put us out of our misery.

'Shelley. Can you wait behind?' The gruff voice of Inspector Retford echoes around the room as we get to our feet.

'Why?' She looks bewildered at first, then close to tears. 'I'm not feeling too good. I need to get out of here.'

'She's on antibiotics,' I say. 'She's not well. Surely she can have some food before she answers any more questions?'

'If you could make your way out, please.' Inspector Retford completely ignores me.

Why are they keeping her behind? She would be the last person out of our group that I'd suspect of knowing anything. Maybe they're just wanting to clarify her statement about finding the door unlocked. She sinks into her chair as everyone leaves the room and heads towards our stacked cases in the hallway.

'You know where we'll be when they've finished speaking to you,' I say, squeezing her arm. 'I'll get you some lunch if you don't get your bag back for your purse. How long will she be?' I say to Inspector Retford, my conscience prickling at me. 'Can I wait for her?'

'No. Like I said. Make your way out, please.'

'What do you want to ask me?' I can hear the wobble in Shelley's voice and her eyes are larger in her face than normal. 'I've told you everything I know.'

'It'll be fine.' I try to smile at her. 'They'll just want to ask you more questions, maybe about the door being left open.'

'I'll see you shortly.' She looks terrified. I would be if they were keeping me behind. What do they want to question her about? We're still no closer really to being told what has happened to Caitlyn.

. . .

As I get down to the main entrance, the police officer guarding the door raises the cordon for me to leave. The glare of daylight hurts my eyes – it's the first time I've seen the outside world since yesterday afternoon. I can see the pub on the corner and know the officer will keep an eye on that doorway as well. I hurry to catch the others up, though I don't know why I bother. It's not as if any of them think much of me. They haven't got very far.

We're an eclectic bunch. Other than Karen, no one has any make-up on, we're all dressed in either gym stuff or baggy trackie bottoms and hoodies. I don't even think I've brushed my hair today. I hope it's not an upmarket pub. With a name like *tavern*, it probably isn't.

The fresh January air is a luxury I will never take for granted again. I don't want to speak to the others as we trudge along the street towards the Dublin Tavern. I feel as though they're all blaming me. Once again, I wonder why I've caught them all up.

Now we're out of that building, the fog in my brain lifts. Adele and Mari walk together, Annette and Emma, then Karen, Michaela and Lucy. I'm on my own. I'd normally be walking alongside Caitlyn and Shelley. I feel the freeze of tears on my face. In the cold light of day, I realise that I'm never going to see Caitlyn again. I stare into the sky, wondering if she's somehow up there, watching us. What light would she be able to shed on what's happened to her? This time twenty-four hours ago, she was by my side; she was getting married and I was going to be her chief bridesmaid. I don't know how I'm going to get through this. Shelley pops back into my thoughts. I hope to God they let her out soon.

I'm first through the door and stride towards the bar. The Dublin Tavern is neither upmarket nor a dive – it is somewhere in the middle. Luckily, not a place we need to look any more dressed up than we are to blend in. 'Do you do food?' The barman nods towards a propped up menu. I glance at it, then hover my finger above the first item. 'I'll have that please and a gin and tonic. A double.'

'Where will you be sitting? So we can bring your sandwich over?'

I point towards a large table. 'There.' I watch as he pours my drink. Such a normal scenario. A Saturday afternoon pub in Dublin. Caitlyn liked gin when she used to drink more. All the flavoured ones. The realisation that she's gone forever keeps knocking me over like a double-decker bus.

I take a seat in the corner and await my sandwich. I couldn't face more than that. My stomach's churning and I hope I can keep the sandwich down. I look towards where Mari is intently studying the menu. Everyone else is bustling around one another, ordering food and drinks, clearly relieved to be let out of that awful apartment. No one in here would think we've just been freed from what amounted to being in police custody. Emma was right – no way could we stay another night there. She looks dreadful. I think she'll be the hardest hit by all this. She adored her sister. I'm glad to see that Annette's taking care of her – it must be a struggle for her too. For Karen, Michaela and Lucy, it seems to be business as usual – especially Michaela. I watch as she laughs with a man who's standing next to her at the bar. Even as Karen and Lucy walk away, she continues talking to him. How could she be thinking of chatting up some bloke at a time like this?

One by one, everyone joins me and we just about squeeze around the table. Mari and Adele are the last ones to sit, and for a moment I wonder if they're going to sit somewhere else. To an onlooker, we almost look like a bunch of friends here to enjoy a Dublin weekend. With our cases, we could be new arrivals or a party about to leave. Little does anyone know that we're awaiting further instruction from the police on when we can or can't get a plane back to Leeds.

NINETEEN

SERGEANT WHINSTABLE

'My name is Sergeant Whinstable and I am conducting this interview with my colleague, Inspector Tina Hobbs. The interview is being conducted at Bridewell Gardaí Constabulary in Dublin. Also present is...' I gesture towards the demure-looking woman in front of me.

'Shelley Watts.'

'And her representative.' I nod to the man towering beside her, making her look even smaller than she is.

'Andrew Brighton, of Davis and Partners, Solicitors.'

'Shelley Watts, we have arrested you on suspicion of your involvement in the death of Caitlyn Elizabeth Nicholson. Before we proceed, I am going to read you your rights again.' I should be able to say these in my sleep, but I always have to refer to a script. It's imperative that they're word perfect, anyway.

'This interview is commencing at 4.42 p.m.' We've got her into the interview room in good time, considering how busy things are today with the match and the protest. It couldn't have been a worse day in terms of our personnel to have had to be diverted to a suspicious death, where it has been necessary to speak to nine women. But on-call solicitors are often less tied up at the weekend too – obviously we're not having to wait for them to finish in court or leave office meetings.

Through the small window in the corner of the room we're in, I can see it's dark now and wonder where on earth the day has gone. It's passed in the blink of an eye in one respect – but in another it's dragged on forever and shows no sign of ending anytime soon.

Shelley's eaten a sandwich and had a drink. She looks more human than she did when we were putting her into the car. She's pregnant, so we need to treat her according to protocol. She was sick before we left the apartment and I have to admit, I felt sorry for her. Obviously, I can't let that show and have to remain professional. I'm relieved to have been able to change my shirt when we got back to the station. I'm not used to having to interview for hours on end in spaces like that room in the apartment. I must have stunk, but Tina was too polite to say so. Not like my wife. She never tires of putting me down. And then she wonders why I hit the whiskey every night.

'Do the others know I've been formally arrested?'

'No. When asked, you declined to have anyone informed of your detention,' Tina reminds her.

I take a deep breath. We might as well get this show on the road. It's going to be at least a couple of hours before I get out of here, and there's a pint with my name on it. 'Shelley. Evidence has come to light which implicates you as a suspect in the murder inquiry we are conducting into the death of Caitlyn Elizabeth Nicholson.'

'What evidence?' She fixes her stare on me. I don't think I've ever seen a woman with such large eyes. Despite being shattered and ill, she's very attractive.

'I was hoping you might tell us that. What do *you* think we might have found to implicate you?'

'You don't need to answer that.' Her solicitor is a dominant presence in the cramped interview room. He must easily be six and a half feet tall. 'It's up to the Gardaí to let you know what evidence they've got, not to ask you what you think they've got.'

I reach into the box beside me and pull out the first evidence bag. 'Firstly, Shelley, these strands of hair were found at the side of Caitlyn's hand. We took a sample of DNA from you at the point of arrest, so we're waiting on the results from that to confirm our other findings.'

'You're going to have to do better than that.' Andrew Brighton laughs. 'How many of them were there in that apartment? Ten?'

I frown at him and look at Shelley.

She sits straighter in her seat, whilst also seeming to relax, and flicks her fringe from her eyes. 'All our DNA would have been in Caitlyn's room. Everyone went in there after Adele had found her. Plus, I was the one who decorated her room. I was at the apartment for nearly three hours before the rest of them arrived yesterday. My DNA will be all over the place.'

'The hair is a clump and looks as though it has been pulled from the roots,' I continue. 'We'll be asking a Garda doctor to examine your scalp after this interview whilst we wait for the DNA results.'

'You can examine whatever you want.' Her eyes are still fixed on mine.

It's the first time I've detected any attitude from her. It won't do her any favours. 'That's not all that has been found. Fingerprints, matching yours which we also took at the point of your arrest, were found on a glass she'd drunk from.'

'That means nothing. She'd probably picked up a glass I'd been drinking water from earlier in the evening.'

'We'll return to that.' It's my best piece of evidence and I'm saving it. 'The next piece of evidence I would like to present is a log of calls, obtained from your mobile phone over the last two months. And also a transcript of text messages.' I slide two pages towards her across the table. 'Do you agree,' I point to a number at the top of the page, 'that this is your mobile phone number, Shelley?'

I watch her as she leans over the page, visibly paling as she realises what we've got. 'This doesn't prove I had anything to do with Caitlyn's death though.'

The solicitor pores over it for a moment and writes something down, obviously not knowing the connection we've made at this stage.

'But it proves that you were having an affair with Caitlyn's fiancé, Benjamin Mortimer, doesn't it? As do all the photographs we have found on your phone of the two of you together.' I take some more pages from my folder and lay them out, one by one, in front of her. There's no denying how happy she looks, in the arms of the good-looking bearded man who was engaged to her friend. Women are a strange breed.

She stares down at the pages, then up at me. There's a look of defiance in her eyes. 'Ben and I really didn't mean for anything to happen. It was because we were spending so much time in each other's company. When we were looking around the shopping centre for the engagement ring, everyone assumed Ben and I were a couple. At first that felt awkward, but it planted the seed and everything else followed. The last thing I wanted to do was to hurt Caitlyn.' Her eyes fill with tears now. She's probably responsible for the death of her friend, and she's crying for herself. Any sympathy I had towards her is waning.

'I'm sorry I keep crying. It's the hormones.'

She's blaming hormones rather than grief. 'Ah yes. The baby. Ben's, I take it?'

She appears to hang her head. 'Yes.'

At least she has the grace to look ashamed. I never met Caitlyn before her death – but all I want is to get justice for her.

'You never mentioned that you were pregnant.' The solicitor's deep voice echoes around the room we inhabit. 'How far along?'

He writes her answer down. 'Ten weeks.'

'Does Ben actually know?' I ask.

'Yes. He's known for some time.' I wonder if Caitlyn knew as well, but we'll get to that shortly.

'How does he feel about it?'

'Who, Ben? A bit panicked at first.'

'Why's that?'

'Many reasons. Responsibility, finances...'

'Finances? Doesn't he own his company?'

'Yes, which Caitlyn is involved with too, and is partly why it's all such a mess. If it were to have got out what Ben was up to with me, it would have damaged his reputation beyond repair, particularly considering Caitlyn's cancer.'

'But am I right in thinking she'd gone into remission? Surely that eased the way for you both to come clean about things?'

'Yes, she had, but no, it eased nothing.' She stares down at her thin hands. I notice they're trembling.

'So their wedding was due to go ahead. To save Ben's *reputation*. It seems extreme.'

'I know. That's what I thought. But he had a couple of huge contracts in the pipeline. Ones Caitlyn had started the ball rolling with. That's why he's in London this weekend.'

God. Why do so many things have to boil down to money? 'So where was it going to leave you and the baby? If he was getting married?'

She appears to swallow. 'He was just going to allow some time for it all to go through and for the dust to settle, and then he was going to leave her and be with me and the baby.'

I want to tell her, *That's what they all say*, but instead say, 'And were you OK with this? Waiting around for him to leave the woman who would have been his wife?'

'Of course I wasn't. I didn't want to hurt Caitlyn, and neither did Ben, but you know, you can't help who you fall for. Once it had all started, we couldn't stop. I fell in love with him.' Tears are rolling down her cheeks now. 'God, what a mess.'

'Do you think Caitlyn had any idea that her husband-to-be was having an affair? And that there was a baby on the way?'

Her voice is small. 'I think she would have said something to me if she'd suspected anything.' If this woman ends up in court, we will risk her winning the jury over, particularly if she's heavily pregnant by then. With her long hair and pretty face, I can see what Ben fell for. She exudes vulnerability and femininity.

'Perhaps Caitlyn knew his affair was with you. That's why she said nothing to you directly.'

'No. She was the sort of person who would have had it out with me if she'd suspected an affair. She certainly wouldn't have invited me to her hen party. I was trying my bridesmaid dress on with her the day before yesterday. She would have said something.'

I keep forgetting she was one of Caitlyn's bridesmaids. The plot thickens. I take my next piece of evidence from the folder. 'I am now going to read out a letter that was found in a pocket of Caitlyn Nicholson's handbag. It's dated 1 January – just over three weeks ago. From other items found in Caitlyn's bag, it appears to be in Caitlyn's handwriting, but we are getting that verified.' I clear my throat, look at Shelley and then down at the letter.

If you're reading this letter, I might be dead. I've found out my fiancé, Ben Mortimer, is having an affair with my friend, Shelley Watts, who is also pregnant by him.

I watch Shelley's expression as it changes to one of horrified recognition. It's a shame we can't capture it as further evidence.

Shelley and Ben expected cancer to kill me when they first got together. It is going to kill me, but they don't know that. Everyone thinks I'm in remission. I've stopped all my treatment and could live until around June.

I've heard Ben on the phone to Shelley, promising her they will soon be living as a family and will get my life insurance and critical illness cover. Ben also promised to get me out of the way before the wedding.

I am now worried I'm at risk. He won't leave me so close to our wedding, when I've been so ill.

I have gained and managed many of his company's customers and investors, and have made good relationships. Ben treating me callously will bring his reputation into jeopardy.

If I'm injured or worse, between now and the wedding, they should both be questioned.

Signed, Caitlyn Nicholson (1st January)

'She was terminal? But why didn't she say?' Shelley's former expression of horror has changed to one of confusion.

'I might be making assumptions here, but perhaps she felt as though she couldn't trust you.' I want to laugh at my irony. Tina gives me a sideways look as if to say, *Cool it.*

'But...'

'Shelley,' says her solicitor. 'It might be useful for us to talk alone at this stage.' He places his pen on top of his notepad. 'Have you finished presenting your evidence to my client?'

'I haven't, actually. Are you all right for me to continue or do you want to pause and speak to your solicitor?' I direct the question at Shelley.

Andrew Brighton, or whatever his name is, turns to her now. I notice that he's got so much wax or gel on his head that his hair doesn't move as he does. It glistens in the overhead fluorescent lighting. I remember when I used to make the same effort with my appearance. There isn't much point anymore.

'I suggest we speak after Sergeant Whinstable here has finished presenting his evidence, so we know exactly what we're dealing with. Is that all right with you?'

'Yes.' She lowers her eyes to the table.

I slide the next evidence bag from the box beside me and place it gently on the table between us all. 'Shelley. I'd like you explain to me how this vial, containing the traces of a so-called date-rape drug, namely gamma-hydroxybutyric acid, was found in your handbag in the apartment.'

She stares at me.

'Samples have been taken to confirm our suspicions that it was ingested by Caitlyn, as it was present in a glass on her bedside table. The glass which is covered with your fingerprints.'

'I know nothing about any date-rape drug.' Her voice is definite as she points at the vial. 'And I know nothing about that. Someone must have planted it in my bag.'

'I suggest,' I look from her to the solicitor, 'that between you and Ben, your plan for your part in this was to ensure that Caitlyn was drugged and drowsy, and for the door to be left unlocked, which you conveniently blamed Jennifer for. Then, for Ben's part, he would enter the apartment whilst everyone else was asleep and ensure Caitlyn never woke up. Perhaps you hoped that because you were so far away from home, we would never suspect Ben.'

Tears are pouring down her cheeks. 'We might have done a lot of things, but we'd never do that. *To plan to murder her!* Oh my God. I can't believe you're accusing us of this. I was just biding my time until Ben left her – you've got it all wrong.'

'What about this?' I place another bag in front of her, containing a ring which catches under the lights.

'That's Caitlyn's engagement ring.'

'So what was it doing in your handbag?'

'I'm not sure. Maybe she gave it to me to look after. It had got too big for her with all the weight she had lost. I can't remember. I'm sorry.'

'We've also got Ben on CCTV landing at Dublin airport and arriving at your apartment in the early hours. I'd say your plan was very carefully drawn up.'

'That's not possible. He's been in London. You can't have.'

'And we have evidence placing him at the scene which we will shortly be speaking to him about.' I pause for a moment, considering whether to change tack. 'Shelley. I have to say that you'll save yourself a lot of trouble by telling us what you know. If this goes to trial, you don't want to be having your baby in prison. Perhaps Ben talked you into this? Maybe it was all his idea?'

'I object to this line of questioning.' Andrew Brighton frowns at me.

'I know nothing. I want to go.' She grips the table and stares at me, desperation in her eyes. She looks as knackered as I feel. 'Please! I've answered all your questions.'

'I'm afraid you can't go anywhere yet, Shelley. May I remind you you're under arrest?'

'Are you actually intending to charge my client?'

'We're going to put it in front of the Public Prosecution Service shortly, and then we'll let you know.'

'I can't go back in that cell. You can't make me! I'm pregnant. You can't treat me like this!' Shelley flings her chair back and turns it towards her solicitor. 'Isn't there anything you can do? I don't feel well!'

I remember my wife being pregnant both times, in happier days. She was as sick as a dog. Something softens in me. 'We'll bring you a drink and some food, Shelley. It shouldn't be too long before the PPS let us know what they want us to do. We'll take your condition into account and this should speed things up.'

She nods, looking defeated. 'What about Ben? If you're accusing *me* of this, then I take it he's been arrested as well?'

'Yes. He's being interviewed in London. Which is why, if you are implicated in Caitlyn's death, even if you've been coerced into something, you're better speaking about it now, and telling us what you know before things go any further. To admit guilt is always better than being found to be guilty.'

I wait for her solicitor to say something but to my surprise, he doesn't. The silence between us all hangs for a moment and feels so loaded with tension that I feel sure she's going to confess.

'If you don't mind.' The solicitor slides his chair back with a scrape, breaking the silence. 'I'd like some time alone to speak to my client.'

'This interview is terminated at 5.21 p.m.' I press the end button on the recording equipment. God, what a day.

TWENTY

DI MEXBOROUGH

'Sure. Right, if you could send me copies of all your evidence, especially the transcripts of what you've got so far. And anything else that might be useful.' I glance through my office window to see who's around. 'I'll get my officers to bring him in whilst I go through it all. Yes, I'll keep you informed.'

I sigh as I replace the phone in its holder and stride towards the door. I curl my head around the wall into the open-plan area which is buzzing with voices, phones and keyboards tapping. 'As if we weren't busy enough today.' Joe and Sam glance up as I speak.

'What's up, sir?' Sam puts his pen down.

'I need you to attend at the London Parkway, both of you, please.' I nod towards Joe, deliberating with myself as to whether I should send additional officers with them. I dismiss the idea. After all, our person of interest is amongst his business associates. He's unlikely to want to draw further attention to himself.

'If you could bring in a Benjamin John Mortimer. He's the manager of...' I glance down at my notepad, 'a company called Mortimer's Apparel UK Limited. I'm told he will be in the conference suite.' I pause for a moment to give Sam a chance to write this down. 'There's apparently a photograph of him on his website, so take a look at that before you set off. The suite he's using at the hotel is booked for another couple of hours.'

'Right you are, sir. What are we bringing him in for?'

'Suspected murder.'

Joe's head jerks up. I remember when I was a new officer, hungry for the exciting jobs, as I thought they were back then. I've got to an age and a point in my career where I've dealt with so many murders, they've almost become commonplace. Not that I've ever hardened to them, I've just become more thorough. And determined to get justice for the victims. Each one is an individual with a worthwhile life and people who loved them. Most of the murders I've encountered have occurred within a domestic setting. I'm always amazed by the darkness that exists in situations where people are supposed to love and look after each other.

'If you could take our man away from everyone else, perhaps to a side room at the hotel before you speak to him.'

Sam nods. 'Can you say whether he'll come quietly, sir?'

'He's at the hotel on business so it's likely he will. I can't imagine he'll want his associates knowing anything. We're going to be questioning him in relation to the death of his fiancée, Caitlyn Nicholson.'

'Caitlyn Nicholson,' Sam says slowly as he scribbles this down.

'She's been smothered to death in Dublin, whilst on her hen party. He's a suspect, but he doesn't need to know that yet. Just let him know that there's been an incident involving Caitlyn Nicholson and we need to speak to him about it.'

'And what if he *doesn't* come quietly, sir?'

It's a good question. 'You'll have to arrest him then.'

'What grounds should we give for arrest?'

'Try to bring him in first. I want his reaction to the allegation on record. But if it comes to it, you'll have to say it's in connection with the death of Caitlyn Nicholson. Before making the arrest, tell him that we have discovered her body, then watch and note his reaction carefully.'

Joe's looking nervous, but I know Sam will take this in his stride. He's one of my best officers. Joe's still learning the ropes. 'Let me know when you're on your way back here. I'm going to go through the evidence they've sent me whilst you're bringing him in.'

'Where do you want us to bring him, sir?'

'We'll get him straight into an interview room and break the news about his fiancée, all recorded, of course. Then I'll formally arrest him and see if he wants a solicitor. We'll take it from there.'

'Sir.'

As I return to my office, Sam's already tapping on his desktop, presumably looking for the photo of Ben Mortimer. Within a few moments, I watch them head towards the office exit.

I turn to my computer where the details are coming through from Dublin. They've got people working on the interview transcripts that should be with me shortly, but there are plenty of photos for now, and the main report. I watch as more information filters through – another photo of bagged evidence, CCTV stills, a call log, then a message log, an outbound flight, an inbound flight, another photograph, then the first transcript. I see post-death photographs all the time, but this one gets me. Caitlyn is the same age as my daughter, Jess, and with her blonde hair, has a look of her. Jess is getting married this summer. What a senseless waste of life. Who could do such a thing? Some cases get to me more than others, and this is shaping up to be one of those.

The Dublin force has already arrested one member of the hen party and are currently interviewing her. Sergeant Whinstable was on his way into the interview when he rang me. Hopefully, by the time Mortimer is brought in and has waited for representation, I'll be given the gist of whoever they've arrested and what's been said in interview. I'd better ring Ruth – it looks like I might be late this evening.

'DI Mexborough.'

'We're on our way back, sir.' The voice of PC Joe Harris echoes through my phone's loudspeaker an hour later.

I lower my voice, aware that what I say will carry in the silence of their car if I speak too loudly. 'Has an arrest been necessary?'

'No, sir.'

'I'll meet you in the custody area. Good work. How long will you be?'

'About fifteen minutes, sir.'

That's something anyway. At least I'll get to witness Mortimer's reaction first-hand when I give him the news of Caitlyn's death, also we'll have it on record. More transcripts are coming through – I've got the first four interviews as well as their accompanying notes. I've plenty to be getting on with, but for now, I'd better get down to the custody suite and make sure there's a room ready.

I'm behind the counter with the desk sergeant when they bring him in. He looks young for forty. Not a grey hair or wrinkle in sight. It wasn't like that for me when I was his age. He must have had an easier life. I'm surprised also at his pristine beard. He hasn't got one in the pictures on his company website. I've yet to look at his social media profiles to see what they turn up about him.

'Benjamin Mortimer?'

'Yes. What's this all about?' There's an air, just an air, of worry about him. 'I've been told Caitlyn has been involved in an "incident". Is she all right?'

'We'll let you know what's happened in a few moments. But before we go any further, I have to ask whether you require legal representation whilst we speak to you?'

Now he looks worried. 'Do I need it?'

'Only you can decide that.'

'No, not for now. I just want to know what this is about first. What was so important that you had to bring me here, rather than speaking to me at the hotel?'

'Perhaps we should have our chat and then we can take it from there. Joe, you can get back to what you were doing before I interrupted you, and thanks for your help.' I nod at each of them. 'Sam, will you sit in with us?'

'Of course, sir.'

I make my way around the desk. 'Which room did you say was free, Sarge?'

'You can have room two.' He looks up at the board. For a Saturday afternoon, it's not too bad. 'It's all set up in there.'

'If you'd like to come this way.' I sweep my hand towards room two.

'Take a seat, Benjamin.'

'It's Ben,' he says, flatly.

I follow him in, then Sam follows, our heels all clicking against the hard floor. 'I'm going to hit record on the machine,' I tell him, 'as we need this conversation on record.' I glance at Ben's face as I wait for the beep. He looks concerned, but otherwise, he's not giving anything away. 'The date is Saturday the twenty-fifth of January, and the time is,' I check my watch, '4.52 p.m. We are conducting this interview at the City of London police headquarters. My name is Detective Inspector Tom Mexborough of the City of London Police Division and I am joined by...' I nod at Sam.

He clears his throat. 'Police Constable Samuel Morrison of the City of London Police Division.'

'Also present in the room is...' I look at Ben. 'Can you give your full name and date of birth, please?'

'Benjamin John Mortimer.' As he gives me his date of birth, I feel a pang of envy. I'd like to be that young again.

'And your home address?'

'Thank you,' I say, after he has finished speaking. Yorkshire. I didn't think he sounded like he was from around here. 'As my colleague PC Morrison has already told you, we need to speak to you in connection with an incident involving your fiancée, Caitlyn Nicholson.' He smells of leather and expensive aftershave. He's certainly not our run-of-the-mill murderer, if such a thing exists. My time in the force has shown me not to make assumptions or form stereotypes. 'When you arrived at the station a few moments ago, we asked whether you required a legal representative, which you declined for now. Can you confirm that please?'

'I thought you just needed an informal chat with me. That's what *he* said.' His irritation towards us flashes from his eyes as he jerks his head in Sam's direction.

'For the benefit of the recording can you clarify that you have declined to have legal representation at this stage?'

'I don't know yet. It depends on what you've got to tell me.'

'Am I OK to continue, Ben?'

'Yes. Can we get on with it?'

There's a smarminess about him I don't like. And I feel scruffy in comparison. Though he owns a clothing company, so I guess he's got to look the part. I left the house just after seven this morning, so it's no wonder that neither my clothes nor my brain are all that sharp. But no matter how suited and booted he might be, first impressions and the condescending way he's looking at me, say he's a complete sociopath.

'OK, Ben. I have to begin by reading you your rights. You have attended here, at the City of London police station, voluntarily, to assist us with an investigation concerning your fiancée, Caitlyn Nicholson.'

'Are you going to tell me what the hell this is all about?'

I'd better move with this. 'Ben. When was the last time you were in contact with your fiancée, Caitlyn Nicholson?'

He pauses, as though trying to work it out. 'Yesterday morning, whilst she was packing for her hen party in Dublin.'

'At the home you share at Yeadon, in Leeds?'

'Yes.'

'And have you spoken at all since she left?'

'Erm. No.' He half tugs, half strokes his beard as he answers. I might have to grow one myself. They look therapeutic. 'She tried ringing me last night. But I was busy.'

'And what time was that?'

'Around nine p.m.'

That ties in with what I recall seeing on her call log. 'And there was nothing since. No messages or anything?'

'She left me a message, telling me to ring her. I should have messaged or rung her back really, but I've got a lot going on right now and it went out of my head. You know how it is.'

'Have you been in touch with any other members of the hen party, since they left Leeds yesterday? I gather there are some of your family members amongst them?'

'Yes. My mum, sister and daughter, but no, I haven't spoken to any of them. They're on a hen party, aren't they? They don't want me bothering them.'

I take a deep breath. Here we go. 'Ben. I'm afraid I've got some dreadful news about your fiancée, Caitlyn.'

I watch him carefully. His expression is unreadable – it's still one of arrogance, rather than guilt. 'What? Tell me!' Despite his words, I can't work out if what I'm about to say will come as a shock.

'Ben.' I glance across the table at Joe. 'The Dublin police force were in touch with us a short time ago and I'm sorry to be the one to tell you that the body of your fiancée was found earlier today.'

'*Body?*' He stares at me. 'You're joking – right?' His knuckles turn white as he grasps the table.

I almost feel like saying, *Is this something you think I'd joke about?* His face is tight, still emotionless. 'She was discovered at around ten-thirty this morning.'

Ben looks at his wristwatch. Rolex. I always notice these things. 'That was hours ago. Why am I only just being informed?' His voice hardens. 'Why has no one let me know before now?'

Hmmm. Interesting reaction. Not disbelief, shock or grief. Just anger at being the last to know. 'We needed to conduct some preliminary enquiries before we got in touch with you.'

'I had a *right* to know. Straight away. I'll be taking this further.'

Here I would expect some sort of reference to Caitlyn being his *wife-to-be*, not threats of further action. 'We've let you know as soon as we could. I'm truly sorry for your loss, Ben.' I say this, hoping to jolt him into the reality of what I've just told him.

'But how? She was in remission from cancer. When did she *die?*'

Despite the emphasis on the word *die*, he really seems to be taking this in his stride. I've witnessed grown men wailing and throwing themselves around, quite rightly, when given news of this magnitude. 'Caitlyn was found in her bed. We believe she died during the night.'

'During the night? And she was only found at half past ten this morning? I can't believe my mum, sister or daughter didn't let me know – nobody.'

'As far as I know, the other members of the party had their phones seized for inspection. They wouldn't have been allowed to contact you, especially whilst they were being questioned themselves.'

'Questioned? But how did she die? I don't understand it.'

There's no wobble in his voice whatsoever. Just incredulity.

Not the reaction I usually get when I break news of a death to loved ones. 'She was suffocated, Ben. In her sleep.'

'What do you mean, "suffocated"? You mean with a pillow or something? On purpose?'

Right. Time to get the ball rolling. I take a deep breath. 'Benjamin John Mortimer. I am arresting you on suspicion of the murder of Caitlyn Elizabeth Nicholson. You do not have to say anything, but it may harm your defence if you do not mention, when questioned, something which you later rely on in court. Anything you do say may be given in evidence.'

'You're arresting *me*! But how can you? I'm here, in London – she's in Dublin! It's logistically impossible!'

'Would you like us to sort that legal representation for you now, Ben?'

TWENTY-ONE

DI MEXBOROUGH

I lift my glasses and rub at my eyes. I've read through all the transcripts apart from the latest one for Shelley Watts.

Ruth wasn't too happy at me saying I wouldn't make it back in time for our meal later, and despite my suggestion that she should invite a friend in my place, she's going to cancel the table. I feel bad letting her down, yet again, but she should be used to it, really. I can hardly tell a suspect and a colleague, *Never mind that I'm in the middle of interviewing a murder suspect, I've got to go now – I've a table booked at half-past eight with my wife.*

'Mortimer's solicitor has arrived, sir.' Sam tucks his head around my door. 'I've put them back in room two.'

'Which firm?'

'Collins and Smeaton.'

I let out a low whistle. 'Charles Smeaton?'

'That's the one.'

'No expense spared there, then. I can't imagine they'll be speaking for too long. Mortimer doesn't know what we've got on him yet, so there won't be a great deal for them to discuss.'

'What *have* we got on him, sir? I could do with knowing more before we go in. I know you'll be interviewing, but so I know what to concentrate on in my notes.'

I slide the folder towards him. 'Have a seat, Sam. It'll take you some time to make your way through that lot. Oh, the Dublin station is coming through again.' I grab the phone. 'DI Mexborough.'

'It's Sergeant Whinstable again from Bridewell Gardaí in Dublin.' I'd have known from his accent even if he hadn't announced himself. 'We've just completed the interview with Shelley Watts. I thought I'd ring with an overview whilst her transcript is being processed.' There's a weariness to his voice. I know he's done a lot of interviewing today, and it is one of the most knackering parts of the job. Interesting, but intense. Well, I say interesting – it depends on the case. Now that I've met Ben Mortimer, I am intrigued by this one. He's one hell of a cool customer. I feel certain of his guilt already, especially with the evidence I've seen, but now that's for the DNA to confirm and for the courts to decide.

'Thank you. I'd appreciate that. We've brought Mortimer in and he's currently with his solicitor.'

'I thought you'd need more on Shelley's responses to the evidence before you interview him. We'll get the transcript to you shortly, but here's the gist for now.'

'That would be helpful. This is one of the bridesmaids we're talking about, right?'

I grab a pen from the pot and rummage for a sheet of paper amongst my cluttered desk. One of these days, I'll have it more organised.

'Yes. First, she's admitted to the affair with Mortimer. She couldn't deny it. It was in black and white on her phone. It sounds like it's been going on for around eight months. She's denied all connection with Caitlyn's death. The evidence we've presented her with has been planted, she suggests.'

'There's rather a lot of evidence for it to have been planted. Not just that, they've got motive, her and Mortimer, circumstantial and financial. And they've certainly had the opportunity. Have you countenanced the possibility she was coerced into things?'

'Yes. We've been down that line of questioning. She's dismissed it out of hand. How do you think the evidence will hold up, sir? I've only just put it through to the Public Prosecution Service. Have we got enough for a charge?'

'The forensics from the bedroom could be strong evidence. The empty vial and engagement ring amongst her possessions is also strong. Less so is the CCTV footage.' I run my pen down my page of notes as I speak. 'Whilst it certainly looks like Mortimer, it's ambiguous. But it's certainly presentable, and we can look to get more. Has Shelley Watts's pregnancy been confirmed?'

'Yes. When she first arrived.'

'You've brought in the pregnancy liaison officer, haven't you? Everything must be done by the book here.'

'Yes, sir. There's been a female officer present all along as well. I's and T's are dotted and crossed.'

'What's happening with the other women in the party?'

'We released them from the apartment for food and drink. We know where they are and I've officers on patrol in the streets monitoring them all. They're all staying in Dublin. For tonight, at least. We've got hold of their travel documentation and will bring them in tomorrow for statements and fingerprints.'

'Right you are. Well, let me have the final transcript when you get it. I'll call you when I've finished interviewing Mortimer. Will you still be around?'

'Yes. I'll hang around until we've had a charging decision and I've heard from you.'

'Obviously, we'll have to hold them tomorrow and hopefully get them in front of a court on Monday.'

Mortimer looks different than he did earlier. Stripped of his personal effects, including his posh watch, tie and shoelaces, he's started to look rather unkempt. His time in a cell has taken its toll already.

His eyes don't leave my face as I take my position in front of him, though his expression is softer than it was before. Something has certainly shifted within him. Sam follows and sits beside me. Charles Smeaton nods in my direction. I know him vaguely from the golf course, and that's where we go to dust this sort of thing off. This isn't the time to exchange pleasantries.

Charles's reputation goes before him for getting the most lenient of sentences for the worst dregs of society. He's a shit-hot criminal solicitor, adept at finding loopholes, though I don't know how he sleeps at night. Some right cases have walked free because of his intervention.

'Right. We'll get straight on with it.' I place the evidence folder in front of me and set the recording going. I repeat the allegation, and I've read the rights so many times before, I could recite them backwards in my sleep. We all introduce ourselves. I glance at the wall clock. 'The time is 6.13 p.m.,' I say, in conclusion to the introductions.

Ben sits, drumming his fingers against a plastic cup of water. His earlier incredulity seems to have turned into agitation.

'Ben,' I begin. 'You've chosen to have a solicitor present. If at any stage you wish to speak privately together, please let us know. We will pause the recording and temporarily leave the room.'

'I want to know why you're even thinking what you're thinking of me.' His spittle hits me across the table. 'I wouldn't hurt a hair on Caitlyn's head. And how could I have done? I've been here in London. How I am expected to have got to Dublin and back in the middle of the night from Yorkshire, then arrive here in London to do a day's work, I don't know.'

'So there's nothing you want to tell us before we get started?'

'No. Nothing.' He shrugs and his voice rises.

The solicitor is writing on his pad. We've barely said anything yet, so God knows what he's writing about. I suppose he needs to look as though he's earning his five hundred quid per hour, or whatever ridiculous amount his company charges. I think I missed my chance in life. I should have made a killing as a hot-shot solicitor, rather than as a public servant in the police. I've been at the top of my pay scale for years.

I adjust my position so I'm turned squarely towards Ben. 'When did you arrive at the London Parkway Hotel?'

He visibly relaxes as I give him a straightforward question to start with. 'This morning. At half past ten.'

'You travelled from Yorkshire, from the home you share with your fiancée, Caitlyn?'

'That's right. I got the train down here. Leeds to London in less than two hours.' He's stroking at his beard again. Maybe we should have a body language expert in here. What would they be able to ascertain about a 'beard-stroker'?

'What time train did you catch?'

'The one that's a few minutes past eight.' He rubs at his head. 'I was at King's Cross for ten and jumped straight in a taxi to the Parkway.'

'Busy morning. Then what?' It's all a bit tight, but it's perfectly doable.

'I had a coffee when I arrived at the hotel, and then I've been in a meeting since eleven. I'm sure you'll have checked that.'

'What was the meeting about?'

'It was a business meeting.'

'Can you elaborate on that, please?'

Something in Ben's face tells me he'd rather not.

Charles Smeaton clears his throat. 'I cannot see what relevance the ins and outs of my client's business meeting has on what you've brought him here for.'

I meet Charles's eye across the table. 'It's important for us to establish facts around all aspects of your client's life in order to build a true picture of what has happened.' I load as much authority as possible into my voice. 'This includes financial and business circumstances that may have influenced his motivations. At this stage, we don't need to go into too much depth, but if this interview were to lead to charges being brought, there will be areas which will need probing more fully. I'm sure you can understand.' I give him what I hope comes across as a knowing look.

Charles nods towards Ben. 'If you just give DI Mexborough an overview of what your meeting was about.'

Ben clasps his hands together. 'It was more of a presentation than a meeting. I directed part of the day at current investors, the other part at potential investors.' His shoulders sag and he looks down at his hands. 'Caitlyn was supposed to be with me today – this is normally her arena, but her hen do was arranged and neither event could be moved.'

'Why did you come to London this morning? Why not last night? Particularly if your fiancée was away for the weekend?' I know what I'd have done in his shoes.

'I was at the office in Leeds until late last night. I had figures still to prepare which had to be up to the minute. I'm booked in at the Parkway tonight. I was planning a swim and a meal. I'm knackered.'

You will be, I resist the temptation to say. *Being up all night on a round trip to Dublin is bound to have taken it out of you.*

The word *was* is telling, as though Ben's accepted his fate. It's time to ask the all-important question: 'Ben, where were you at three this morning?'

'At home, in my house in Yeadon, asleep.' His gaze is steady and unwavering. I can see how his business associates might fall for his patter.

'Were you on your own at home?'

'Of course I was!' His voice rises again.

'But there's no one to vouch for your whereabouts?' I roll my sleeves up. It's getting warm with four bodies in here. And because it's January, the heating's pumping out everywhere. It's that awful dry heat that makes you choke.

'No one can vouch for me but that's where I was. Until I left early this morning.'

So there's no alibi. Another factor in our favour.

'Have you made a note of all that, Sam?' I speak to Sam, but my eyes don't leave Ben's face.

'We'll be checking train ticket purchases, taxi records and CCTV both at Leeds and here in London, Ben, so you need to be certain of what you're telling us.'

'I am.' His voice is steady and his eyes don't leave my face either. Jeez – looking at this man, it's easy to believe he could pass a lie detector test. Even when lying.

'How did you get to the train station in Leeds this morning?'

'By taxi.'

'Which firm?'

'I, um, can't remember. I'd have to check.'

'Were you picked up from your home address?'

'Yes.'

Sam's scribbling something down again – probably a reminder to check Ben's phone log for a call to a taxi firm.

'For the benefit of the recording, I am now showing Mr Mortimer two photographs.' I slide the first two exhibits across the table. 'One is of a man, matching your description, Ben, and using your identification, namely your driving licence, to board a flight from Leeds Bradford airport to Dublin late last night. The other is of a man, matching your description, who we also believe to be you, again, using your driving licence to board a flight at Dublin airport early this morning.'

He stares at the photographs for a moment before picking one up for closer scrutiny. 'This is impossible. Granted – that looks like a coat I wear, but it's impossible to see anyone clearly. Not with the hood. You can't charge me based on this photograph.'

I continue. 'I am now presenting Mr Mortimer with a printout, showing that the tickets used for the inward and outbound flights from Leeds Bradford to Dublin were purchased from the internet provider address at his home.'

'But I didn't buy them. It isn't me. What is it you're accusing me of?' He glances at Charles as if to say, *Do something*.

The solicitor reaches for the CCTV photographs and studies them intently. 'In my opinion, Detective Inspector,' he says, 'my client is correct. You'll have to get better photographs than those to have any chance of any allegation sticking to him.'

'How do you explain the tickets being bought from your computer at home and your driving licence being used as identification at the airport?'

'I don't know. Someone must have broken into my house.'

'And bought tickets using your computer?' I load as much scepticism into my voice as humanly possible. 'All at the same time as *borrowing* your driving licence?'

'When were the tickets bought?' Charles Smeaton loosens his tie.

I look down at my printout. 'Twenty fifty-three last Monday evening.'

'Well, that rules me out then.' Ben smirks.

I wouldn't expect anyone who has just lost their fiancée to *smirk*, and I'm disliking him more by the minute. My daughter, Jess, again enters my mind and I wonder about Caitlyn's father, if she has one. No doubt he will have been preparing to walk his daughter down the aisle, like I am in the summer. Instead, he's likely to hear that her fiancé and bridesmaid have conspired to bump her off, and for what? So they could save face and finances whilst carrying on with their sordid affair?

'I was at the gym. You can ask Shelley – Caitlyn's friend. She works there.'

'We'll come to Shelley in a moment.' I watch Ben's expression as I refer to her. Something in his face darkens. 'Which gym do you attend?'

Sam makes a note of his answer. He'll be having a late one, too, with the checking of all the information that's going to be required. Things aren't nearly secure enough for Ben to be charged yet. There's more work to be done – both here, and in Dublin.

TWENTY-TWO

DI MEXBOROUGH

I stretch my arms out in front of me. I'm as stiff as a bookend. 'So, Ben, to clarify once again, as you didn't answer last time, you're saying that on Monday night, at 20.53, whilst you were at the gym, someone broke into your house, bought some flights for Dublin on your computer, which they would have needed passwords and your payment details for, took your driving licence *and* stole your jacket?'

'I don't know what's happened, but I didn't book any tickets for Dublin.'

'Was Caitlyn not at home?'

'Yes, I believe so. I don't know for certain, but what I do know is that I did not go to Dublin last night. *Why would I?* I was at home and then here, in London, first thing this morning, like I've already told you.' A desperate edge to his voice is coming through now. Good. We've finally shaken him from his perch.

'You certainly had time between the time you landed at Leeds Bradford Airport to then make an 08.00 train. How far do you live from the airport, Ben?' I glance down at his address on my sheet but I'm none the wiser. I've never been to Leeds Bradford airport.

'Not far.'

'I don't know Yorkshire very well, so you'll have to enlighten me where Yeadon is, in relation to the airport.'

'The airport is in Yeadon itself.'

'So it would be fair to say you live close to the airport?'

'I'm admitting to nothing because I've done nothing.' His northern accent reminds me of Ruth's father who was brought up in York.

Charles Smeaton, in contrast, speaks the most proper of Queen's English. I fall somewhere in the middle. Posh enough to get by in court but 'common' enough to level with the suspects we bring in.

'For the benefit of the recording, I am now showing Mr Mortimer a photograph of a glove, found on the floor of the bedroom where Caitlyn was killed. Does this glove look familiar, Ben?'

He takes the photograph from me. 'It's just a glove. Caitlyn was always borrowing things like that from me. She'd lost so much weight and was often cold.'

'But you can confirm it's your glove?'

'Probably. So what? Like I said, it's just a glove and not exactly distinctive.'

'In front of me, I have the report of some DNA analysis from the crime scene. Some hair was found in Caitlyn's bedclothes, which is currently being compared to your DNA on our system.'

'How do you have my DNA?' He looks at Charles as though he might have the answer.

'You must recall being brought in to the station in 2005 for a public order offence.'

'They only gave me a caution.' His expression darkens again.

'We would have requested a sample from you for the database. Anyway, like I said, your DNA is currently being scrutinised against some other findings from Caitlyn's room, therefore if we're going to discover anything, the information is better coming from you first.'

'I can't tell you anything.'

He's taken the news of Caitlyn's death far too well, and I've noticed that he has effortlessly slipped into referring to her in the past tense. I slide another two photographs towards him; one is of him at the end of the street where the apartment is, standing outside a pub called the Dublin Tavern. Then he's been picked up again near the entrance of what must be the hen party apartments. Granted – he's huddled inside a thick hooded coat, and the beard provides further obscurity, but there's no mistaking that it's the same person at the apartment in the middle of the night as the one that has been captured on camera at both airports.

'It's someone who looks like me. I've told you, I can't be in two places at once. I was at home, then here, in London.'

'There's a few coincidences here, Ben. I feel they're stacking up.'

'So you've a glove and a half-arsed photo, so far, as evidence against my client?' Charles says. I'm unsure whether it's a statement or if he's asking a question.

'Also fibres from the coat he was wearing.'

'I've already told you that Caitlyn was always borrowing my stuff.'

'The same coat has been recovered from your address at Yeadon in Leeds this morning, which would suggest you briefly returned home after your return from Dublin.'

'How many times do I have to tell you? That's not possible. None of it is.' But Ben looks worried now. 'I've been nowhere near Dublin.'

Charles continues, seemingly undeterred by this latest evidence. 'I would suggest that the victim would have fought back under the circumstances you allege. There'd be skin under her fingernails if someone had been trying to kill her. Namely, my client's, if that's what you're accusing him of.'

'Not necessarily,' I say slowly as I prepare to reveal another weapon in our arsenal. 'In this instance, Caitlyn had been heavily drugged with GHB. She'd have been totally out of it and in no fit state to fight back against anything or anyone.'

'That's the date-rape drug, isn't it?' Charles writes something down. 'From what I know of that, it's undetectable a short time after administration, therefore I'd be interested to know how you are evidencing this.'

'It can't be detected in blood after a few hours, but there's a new hair analysis test that can pick it up. We should have the results in a few days. There were traces of it in a glass on Caitlyn's bedside table.'

'Oh my God.' Ben slides forwards in his seat. 'The plot thickens. So now you're saying that not only did I get to Dublin and back overnight, then down here to London this morning,' he rakes his fingers through his hair, 'I also administered a date-rape drug to my fiancée whilst she was enjoying her hen party, before smothering her to death.'

'We're not saying it was you who personally administered the drug. In fact, the empty GHB vial was found in the possessions of Shelley Watts, along with Caitlyn's engagement ring.'

'Her engagement ring? Maybe Shelley was looking after it. Caitlyn had lost weight and was always worried about losing it.' A sadness enters his eyes for the first time since I've met him.

'That's as may be, Ben, but I have to say, that *everything* is pointing to the fact that you planned and executed the killing of your fiancée along with Shelley Watts.'

'That's not bloody true.' I've finally managed to shake his composure. 'OK, I can't deny that Shelley and I have been seeing each other, but we hadn't planned to bump Caitlyn off. Oh my God!' He slaps the palm of his hand onto the table. 'Why won't you just believe me?'

'I know how manipulative some women can be,' I begin, like a dog with a bone whilst I've got him on the back foot. 'Maybe you were talked into this? Given some sort of ultimatum?'

'You're not listening, are you?' He's shouting now. 'Caitlyn's death is absolutely *nothing* to do with me!'

I will not react to him – I'm going to fire our next piece of evidence instead. 'I'm now going to read out a letter found in the handbag of Caitlyn Nicholson. It was discovered in her belongings during the search that was conducted this morning.'

Ben sits, as still as a rock, as Caitlyn's words, in my voice, echo around the interview room. It will have to be verified as Caitlyn's handwriting, but it's certainly a vital piece of evidence. The poor girl. Hearing her words verbalised makes me want justice for her even more.

'I had no idea Caitlyn was terminally ill.' Ben drops his head into his hands as I get to the end. 'None whatsoever.' He seems more moved by this realisation than he did by the news she is dead.

I feel like saying, *Perhaps you could have saved yourself a lot of trouble if you'd known. Plus an air fare to Dublin.* It was the letter that was the final nail for me, when I was going through the evidence. There's no reason to suspect that the handwriting is anyone's but hers. The CCTV stills wouldn't have convicted him alone, but the accumulation of evidence, once the forensics confirm it, which they hopefully will, is very much stacked against him and Shelley. Ultimately, it will be up to a jury to decide, but it's my job to get the case there, in front of them.

I glance at one of the photographs as I replace them in my folder. There's little doubt it is him, the height, build, beard and facial features. Both Leeds Bradford and Dublin are only partially facial recognition controlled – he's obviously used the control area where it's staffed, rather than the automated control. Probably because he was travelling on photo identification rather than with a passport.

'OK, so Shelley and I are together, and it's become more than just seeing each other,' Ben admits. 'But I had no idea that Caitlyn knew about it. I'd told her I wanted to call off the wedding, but not that I was having an affair. It would have broken her heart. And I don't know how she found out about Shelley's pregnancy.'

'*Shelley's pregnancy?* The baby is yours, isn't it?'

His expression darkens again. 'As far as I know.'

'It's just, with you referring to it as *Shelley's* pregnancy. How do you feel about becoming a father, Ben?'

'I already am a father. I have a seventeen-year-old daughter.'

'Did you and Shelley *plan* to become parents?'

'Not at all. It seems to be the story of my life, women deciding for themselves that they're going to have a baby with me. It happened with my daughter Lucy. Anyway, this isn't relevant, is it?'

'How do you feel about the fact that Caitlyn had found out? Not only about your affair with her friend, but about the baby as well?'

'Gutted. She'd talked about having eggs harvested prior to her cancer treatment, and I'd put the kybosh on that. I really didn't want any more kids.'

'Why didn't you just call off your wedding?' This is the bit I really don't understand. If my daughter's fiancé had any doubts about marrying her, I'd rather Jess suffered a broken heart in the short term. I'd look after her in the same way I'm sure Caitlyn's family would have looked after her. To think she was coping alone with a terminal cancer diagnosis as well. 'There's no denying she'd have been upset but...'

'I tried. I really did. She made threats about ruining me if I did. She could have done as well. I gave Caitlyn a lot of control within the business. I've been an idiot. It was struggling anyway. Any damage to my reputation would have finished me. She came across as all sweetness and light, Caitlyn did, but she could be really conniving.'

'So you thought you'd just kill her instead?'

'Are you going to listen to me? I. Did. Not. Kill. Caitlyn. Maybe Shelley did it on her own. She had every reason for wanting Caitlyn out of the way and getting me all to herself. Particularly since she became pregnant.'

I think no more highly of Shelley than I do of Ben, but right now, as I look at the arrogance in his face, I can't believe that he's trying to wriggle out of this and pin the entire blame on his pregnant girlfriend. They're both as guilty as sin. In it, up to their necks. All we need is the forensic confirmation, then the Crown Prosecution Service will let me charge him. I think there's enough here.

'I'd like a copy of these documents, if you don't mind.' Charles points at my folder. 'And I'd like a few minutes with my client. He's answered your questions. Personally, I don't believe you've got enough to charge him, so if you'd like to get a decision on that as soon as possible, we'd be very grateful.'

'I'll be putting it all in front of the CPS as soon as the DNA results come back.' I slide the letter back into the folder. 'We'll leave you to speak and then Ben will be returned to a cell until we get a decision.'

'Will it be tonight?' Ben raises his head from his hands.

'It's unlikely.'

'Can I just return to the hotel?' His tone suggests a climb-down from a moment ago. 'You know exactly where I'll be. Look, I've not even eaten since lunchtime.'

'I'm sorry. It doesn't work like that. I'll see that someone brings you something to eat – and a drink, of course.'

'What about Shelley? Have they charged her?'

'I can't tell you that, I'm afraid. Is there anything else you would like to tell us before we end the interview?'

'No.' He folds his arms. 'There isn't.'

'Is there anybody you'd like informing of your continued detention?'

'No.'

'In that case, I am terminating this interview at 6.50 p.m.' I stop the recording and rise from my seat. 'I'll leave you to speak with your solicitor before you're returned to the cell.'

'You've given me the news that my fiancée is dead, and now you're treating me like an animal.' His eyes narrow. 'I will take action against you after this. That – I can promise you.'

TWENTY-THREE

JEN

I need to keep a clear head, so I stopped at three gins. It's nearly seven o'clock. Everyone seems subdued, having run out of things to say. We're still waiting to hear what is going on and what happens next. 'We've been here ages.' I push sugar lumps around the bowl with my spoon.

It's sinking in that my best friend has gone forever. After going into remission, Caitlyn had her whole life ahead of her. This has got to be the worst day of my life. I look around the pub in an effort to distract myself from the fresh wave of tears that is burning my eyes. Crying in the middle of the pub will only draw more attention to us. It's Saturday night, and as I notice other women my age, drinking and enjoying themselves, I wonder whether I'll ever have an enjoyable evening out again.

Despite trying to act normally, we must be raising questions amongst the bar staff. We're probably not their usual clientele, hunched miserably here in the corner with our cases. Still, we've been intermittently spending money behind the bar in the time we've been here, so they can't ask us to leave. Not that we could go anywhere, even if we wanted to. I wish I had my phone to pass the time with. I wonder if the police are still keeping an eye on us and whether we really would get arrested if we tried to leave here. The not knowing what is happening is killing me.

'Do you reckon the police are even coming back?' Emma is hunched over the table. She has veered between explosive bouts of tears and eerie introspection whilst we've been here. I think everyone is still shell-shocked and also exhausted now. We haven't got a phone between us, so we can't check on anything, or make any arrangements. All we can do is wait.

Adele and Mari have sidled onto the next table. They're still not speaking to me. It's ridiculous, given that we're all in this situation together. Hopefully, I'll never have to see them again after this. Then it dawns on me that there'll be a funeral to face, so I'll have to see them once more. God, I wish I could stop myself from thinking. My mind is spinning like a children's roundabout – I'm driving myself nuts.

I'm worried sick about Shelley. I can't believe she would somehow be involved with what has happened to Caitlyn. But why else would they have kept her for so long? She obviously knows something. And how can they just dump us here, not letting us know what's going on, or when we can get a flight back to England? I'm panicking in case we can't find anywhere to stay. I agree with Emma – we can't return to those apartments, but if it's left too late to find anywhere else, we might have to.

I must be telepathic because, right on cue, Inspector Hobbs and Sergeant Arthington appear in the pub doorway. The noise level in the pub plummets as they do a sweep of the room. Then, spotting us, they head towards our table. Everyone is staring at us and we might as well give up our attempts at keeping a low profile. I suppose that a sudden police presence in a pub is going to put a dampener on *any* conversation.

'What's going on?' A barman follows them as they take a seat at our table. He eyes our group with suspicion.

'Just carry on with your evening,' Inspector Hobbs says to him.

'We just want a quick word with these ladies about a private matter, and then we'll be on our way. It's nothing to worry about.'

He frowns but leaves us to it. The volume in the pub gradually cranks up again.

Mari and Adele squeeze themselves back onto our table. We're all leaning into the middle. I'm desperate to hear what the police have got to say, but I don't want anyone else in the pub listening in. Until we know what's going on, this can't get out.

'Right. Obviously, it's difficult to say too much in here.' Inspector Hobbs frowns at the man who is watching us from the next table. It's the one Michaela was chatting up earlier. 'Firstly, I must apologise for keeping you all waiting for so long. We uncovered more evidence and needed to investigate it more fully before we could come back to you. We've also been interviewing.'

'Where's Shelley?'

'Before I get into any specifics, let's deal with the practical elements first. We've spoken to each of you this afternoon and recorded every conversation. Next, we must take detailed individual statements, and ask you to provide us with elimination fingerprints at the station.'

'Tonight?' I can't face any more tonight. There's no way I can bring myself to attend at the police station.

'No, tomorrow.'

I let out a long sigh of relief. 'But what are we supposed to do tonight? None of us feel able to return to the apartment, even if we could.'

'Actually, we've spoken to the landlord. You can stay in some ground-floor accommodation, given the circumstances you're all in.' She smiles, as though she's solved the problem for us.

'Well, I'm going to find a hotel. I'm not going back there, no chance.' I've already decided that I don't care what the rest of them are doing. I'm done with it.

'Me too.'

'And me.'

'I can't afford a hotel,' Adele says. 'I had to scrape the money together to come here. I'm a single mum.'

'I'll lend it to you.' Mari rests her hand on Adele's arm. 'We don't want to go back there tonight.'

'They have accommodation here.' Inspector Hobbs raises her eyes upwards.

'I've seen enough of this place as well.' I wouldn't stay here if you paid me. I remember from last night that there's music and carrying on well into the early hours. I could hear it going on until after 2 a.m. *Last night*. What I wouldn't give for it to still be last night.

'Well, if you could let us know where you're going to stay.' Sergeant Arthington positions her hat back on top of her head. 'I think it would be best to speak to you there rather than here. More privately.'

'Well, that's just it.' Michaela's voice is highly pitched. 'How are we supposed to look for somewhere to stay, when we've no phones to book anything?'

'Can you recommend anywhere?' As if I'm asking the local police for a hotel recommendation. To say I can't believe how this weekend has turned out is an understatement.

'There's a Marriott nearby,' Sergeant Arthington replies. 'It's cheap and cheerful – and usually has plenty of vacancies, especially at this time of the year.'

'So when can we have our phones back?' I'm surprised it's taken Lucy so long to ask. She's just taken the words from me.

'As soon as possible,' Inspector Hobbs replies. 'The Marriott is two streets away.' She points in the direction we should be heading. 'Get checked in there if you don't wish to stay at the apartment, and we'll follow you there in a few minutes.'

Well, thank goodness for that. But I stop myself from saying the words out loud. I just need to get out of here. The vision of Caitlyn in that bed this morning won't leave me. It's tearing me apart, imagining her now, either getting pulled apart by some pathologist or closed up in a mortuary fridge.

All eyes are on us as we rise from the table and head towards the door, wheeling our cases, followed by the two police officers. We must be a perplexing sight. I take some more directions to the hotel from Inspector Hobbs and lead the way there. 'What sort of rooms are we asking for?' I turn to the rest of the group then immediately regret my words. I should let them all organise themselves.

'Do you want to come in with us?' Emma links my arm. I notice Annette nudge her as if to say, *I don't want her in my room.*

I resist the urge to tell her I'd rather gouge out my own eyes than share a room with Annette. 'Thanks, but I just want time to myself after the police have gone.'

'I wish we could go home tonight.' Karen sounds more like Lucy than a supposedly mature woman in her sixties. This day is feeling as though it will never end. 'We'll get a three if they've got one for myself, Lucy and Michaela.'

'Are we sharing?' Mari seems more enthusiastic about sharing with Adele than last night. Yet they're both still looking at me as though I'm something to avoid stepping in.

Adele nods and we make our way through the brightly lit foyer of the Marriott, towards the reception area, which is completely empty. I guess most people will have checked in and gone out for the evening. Most normal people.

'Have you got a single, two twins and a triple room available – for tonight?' I ask the immaculate receptionist, keenly aware of my dishevelment. The plan for today was a spa and facial, so I've not even showered or brushed my hair. Then the fact that my best friend is dead steamrolls over me, and I'm totally ashamed for even thinking about my hair. I can't wait to have a lie-down and just be alone with my thoughts.

'Let me have a look for you.' I can't help but notice her impeccably manicured nails, painted a similar colour to that Caitlyn was wearing as she taps on her keyboard. 'Will you all be requiring breakfast?'

'I will, in the single room. If I could just reserve that for myself and everyone else can make their own bookings.' I'm ready to drop now. I can't take much more today. I hope the police won't be long before getting here.

TWENTY-FOUR

JEN

'Yes, we've got the rooms you require available.' The receptionist's voice is bird-like. 'If I could just swipe a card for each of them.'

'Are you serving food this evening?' My belly is griping – all I've eaten today is the sandwich in the pub.

'Yes. Until nine p.m. You can place an order any time before then.'

'Thank you.' I slide my payment card towards her. 'For the single room. Do you have a bar?'

'Just through there and turn left.'

'Thank you.' Thank God we're sorted for tonight. I turn to the others. 'I'm off for a gin. Keep an eye out for our visitors and bring them through.' I've asked enough questions and taken enough charge. I need a drink, I need answers, then food, a shower and sleep. I need my best friend back too, but she's been taken away from me forever. Tears stab at my eyes again as I follow the corridor in the direction the receptionist pointed me in.

I sink onto the comfy sofa by the window and watch as the police car pulls into the car park.

I take a large swig of gin and momentarily close my eyes. I'm so relieved we can settle down for the night, though how much sleep I'll get, I don't know. I'll probably be out like a light to start with but will no doubt wake after a couple of hours and spend the rest of the night staring into the darkness, wondering what the hell happened to Caitlyn. And what about Shelley? I hope to God she's OK and that the police will let us know what's going on with her.

One by one, the others join me, all deciding to wait to get a drink until after the police have spoken to us. No one seems to want to miss a word. The policewoman who is a sergeant has left her hat and jacket in the car this time so they don't stand out as much as they did in the pub. The other one might be plain clothes, but you can tell she's a detective a mile off.

The lounge is vast enough that we can take up the corner without being overheard. Not that there are many people around. Most visitors to Dublin on a Saturday night will be out enjoying themselves in town. We'd planned to spend this evening having a meal and then checking out the vibrant Temple Bar area. We should have been having the time of our lives.

'OK,' Inspector Hobbs begins. 'First, I'd like to say how sorry we are about the loss of your friend and sister.' She nods towards Emma and Annette as she says the word *sister*.

'Also,' Sergeant Arthington adds, 'like we've said before, we're sorry that you've had so much waiting around for the last few hours. Our enquiries are ongoing, but we're now able to tell you where we're up to.' She looks at her colleague.

'Caitlyn's death will shortly be reported in the media. She won't be named yet, as we're not looking for anyone else in relation to her death.'

'Anyone else apart from *who*?' Karen asks.

'Will it just be on the news here, or in England?' Annette's been quiet for a while, so I'm surprised to hear her voice. She's probably thinking of letting their dad know. I'd suggest leaving him in blissful ignorance for as long as possible.

'Just here in Dublin, for now, as we're making requests for any witnesses or owners of CCTV or dashcam footage to come forward. Eventually, with Caitlyn being English, it will be reported there too.'

'Can I ask if you'll give us the chance to let our dad know first?' Annette adds. 'Really, because he's in poor health, we need to tell him face to face.'

'What about Shelley?' Lucy asks, not giving the police a chance to reply to Annette.

She's evidently not been released, or they'd have brought her back to stay with the rest of us.

Inspector Hobbs appears to swallow as she looks over our little group. 'All I can tell you is what is about to be reported – that a twenty-nine-year-old woman has been arrested on suspicion of murder.'

'WHAT?' Emma's voice is a shriek, and she slaps her hand across her mouth. 'She can't have been! Why?'

My own heart rate feels like it's doubled. Shelley! Arrested! Oh my God!

'We can't say more than that to you at this stage. We can only tell you what's about to be reported in the media. She won't be named yet; what they will report is that a twenty-nine-year-old woman and a forty-year-old man have been arrested and are being questioned in connection with the suspicious death of another twenty-nine-year-old woman.'

'*A forty-year-old man?*' It's Michaela's turn to shriek now, and the few people that are nearby turn to us.

I think we all suspect which forty-year-old man is being referred to. I won't believe it until I hear it though. I feel sick. All eyes rest on Sergeant Arthington as we await her answer.

'The other suspect was arrested in London earlier. We have

evidence that implicates both parties. Like I said, we're not looking for anyone else at this stage.'

'Ben's in London.' Karen's hand flies to her mouth. 'He couldn't have been in two places at once. You've obviously made a terrible mistake.'

'I'm so sorry. I know this is a lot for you all to take in.'

'What evidence have you got to arrest my brother?' Michaela stands and walks around the back of her mother, resting her hands on her shoulders. 'Look, we've got a right to know why on earth you think Ben could be involved with this. We're his family.'

'There will be more information in due course, but I'm afraid that is all we can say for now. I'm really sorry. This must be very difficult for you.'

'Is he allowed to make a phone call? Can he ring us here?'

'We offer anyone in custody the right to make one phone call.'

Karen moves her chair next to Lucy, who looks distraught. Tears are rolling down her cheeks. 'What are my friends going to say? No one will want to come anywhere near me if they think my dad could murder someone. He wouldn't. I know my own dad. No way.' It's the first time I've seen her show any emotion about anything, albeit concern towards herself. She's normally so aloof.

Karen hooks her arm around Lucy's shoulder and draws her in. I suppose it's a typical seventeen-year-old reaction. What everyone will think. It will certainly mark her out at college. Her dad arrested on suspicion of murdering his fiancée.

I gulp the rest of my gin straight down. My best friend is dead, allegedly killed by her husband-to-be and one of her bridesmaids. I used to know Ben, *really* know Ben, and whilst he might be selfish and a bit of a lad, I feel that there has to be some mistake here. And Shelley? Well, my brain hasn't even processed that yet. That they would be behind Caitlyn's murder doesn't compute. But the police wouldn't be holding them without something significant.

I need to be alone. With my shock. With my memories. And away from this lot. I've seen enough of them all to last a lifetime. The biggest mistake I have ever made was organising this hen party.

'We'll leave you to get some rest now.' Both officers get to their feet. 'If you could report to Bridewell Gardaí at eleven o'clock tomorrow morning, we will get the statements done, along with taking your fingerprints and a DNA sample.'

'But why?' Mari asks. 'The rest of us aren't under any suspicion, are we?'

'It's for crime scene elimination purposes.'

Sergeant Arthington adds, 'Then when you have your documentation and if we finish with your phones, as far as I know, you'll be free to leave. But we'll confirm that tomorrow.'

How can I leave Shelley here? I really think there's been a mistake. They'll get more evidence and realise that. 'What will happen to Shelley? Will she be locked up all weekend?'

'If the suspects get charged, they would be in front of magistrates on Monday morning. That will decide whether bail is granted.'

'Is Shelley all right? She wasn't very well earlier.'

'Like you should even be bothered after what she's accused of doing to my sister.' Annette spits the words out like gristle, her hand resting on Emma's shoulder. Emma hasn't stopped crying since the police arrived.

'And you lot.' She sweeps her gaze over Lucy, Karen and Michaela. 'You could at least try to look more ashamed at what a member of your family is accused of doing, instead of acting like victims yourselves.'

'Innocent until proven guilty,' Michaela snaps.

'He's been bloody arrested,' Annette replies, flatly.

'Will my dad be allowed out?' Lucy's voice is small and her eyes wide. Her grandmother tightens her grip around her shoulders, and I notice Michaela is glassy-eyed with her arms around herself as though giving herself a hug. Much as I don't like them, it's true what they say about the families of perpetrators of crime being victims too. They have to live with the stigma, the finger-pointing, and the gossip. That's if it really is them. To be honest, I still think there's some other explanation.

Inspector Hobbs's voice is gentle. 'It will be the same for both people who are in custody. But in the man's case, the court in London will decide whether he will be released or remanded.'

Lucy looks from Inspector Hobbs to Karen. 'What does that mean?'

Michaela reaches over Karen and takes Lucy's hand. 'Remanded means they'd send him to prison until the court date. But we're jumping ahead here – he hasn't been charged yet.'

'He's done nothing wrong! He wouldn't.' She buries her face in her grandmother's scarf. 'You've made a mistake.'

I stride away from the table, grateful as the conversation and the crying becomes more and more distant. I can't be part of it anymore. I've had enough. I buy a bottle of wine and order a lasagne to be brought to my room. That should knock me out enough to sleep. Nothing else can alter tonight, and I can hardly bear to contemplate what fresh misery and stress tomorrow will bring.

I force a weak smile as I walk past the receptionist towards the lift.

'Enjoy your evening.' She waves, obviously noticing my wine bottle and single glass.

'My friend was murdered last night. I'm drowning my sorrows.' I get a weird sense of satisfaction watching her smile turn to a look of horror.

'Gosh. I'm sorry. That's absolutely awful.'

'It'll be on the news soon. She was getting married next month. Her fiancé and one of her bridesmaids have been arrested for it.'

'Oh my God.'

I walk towards the lift, tapping my pocket to make sure the key card for my room is still there. In just a few moments, I can shut out the world.

I let myself into my room, kicking my shoes off with relief. Never has a bed looked more inviting. We would have been better booking in here than that poxy apartment. Maybe it wouldn't have happened then. Maybe if I'd insisted on sharing with Caitlyn. Maybe if it had been me who'd gone ring shopping instead of Shelley. What a mess, what an absolute bloody mess. I unscrew the top from the wine bottle and pour myself a generous glug. I can ask myself all the *maybes* in the world, but nothing I say or think can change a thing.

Caitlyn knew Ben was having an affair. Never in a million years would I have expected it to be with Shelley. It must have started when they were supposedly shopping for Caitlyn's engagement ring last year. Surely they wouldn't have been involved prior to that? She even helped him plan the marriage proposal. It's madness. It was Shelley who accompanied Caitlyn to her appointment when she got her diagnosis. How could she do what she's done to her?

I nearly slop my wine as a knock at the door jolts me from my thoughts.

'Your order, madam.'

'Thank you.' I take the steaming plate and put it to one side. I'll try to eat some soon. For now I need the wine more than the lasagne. I'm just grateful it was only room service, not the police or one of the others.

For any initial enthusiasm she showed, Shelley's never seemed overly happy about any of the wedding preparations, now I think about it. At first, I thought she had either gone off Ben, or was peeved at not being chosen to be the *chief* bridesmaid. She was judgemental about everything from flowers to shoes, and I've even wondered if she was jealous because marriage was happening to Caitlyn before her. Though who could be jealous of Caitlyn's life, I don't know. She's been so poorly, fighting the same disease that killed her mother.

Now I know that Shelley's jealousy stemmed from having it away with the groom-to-be. Then there'd been the hen party itself. She'd been quiet since we set off. I put it down to the not drinking after she told us she was on antibiotics. After all, we all loosen up once we've had a drink. Is she really on antibiotics? Some new cogs turn inside my mind. I put my glass down. Or is she not drinking because... Because she's *pregnant*! The realisation that this is what it is almost winds me. No!

One of the last things Caitlyn said to me re-enters my mind. *The woman he has been seeing is pregnant.* Oh my God! Poor Caitlyn. She'd been told that her treatment probably meant she couldn't have children. Poor, poor Caitlyn. What did she ever do to deserve how they've treated her? I wonder whether I'll tell the others about her being pregnant. How utterly ironic after the conversation I had this morning with Karen, about Ben not wanting any more children. When life still seemed normal and I thought Caitlyn was alive, either sleeping or having gone for a walk.

What I'd give to turn the clock back to last night. Protect her from two of the people who were supposed to love her most in the world. I finally let the tears slide down my face. Caitlyn was in remission. She had fought for her life and won. She wasn't even thirty years old and could have had the world at her feet. Her whole life was in front of her.

I don't know *how* they have done what they are accused of

doing, but that will come out soon enough. I refill my glass, vowing to stay in Dublin until we know exactly what is going to happen. I will be in that courtroom to look Shelley in the eyes.

TWENTY-FIVE

JIM

I knew Caitlyn as a young girl. I lived with my nan, four doors down from the Nicholsons. Nan was the only one who'd have me. No one else gave a shit after my mum died, and my dad had left years before. I don't know if he's alive or dead, and I don't care.

She was all right, was Caitlyn. Probably the only lass I've ever really cared about. Not in that way, mind – I don't go in for relationships. Bit of a lone wolf, me. It's the safest way to be. But Caitlyn was about the only person who ever gave me a chance. Everyone else in our street thought I was scum.

Admittedly, I've done some pretty dreadful things in my time. Caitlyn was too young back then to understand about the robberies, the drug trafficking and the times I was paid to take people out. As she grew older, she never questioned the stretches I was away at Her Majesty's pleasure – she just welcomed me when I came back. I'd often find her on my garden wall, waiting. Somehow, she seemed to know when to expect me. She never came into the house, that would have caused the curtain twitchers to make their small-minded assumptions, so we'd always sit on the garden wall, talking about everything under the sun or playing chess, which I taught her. Eventually she could beat me.

I remember one day, her sister, Annette, appeared on the pavement in front of us whilst we were in the middle of a game. I'd smiled at her, expecting her to be as pleasant as her sister, but she'd stood, hands on her skinny hips, and stared at me with an expression I'd come to know well over the years from other people. She had a look of Caitlyn but wasn't anywhere near as pretty.

'Why on earth would you want to hang around with this weirdo? Surely you've got more decent friends than him?'

'Do one, Annette, and never call my friend that again.'

'When are you coming home?' Annette had looked back at me then, her top lip curling.

'When I decide to. Go away.'

With that, Annette brought her fist underneath the chessboard and thumped it, forcing the pieces to fly in all directions. One of the kings ended up down the drain. Annette and Caitlyn ended up rolling around on the floor. I had to break them up. As she'd stormed off, Annette had vowed to get their father to put an end to our friendship. But nothing ever seemed to come of that.

When Caitlyn moved away to uni, we lost touch. I really missed her, which was an alien thing for me. I'd only ever cared about my nan. I'd sometimes bump into Emma, the nicer of Caitlyn's two sisters, and she'd tell me how Caitlyn was getting on. Then I noticed them all leaving for her mother's funeral a few years ago. Afterwards we caught up, with a few beers, over my nan's garden wall. Caitlyn had found out, by then, what I'd been capable of when I was younger, and the trouble I'd been in, but said nothing changed her view of me.

'I know you've done everything to turn your life around. People change,' she had said. 'I know who you *really* are.' She had smiled and squeezed my hand.

'You're great, you are.' It wasn't often I gave out compliments. 'You're the only person other than Nan who's thought anything good of me.'

'Well, you've always been a brilliant friend to me too. Promise me that no matter what, we'll always be friends.'

Granted, it wasn't a conventional friendship. We were from totally different backgrounds with quite a few years between us, but sometimes in life, people just hit it off with one another. 'Course we will,' I replied. 'Unless you go clearing off again like you did when you went to uni.'

Nearly a year ago, I bumped into Emma and discovered that Caitlyn had cancer, and was having a really tough time. I was initially gutted that she hadn't told me herself. Friends are supposed to support each other. However, I knew I'd see her at some point and felt sure, deep down, that she'd beat it. The next time I bumped into Emma, she told me that Caitlyn had got engaged and I thought, *lucky man*, whoever he is. Selfishly, I hoped she wasn't planning to move away with him. Turns out he's a bit of a bastard.

I didn't see Caitlyn after Emma told me either piece of news, but we had one of those friendships that can be picked up and put down, and never changes.

When she finally came to see me at the end of last year, I was shocked by how fragile she looked. I was so stunned I couldn't even bollock her for not getting in touch with me for so long. Not just thin, but gaunt and dark-eyed. Even her hair had lost its shine. 'You don't look like someone who's about to get married,' I'd said. 'You looked happier at Nan's funeral.'

'There's nothing they can do.' She had sunk onto the garden wall in her usual spot. 'My cancer's back and it's spread. I had an appointment last week and I've got a matter of months to live.'

'Oh God. I'm so sorry, Caitlyn.' I'm never any good with these things. What can you say to someone who's been told they're terminally ill? Especially someone you think the world of. I had to swallow my pain and put her first.

'I'm going to die, Jim.' She turned to me then, her eyes large in her face, as though she expected me to perform some miracle. I would have gone in her place if I could.

'No, Caitlyn. No. You're not. You're going to keep fighting. You're not someone who gives in. You never have been.'

'I could do with one of those if you've one going?' She pointed at my bottle of Beck's.

'Sure. I'll be back in a sec.' I was glad of the excuse to leave her for a moment. It was obvious from her appearance that she was very ill indeed, and it was unbearable to see her now, such a shadow of herself. I needed a minute away from her to pull myself together. The last thing she needed was me falling apart in front of her.

'Have they said exactly how long you've got?' I opened the bottle with my teeth and passed it to her. 'Things can change. There are new treatments all the time.'

She swigged from the bottle like she really needed it. 'They've said six months, tops. You're the only person I've told that it's terminal. You must keep it quiet.'

'What? You've not even told your fiancé?'

'No chance. He's the last person I want to tell. Look, what I've told you and what I'm about to say to you – I'm trusting you. Not a word to anyone. Not my sisters, my dad – anyone.'

'How long have you known me? You can trust me with anything.' Although I wondered what on earth she could be about to say. How could it be any worse than what she'd already told me?

'Ben's been carrying on with one of my bridesmaids – Shelley. I've been watching them for a while.'

'Oh, Caitlyn. You're joking.'

'Apparently, she's like a drug to him. I overheard him telling her that on the phone. It's the sex, as far as I can tell. I'm certainly not up to it anymore.' Her gaze remained downcast.

'Do they know you know?' It's the first time she'd ever mentioned sex in front of me. It didn't feel comfortable. Like I said, our friendship couldn't be any more platonic.

'They think they're being discreet.' She stretched her legs out in front of her. 'I've also overheard him telling her he wants to call our wedding off. But he'll get lynched if he does. He knows everyone will judge him and he's right.'

'Like who?'

'Friends, family, business associates. Look, if I was well, I'd walk away with my head held high and get on with my life, but I'm not, and I can't believe that either of them could treat me like this.'

'How long's it been going on?' I drained my beer and opened another one. She was remarkably calm, considering, apart from clearly fighting back tears. And who could blame her?

'Since she secretly met him to help find my engagement ring. It's ironic, isn't it? Whilst I've been having chemo, she's been screwing my fiancé. I don't know who I feel more betrayed by.'

'Both of them, I would say. They sound like they deserve each other.'

The tears spilled down her cheeks then. Evidently that was the wrong thing to say. 'Since then,' she said, her voice wobbling, 'he's been going away on business more and more, presumably to spend time with *her*. He hasn't even got the decency to come clean about what he's been doing. Neither of them have.'

'That's really rough for you. As if you haven't got enough to cope with.'

'I can't believe it. Me and Shelley have been through so much together over the years. We've been friends since we were sixteen.'

'Are you absolutely sure about them?'

'I got into Ben's phone and looked at his messages – there are texts from her to him a few months ago saying they have to stop. She was feeling guilty, apparently. But anyway, it seems that they can't stop themselves. They've been making an utter fool of me.'

'They're the fools – not you.' I couldn't bear to see her like that. My next-door-but-one neighbour gave us a funny look as she walked past. I suppose it wasn't even noon, and there we were, sitting on my garden wall, drinking beer.

'You haven't heard the best of it though...' Her voice was drowned out by a passing car.

How can there possibly be any more? I looked at her. 'What?'

'To top it all, Shelley's bloody pregnant. Can you believe it?'

'That's terrible.'

'It's so unfair. I'll *never* be a mother. I'll be too busy lying in a coffin.'

I stared at her. Caitlyn, who should have had her whole life in front of her. Motherhood, career, marriage, travel – the lot. 'Are you absolutely sure there is nothing the doctors can do for you? They must be able to do something.'

'Nothing. The cervical cancer was pretty advanced. I was scared after what happened to Mum and left it too late to be diagnosed. I wouldn't admit what was happening to me. I've been an idiot. Everything that could be tried has been. It's pain relief now. Worst case, they're even talking hospices by next month.'

'You're joking.'

She smiled, a weak smile, but it was good to see. 'Is this the sort of thing I'd *joke* about?' The smile vanished as quickly as it had arrived. 'I've always wanted to get married, you know. You should see the wedding dress I was supposed to be wearing – it's beautiful.'

'You'd look good in a sack, Caitlyn.'

She tried to smile through her tears. 'Thanks, but now, all I want is to get back at Ben and Shelley for how they've treated me.'

'Is there anything I can do? I know everyone says that sort of thing in these circumstances, but I really mean it.'

'When you say "anything", do you mean that?' Her head jerked up as she spoke.

'Anything. You just name it.' I glanced up and down the street, wondering what she was going to ask for.

TWENTY-SIX

JIM

I saw hope in her eyes. 'You had that spell of being paid to make people "disappear". Do you remember?'

'I couldn't exactly forget, could I? But that's when I was hooked on... Oh, it doesn't matter. It's all in the past.' I looked at her, wondering what the hell was coming.

'Do you know how you said you'd do *anything* to help me?'

'What is it you're asking, Caitlyn? For me to get rid of your friend? Or your fiancé? Or *both*?' God she must *really* hate them to be considering this. I wanted to tell her to walk away with her head held high, and make the most of whatever time she had left, but the words stuck in my throat. Desperation was written all over her face.

She took another swig of her beer and looked me straight in the eye. 'Me.' Her voice was a whisper and at first, I thought I was hearing things.

'*You?* What on earth do you mean?'

'I'm dying, Jim. I'm terminally ill. So you'll be putting me out of my misery earlier – it's worse at the end, anyway. You'd be doing me a massive favour.' Tears filled her eyes as she looked at me. 'I don't want to end up in a hospice, on morphine, with everyone crying at my bedside. That's what I've got to look forward to. Unless you help me.'

Oh God. She was serious. 'Caitlyn – I—'

'I can't go on any more like this, Jim. My body's riddled with it. I can't eat. I can hardly sleep. I'm puking all the time. And no one gives a shit.'

'I do.' It was true. I really did. 'But, how can anyone give a shit if you're keeping to yourself the news that your cancer's spread and you're terminal with it?'

'I'd tell Emma, or Jen – I trust them both. But to tell *anyone* would mean that I wouldn't be able to do what I need to do.'

'You've got to let your family know. You need looking after now and supporting with this.'

'No one can know I'm terminal. Not with what I've got planned.' There was a fire in her eyes for the first time since she had slumped on my wall.

I noticed how bony her hands were and how much her jeans were hanging off her. If Nan had been alive, she would have dragged her in and cooked her a big roast dinner. She'd have taken care of her. They're the only two people in the world that I've ever thought anything of. I took a deep breath. 'What exactly do you want me to do?'

'I want to cause maximum impact. To get back at Ben and Shelley for what they've done to me.'

'How?' She wasn't making any sense.

'I'm going to frame them for it.'

'For what?'

'For my murder.' She raised her gaze from the floor and looked me directly in the eye again. 'They've been at it for months, Jim. The whole time I've been battling cancer. They've been sneaking off and laughing behind my back. I can't tell you how much I want to make them pay.'

We sat in silence for a few moments. My brain was whirring, trying to compute what she was asking of me.

'The only reason Ben won't call off our wedding is because he'll be vilified for it,' Caitlyn continued. 'His business friends know how ill I've been. All he cares about is himself.'

'Are you absolutely sure no one knows it's terminal? Not even your dad?'

I saw something in her eyes then. Clearly something in my tone of voice had given her hope. 'Definitely not my dad. There's only you who knows *anything*. I can't let Ben and Shelley off the hook. I'll die. They'll live happily ever after with what I leave behind, life insurance, mortgage paid off, critical illness cover, and all that. It would all go to Ben, unless he's in prison, because we'll be married by then. No chance. I've already changed my will to make sure Emma and Annette get everything, including what I put into Ben's business. And obviously I'll see you right for your part. I've got something put by for you.'

Even though it sounded crazy, I understood the force behind her request. 'You seem to have thought it all through.' Though it was making me sick to the stomach. She still hadn't said exactly what she wanted me to do.

'I've squeezed everything I can from Emma and Jen about the hen party arrangements. I've got the date and the apartment details in Dublin.'

'I'm listening. But that doesn't mean I'm going to do it. I've got a lot of thinking to do.'

'They've planned to let me have the biggest ensuite room. I've checked the floor plan on the agent's website, so I'd be able to tell you exactly where to go.' She drained her beer bottle and placed it on the wall beside her.

'I still don't really understand exactly what you're asking of me.' Or perhaps I did, but I needed her to spell it out. Part of me was glad she was confiding in me and asking for help; the other part wished for total ignorance and for life to continue as normal.

'There'd be a decent amount of money for you. Please, Jim.' Despair swam in her eyes. She reached along the wall and placed her frail hand on top of mine. It looked like the hand of an elderly woman, not a young woman of not even thirty.

'I don't want your money, Caitlyn. All I care about is you.'

'Then help me. Look, I'll have taken something, that GHB, which will knock me out beforehand.'

'GHB?'

'It's what's used in date-rapes to sedate people. I won't feel a thing when you hold a pillow over my face.' Her eyes widened, as though silently pleading with me.

'*Hold a pillow over your face!* Caitlyn, I can't do it!'

'It's the last thing I'll ever ask of you,' she replied. 'You'll be helping me, not hurting me. It'll be like an assisted suicide with you as the doc. You'll be saving me from a drawn-out, painful death. When animals are ill, they get put out of their misery. Please, Jim.' She stood and faced me. 'I can't face what's coming. I'll be bed-ridden soon. At least this way, I still have some control over my life.'

'I need another beer. I can't believe you've come up with this.' I bent to the floor for another bottle. 'Do you want another?'

She accepted the bottle from me. 'You're a similar height and build to Ben.' She peered at me in close appraisal. 'You've got the same beard and colouring. Though you'd need to get it trimmed and your hair as well.' She half-laughed and flicked her fingers at my unruly collar-length mop as she sat back on the wall. Her laugh was good to hear for the first time since she'd come along that morning.

'You said Dublin? They'd have my details for the travel, not his. Even if I agreed, I don't see how we could pull it off, to be honest.'

'You'd travel on Ben's driving licence. It looks nothing like him, anyway. I'll get one of his hooded jackets and a pair of his combats. What size feet are you?'

'Eleven.'

'Perfect. You'd just need to make sure they picked you up on CCTV all over the airport and around the apartment in Dublin.'

'It's not that bit that bothers me. That's just details.' God, she had clearly found a solution for everything. 'It's the putting of a pillow over your face that bothers me.' I closed my eyes against the thought. It had been a very long time since I had taken anyone out. It had never really sat comfortably in my past. Perhaps now I was getting my comeuppance.

'I'm dying anyway, Jim. And like I said, I'll have taken some GHB. I won't even know you're there. I'll just stop breathing.'

'OK. Suppose I agree to it. CCTV alone wouldn't be enough to frame him. Especially if there's any doubt whether it's actually him. Which there would be.'

'I've really thought this through. Like I said. I'll plant some evidence in the room. I'll take some fibres from the clothes you'll be wearing and some hair from his comb. Then there are things like a hanky, a glove. And don't forget, the circumstantial evidence will come out. That they've been at it for months.'

'What about prints?'

'Whose? Yours? You'd be wearing gloves,' she replied. 'Don't worry. I wouldn't ask you to do anything where you'd be at risk of being caught.'

'What if the apartment door is locked?'

'I'll make sure it isn't. I won't take the GHB until the others have been in bed for at least an hour. Then I'll drop you a text.'

'Too risky. It'd be logged.'

'What, even if we got hold of pay-as-you-go phones and discarded them after?'

'No. I'll just come at a certain time. Sometime after two a.m.? Will everyone definitely be asleep by then?'

'I would have thought so. We're having a night in that first night. Plenty to drink. I'll make sure of it.' She seemed to brighten then. 'You're sounding like you're in? You've been more easily persuaded than I thought.'

'I haven't made my mind up yet. I want definite proof from you that there's no chance of you being cured – that you really are terminal, before I agree to anything, and even then, I still need to think about it.'

'I've got a letter they gave me. I needed it to get the terminal payment from my insurance company. Anyway, can't you tell how ill I am by looking at me?'

I didn't need to look at her any more closely, I already knew, and misery swelled in my throat like a balloon. 'No. You're still gorgeous. You've just lost a ton of weight.'

'Most brides lose weight in the run-up to their wedding. *Brides.*' She spat the word out. 'It's all gone to shit, hasn't it? If I don't do this, then me and Ben will get married.'

'Why don't you just *not* marry him? Tell everyone what he's been doing to you? Damage his reputation?'

'That's too good for him. Whether I do or I don't marry him, he and Shelley then get the chance to live happily ever after. This way ensures they definitely can't. Even if I let nature take its course and don't get married, he'd likely be able to contest my will. We live together. We're nearly married. Technically, he's my next of kin and we're financially linked. No, after how they've treated me, I'm taking them down.' There's a fierce edge to her voice that I've never heard before.

'I think you'll need more than what you've told me to take Shelley down as well. So far you've only implicated Ben.'

'Oh, don't you worry. I've got it all sussed. When Shelley's stuff is searched after they've found my body, they'll find an empty vial of the GHB in her bag.' She wiped her chin as the beer dribbled down it. 'I'll drink it from a glass she's been using as well, so her prints are on it. I'm also going to leave a note to say I've been worried they were planning to kill me. I'll leave it amongst my stuff and there'll be hair out of Shelley's hairbrush in the bed.'

'God. I can't believe your mind even works like this.' I laughed, despite my misery, then fell quiet for a few seconds. My thoughts wouldn't stop spinning. I can't do this. I really can't do this. 'What if I was to recruit someone else?' I blurted out. 'I really don't think I could bear smothering you with a pillow, Caitlyn. You're my best friend. It's crazy, what you're asking me to do.'

'But – I'm going to prove to you I'm dying.' Her voice became high-pitched. 'You said you'd do it if I showed you proof. Please, Jim. I can't trust anyone else with this. You know I can't. Please!' She grabbed hold of my arm.

'OK.' I closed my eyes and took a deep breath. 'Subject to proof that you're terminal, I'll do it. I know it's not something you can ask of anyone else. When are we talking?'

'Five weeks from now.'

I shivered in the weak December sunshine. 'Get me that proof, then. And anything else I will need. In the meantime, we can't see each other, much as it pains me to say that.' I stood from the wall, sadness enveloping my entire being as the words left me. I'd been so pleased to see her when she'd first shown up that morning. 'If we're seen together, it could come back on me. Much as I love you, I can't do time again. I'm not the person I used to be.'

'I know.'

'And...' My voice cracked. 'I can't bear to see you anyway, knowing what I've got to do.'

'Thank you, Jim.' She flung herself at me then. I don't know how long we stood there. In that moment, I did not even care if anyone was watching. I had forgotten what a hug felt like. The next time we'd be in close proximity, I'd be forcing a pillow over her face.

TWENTY-SEVEN

JIM

I've been repeatedly refreshing the news feed, waiting for it all to break, constantly pacing the house and the garden. Even a few beers haven't settled me down. I haven't wanted to go far from the house, so I took to pacing the street earlier. Really, I just want to get away from here, but I can't. Not yet. Passing by Caitlyn's childhood home was agony. Her dad was sitting in the window, totally unaware of what will soon be coming his way.

Finally, it emerged on Dublin Live.

The body of a twenty-nine-year-old woman has been found in a bedroom of a top floor apartment in central Dublin. The discovery was made at around ten-thirty yesterday morning at the Roundhill Street Apartments.

She is believed to have died during the night as a result of suffocation.

A post-mortem is taking place to determine the exact cause and time of her death, and the identity of the woman is expected to be revealed once her family have been informed.

A man aged forty and a woman aged twenty-nine have been

charged with suspicion of her murder pending the post-mortem results, and will appear before magistrates tomorrow morning. Dublin Gardaí are not looking for anyone else in connection with this incident, but would appeal for anyone who may have witnessed unusual activity in Roundhill Street during the early hours of Saturday, 25 January. They are also asking for anyone who possesses CCTV or dashcam footage in the area to come forward urgently.

Caitlyn's plan has run like clockwork. The police are *not looking for anyone else*. The husband-to-be and the bridesmaid are going to get what's due to them. What Caitlyn wanted to happen. She's got her dying wish.

I hate myself for what I've done, but I did it for Caitlyn. I understand why she asked me to do what I did; however, it will take a long time for the memory of it to fade. And to breathe again, knowing I have definitely got away with it.

She'd planned the whole thing in minute detail. True to what we agreed, we'd kept apart since our discussion last month, except when she was pushing Christmas cards through the doors of all the neighbours.

I got more than a Christmas card though. I got a copy of her Certificate of Terminal Illness, plus a full list of 'instructions'. The ticket to Dublin, she wrote, would be put through my door a few days before she was due to go. She wanted to buy the flights nearer the time.

We'd agreed not to make contact by phone or text either. However, I saw her on Thursday, three days ago, trudging up the path of her dad's house. I'm not normally one for sentiment, but it choked me to know it would be the last time she could spend time with her dad. I just prayed that she let nothing slip.

It was dark by the time she left. I sat in the gloom of my kitchen, watching as she left her dad's before creeping up my path and along the side of the house. I held my breath as there was a soft tapping on the back door. *This isn't what we agreed*, a voice yelled inside of me, but as soon as I'd thought it, I noticed her retreat down the path, this time without the rucksack she'd been carrying.

I left it a few minutes before going out to investigate, wanting to make sure she'd definitely gone. As promised, she'd left the items belonging to Ben – jacket, combats and trainers. Plane tickets. Driving licence. An envelope containing five grand cash, even though I'd said I didn't want any payment. It somehow made the whole thing uglier than it already was. I opened another envelope to find a note, with final instructions and the promise of more cash on 'completion'. I felt sick to my core, but this was clearly what she needed me to do. If she hadn't been dying, there'd have been no way. But she'd struck a chord with me when she said I'd be ending her drawn-out suffering early. I've always believed in the right to die.

I couldn't believe how easy it was for me to get through airport security with Ben Mortimer's driving licence. They checked it against my ticket with hardly more than a cursory glance at me. I had my hair cut and beard trimmed a couple of days ago and have to say that with the clothes that Caitlyn left around the back of the house, I didn't even feel like me, let alone look like me.

Being a Friday, I was pleased there was a late-night pub on the corner of the street where Caitlyn was staying. I needed a couple of whiskeys to steady myself. The place was full of revellers, so I could keep my counsel in a corner. No one bothered me.

I became Benjamin John Mortimer. As I adopted a more than confident stride towards the apartment block, I was him. Ascending ten flights of stairs and stopping at the top to get my breath back, I was him. Slowly walking across the landing and as I tried the door, I was him. It was unlocked, as Caitlyn had promised it would be. Part of me thought I should wait awhile, make absolutely sure that everyone was sleeping, but the bit of me that thought I should get it over with and get out of there won out. I put on gloves, wrapped a scarf around my face and tightened my hood to be as sure as I could be at not leaving anything of myself behind.

Caitlyn was in bed in the room, where she said she would be. I hardly dared breathe as I closed the door behind me. An empty glass on her bedside table caught in the faint moonlight seeping around the blind. I just prayed she had truly knocked herself out, like she had promised.

It was time. There was no going back. A whole myriad of images cascaded through my mind as I approached her. Nan's face. Caitlyn's face as a young girl, Caitlyn's face last month when she had begged me to do this. Yet I couldn't believe I would really get away with it. Still, she was worth doing time for.

The journey back to Leeds was even easier than the outbound one. I longed to shed Ben's clothes, to get rid of the stench of what I'd done. I could hardly believe that I was now on my way back – unchallenged. It was still dark when I got to Caitlyn's house. I watched from the shadows as Ben left the house and climbed into a taxi at twenty past seven. Caitlyn had heard him book the taxi a few days before, when he had specifically stated that it needed to be on time. He had a train to catch to London.

I let myself into the house around the back. She'd told me which drawer the rest of the money would be in. She told me where to leave Ben's jacket, trousers and shoes. Which pocket to leave the driving licence and tickets in, where the police would find it easily.

I quickly changed in the darkness, becoming Jim again as I

replaced Ben's clothing with my own, struggling to button my jeans with gloved hands. Struggling even more to contain my tears as the realisation of what I'd done washed over me, in the same way as the new day was emerging outside. A day Caitlyn would never see.

A LETTER FROM MARIA FRANKLAND

It was my own hen party at the start of 2020, before the world went crazy, that gave me the inspiration for this novel. As I was sitting in the circle in our 'party apartment' enjoying a game of 'Mr and Mrs,' it occurred to me that this would be a great setting for a murder, especially with only a limited number of suspects!

Hen parties bring together groups of women who all hold a different place in a bride-to-be's life, some are more significant than others – they may have known her for many years or not for very long at all. Perhaps some will be attending because they feel obligated rather than really wanting to be there. Yet no matter who they are and where they have come from, there is an assumption that everyone will get along and 'have a laugh' together.

But as *The Bridal Party* shows, this is not always the case! I was incredibly lucky to get my wedding in a year when so many others had to be postponed and luckier still that my awesome hens were nothing like the characters depicted in this book!

I'd love to know your thoughts on the story and would hugely appreciate a review on Amazon or Goodreads – it would be awesome if you could follow me there as well.

If you want to keep up to date with all my latest releases, just sign up at the following link. Your email address will never be shared and you can unsubscribe at any time.

www.bookouture.com/maria-frankland

KEEP IN TOUCH WITH MARIA

mariafrankland.co.uk

facebook.com/writermariafrank
instagram.com/writermaria_f
amazon.com/stores/Maria-Frankland/author/B009UHR6ME

BOOK CLUB DISCUSSION QUESTIONS

1. Discuss possible motivations for murdering Caitlyn, for each character. Who was the most likely to want her dead? Who was the least likely?
2. Has the eventual outcome changed your opinion of Caitlyn in any way?
3. To what extent has justice been done?
4. How could events have taken a different course?
5. Do you think it's possible to die of a broken heart?
6. Choose a character and discuss their flaws, motivations and redeeming qualities.
7. What do you think will become of each of the characters as they move on from this?
8. What are your views on 'right to die'?
9. To what extent is blood thicker than water in this book?
10. How could the story have played out differently if Caitlyn hadn't been terminally ill?
11. Discuss the jealousy that existed amongst the women at the hen party.
12. How has each character changed from the start to the end of the book? What lesson might each character have learned?

ACKNOWLEDGMENTS

Thank you, as always, to my amazing husband, Michael, who is my first reader, and is vital with my editing process for each of my novels. His belief in me means more than I can say.

A special acknowledgment goes to my wonderful advance reader team, who initially took the time and trouble to read an advance copy of *The Bridal Party* and offer feedback on the book.

Massive thanks also to Bookouture, to my editor Susannah Hamilton, who reached out to me after reading this book, and made my publishing dreams come true on my fiftieth birthday. Also to Liz for her copy edits, to Laura for the proof edits and to the rest of the team at Bookouture.

I will always be grateful to Leeds Trinity University and my MA in Creative Writing Tutors there, Martyn, Amina and Oz. My master's degree in 2015 was the springboard into being able to write as a profession.

And thanks especially, to you, the reader. Thank you for taking the time to read this story. I really hope you enjoyed it.